KG MacGREGOR

2014

Bella Books, Inc.
P.O. Box 10543
Tallahassee, FL 32302

Printed in the United States of America on acid-free paper.

First Bella Books Edition 2014

Editor: Katherine V. Forrest
Cover Designer: Linda Callaghan

ISBN: 978-1-59493-407-0

Other Books By KG MacGregor

Etched in Shadows
The House on Sandstone
Just This Once
Malicious Pursuit
Mulligan
Out of Love
Photographs of Claudia
Playing with Fuego
Rhapsody
Sea Legs
Secrets So Deep
Sumter Point
Undercover Tales
West of Nowhere
Worth Every Step

Shaken Series

Without Warning
Aftershock
Small Packages
Mother Load

Dedicated to these wonderful people

Cari and Kathy Robinson
JJ Crabb
Kim Holt
Sylvie Saint-Laurent
Ann de Mooij
Lucy Piper

Acknowledgments

As you read this, be thankful I'm never left to my own devices. Without all the hands and eyes that go into producing a finished book, you'd get dropped words, extra words, dangling participles, plot holes, comical homonyms and characters whose names and features change from page to page.

Thank you to my editor, Katherine V. Forrest, for her insight and expertise, and especially for the confidence she gives me to make each book my own. Thanks also to my two-woman cleanup team—my partner Jenny and longtime friend Karen Appleby. Special kudos to the team at Bella Books, who put on the polish.

The characters in this book are a product of my imagination, as are some of the companies, organizations and venues. The story however was inspired by very real events and circumstances that threaten not only the health of this planet, but the future of our governance.

CHAPTER ONE

So far it was only a few dead fish.

The Gulfstream 280, its tail emblazoned with a blue and green corporate logo intended to convey environmental consciousness, always stirred a sense of awe and self-importance in Cathryn Mack. Travel on the corporate jet was usually reserved for the company brass—vice presidents and chief officers for this and that—but this trip was different. Today she was perhaps the most important person on board.

She'd packed enough business suits and dresses for two weeks in front of the cameras. Plus a few casual outfits for lounging around. Then some yoga wear and assorted lingerie. Cosmetics and vitamins. Four pairs of shoes. And one small, battery-operated tension reliever for the base of her skull. That sometimes doubled as a sex toy. All crammed into two rolling suitcases weighing every bit of forty pounds each.

Juan Merced bounded down the miniature staircase to greet her. He was copilot, cabin steward and baggage handler rolled into one, and she was glad when he relieved her of her load.

"Am I the last one?" she asked. She lived farthest from Houston's executive airport.

"No, we're still waiting for Mr. Bower."

Of course they were. Harold "Hoss" Bower was the CEO of Nations Oil and the rest of the company moved on his schedule.

Cathryn ducked through the doorway and acknowledged her colleagues as she made her way to the back of the ten-passenger executive cabin. All were men. White men. White men with big hats. The oil business in all its clichéd glory.

These men were not really colleagues. As corporate officers, they were superiors in one way or another, including general counsel Gregg O'Connor, the only person on board whose presence rivaled the importance of hers. Over the next two weeks, their combined skills might be worth hundreds of millions of dollars.

While the other executives scrolled through their company-issued smartphones and tablets, Cathryn fired up her laptop. As the company's official spokesperson, she had to read and write press releases without error, and she couldn't do that on a tiny screen, especially one that auto-corrected her thoughts. Her mailbox was brimming already with the pipeline specifications and site information she'd need for the late afternoon press conference already scheduled in Duluth, Minnesota. Her technical assistant, Woody McPherson, was forwarding the available data from George Bush Intercontinental Airport as he awaited a commercial flight. Until he caught up with her tonight, she was on her own.

Hoss's booming voice sounded from the tarmac outside. "Let's get this show on the road!"

As he took his seat in the center of the small cabin, the others swiveled in their leather executive chairs to face him, knowing full well they were in for a wrenching, three-hour business meeting. Cathryn was glad for her position in the last row since she was facing forward. Her stomach had never mastered the art of flying sideways.

Six-foot-five and barrel-shaped, Hoss intimidated most people, even some of the men on the plane, but Cathryn had always found him strangely charming. He'd been up front about why she was promoted from public relations staff to Corporate Communications Director. He liked her long blond hair and youthful looks, and said the press vultures would be more polite to a pretty lady.

Of course, that was eleven years ago when she was thirty-three, and though she still wore her hair long—and kept it blond with a little help—Hoss's prediction that the press would be polite had proven way off the mark. Sure, the financial reporters were fine when she announced robust quarterly earnings, acquisitions and new drilling permits, but crisis communications like today's were different, especially since "the press" no longer meant only newspaper, magazine and TV reporters. Now it included a growing horde of adversarial activists who wrote blogs and newsletters for people who cared a great deal about a few dead fish.

"What's our situation?" he demanded.

Predictably, the executives deferred to Bryce Tucker, Chief Operations Officer and therefore the boss of everyone who should know the answer to Hoss's question. "All we've got so far is a marsh slick covering a little more than an acre. Best guess is that puts us at about ninety thousand gallons."

Nations Oil piped its crude down from Alberta to Hartford, Illinois, where it was loaded onto a barge for transport down the Mississippi River to their refineries in Houston. Today's emergency was a pipeline rupture outside Duluth that had spilled into a lake. Though ninety thousand gallons was a relatively minor event, environmental activist groups would make it out to be a disaster on the scale of Deepwater Horizon in the Gulf or Talmadge Creek in Michigan. Cathryn's job was to mute their efforts with the facts, which weren't nearly so alarming.

"Ninety thousand gallons!" Hoss chortled and slapped the arms of his chair. "Hell, we can mop that up with a few paper towels and be home in time for the ten o'clock news."

"I'm afraid this spill might be bigger than ninety thousand," Cathryn said hesitantly, looking up from her screen to see all eyes turned in her direction. Her mantra for getting ahead in the company was *Don't Make Waves*, but it was clear Bryce Tucker was relying on a rosy report from their local contractor, whose ass was on the line because he was supposed to maintain the pipeline. If these figures from Woody were correct, they could be dealing with a major spill, bordering on catastrophic. "Based on the differential between the two pumping stations, it could be as much as four hundred thousand."

"That's crazy as hell!" Bryce yelled, his face reddening with anger. "Dilbit's so thick it hardly moves when we want it to. It sure as hell ain't going anywhere with the pump shut off."

"Heavy crude," Hoss corrected firmly, scanning the cabin to make certain everyone heard. "Heavy crude, not dilbit."

Dilbit was short for diluted bitumen. Bitumen was tar sands, a thick mixture of sand, clay and water that held dense petroleum deposits, whereas heavy crude had a lower viscosity and flowed more easily. Nations Oil had suffered a rupture two years ago in northern Wyoming, and paid a major fine for transporting dilbit in a pipeline approved only for heavy crude. This pipeline in Minnesota was in the same class, twenty-four inches in diameter and a quarter-inch thick. The company was petitioning the US government for a permit to build the Caliber Pipeline, a stronger conduit for dilbit from Alberta all the way to Houston, but environmental zealots had so far blocked their efforts.

"I certainly hope I'm wrong, Bryce," she said. Crossing Bryce Tucker was never pleasant, but her job was dealing with facts, not temper tantrums. The unfortunate truth was over four hundred thousand gallons of oil were unaccounted for.

Some of that, perhaps even half, could still be sitting safely in the broken pipeline. The sad fact, however, was that the controllers who monitored their pipeline network assumed the alarm had sounded because of a gas bubble. Instead of shutting down the flow, they increased the pressure to push the bubble through, inadvertently spilling even more. There was no telling how much had gone missing, but Woody's latest estimate probably was much closer than Bryce's.

"At least it's a lake and not a river," one of the vice presidents said.

Heads bobbed in agreement. No one wanted to chase crude down a river. By the time the EPA finished with Enbridge, that company's cleanup cost for the dilbit spill in Michigan's Talmadge Creek and Kalamazoo River would top a billion dollars.

Cathryn sent around an information sheet. "Here's what we know about Lake Bunyan. Three hundred twelve acres, stocked with bluegill, trout and largemouth bass. Several dozen species of native birds. Property tax records show ninety-three residential structures fronting the lake—most are probably weekend cabins—one public park with a boat launch and one bait shop. The bait shop owner is the one who reported the spill."

As the jet roared down the runway, Hoss swiveled forward to address Gregg. "I want you to start buying up all that property. Every last one. The sooner we get the locals off our back, the better off we'll be."

Larry Kratke, Bryce's assistant vice president, was already monitoring cleanup operations on his tablet. "We've put three booms in place—two on the lake and one on Van Winkle Creek, which runs out of the southeast corner toward Lake Superior. Two suction dredgers are en route from Grand Forks, ETA about four o'clock this afternoon."

The simplest method for cleaning oil out of standing water was to suction it into a centrifuge and separate it. Once it was spun, the oil was pure, and they could then siphon it into a waiting tanker and return the clean water to the lake. Time was of the essence in cleaning up heavy oil because the diluents would evaporate in a matter of days and the oil would sink to the bottom and mix with the sediment on the lakebed.

"Get two more suction crews and tell them to send in a grab dredger too," Bryce said gruffly. "No, make that two. How many on the repair crew?"

"About twenty."

"Double it. I want them stringing lights and working three shifts. Whatever it takes to get that oil running again."

From Bryce's tone, which was even surlier than usual, he was worried about this spill. So was Hoss, who was staring grimly out the window. If Woody's assessment was correct, they were all in for a long ordeal, much longer than the two weeks she'd planned.

And yet it was hard to complain about anything that took her out of Houston in July.

* * *

"Make a legal U-turn...Make a legal U-turn."

"Knock it off, Marlene. Didn't you see that Detour sign?"

Stacie drummed her fingers on the steering wheel as her smartphone recalculated the route. She'd named the device for her father's second wife, a know-it-all who, unlike her phone, lacked a silent mode.

"In a quarter of a mile, turn right."

"See, I told you."

Only eight miles to Duluth, then another ten to Lake Bunyan, where Israel Kaufmann was already holed up in a vacation cabin waiting for her. It was too early to know what they were sitting on but two things were certain—whichever oil company was responsible for this spill would downplay the damage and then do as little as possible to fix it. That's what BP had done in the Gulf, what Enbridge had done at Talmadge Creek, what Exxon had done in Arkansas and what Nations Oil had done in Wyoming. Why on earth anyone would trust them to build more pipelines was beyond her.

It was a stroke of luck she'd been in Chicago at a green builders conference, since the drive from her home in Pittsburgh would have taken twice as long. Not that she minded her time with Marlene, her only traveling companion ever since an oil company thug snapped the radio antenna off her first-generation Prius. The solitude gave her time to brainstorm strategies for the Clean Energy Action Network, a nationwide organization of activists whose primary mission was to agitate against fossil fuels. They were dedicated and energetic, and she needed to find ways to tap that energy year-round, not just when there was an incident like this one.

To do that, she'd have to take CLEAN to the next level, but something short of corporate. It wouldn't do to have their precious funds eaten up with administrative costs. They'd garnered several friends in high places—congressional representatives and state-level legislators, a few Hollywood types and several technology billionaires, all of whom liked their grassroots approach. What they needed now were more grants, a full-time executive director and professional support staff, and a team of lobbyists to get their message through. She wanted CLEAN to be efficient and effective but without losing its hands-on appeal.

Marlene got her as far as Hermantown before declaring, "*Unknown route*," and Stacie was forced to scroll through Izzy's directions, which she'd tapped into her notes app. Though she detested Marlene at times, it was undeniable the electronic wench had saved a tree or two.

As she drove closer to the lake, the unmistakable smell of petroleum permeated the air. That was typical in the aftermath of a significant spill, but the worst of it usually dissipated within twenty-four hours once the hydrocarbons began to evaporate. This was fresh, as though the oil was still flowing, and that struck her as odd.

When she reached the perimeter road, a Bunyan County Sheriff's patrol car with flashing blue lights was parked in front of a barricade, and a deputy directed all traffic to the left. That told her which part of the lake had been compromised, but it was unthinkable the authorities wouldn't evacuate the entire area soon.

"Second driveway on the right after the *One Lane Bridge* sign," she mumbled to herself from the directions. Shielding her eyes from the late afternoon sun, she crept along until she reached the turnoff. At the end of a dirt drive sat a small rustic cabin, its clapboard siding painted burnt orange and its tin roof dark green. Izzy's car, a white SUV with rusted fenders, was parked next to a small sedan sporting an array of liberal-leaning bumper stickers, and an emblem from the University of Minnesota at Duluth.

No sooner had she climbed out of her car than she was lifted off her feet and twirled around.

"Stacie! I thought you'd never get here."

Izzy was both gentle and burly, like a human teddy bear. For the last eight years they'd been a thorn in the side of energy companies, rallying local communities to demand thorough cleanup and fair compensation in the wake of spills and other disasters. Even more important were their protests against new corporate land leases of public property, drilling or fracking permits, and pipelines. When he wasn't responding to disasters or participating in protests, he loaded produce trucks at his uncle's distribution center north of Minneapolis. This spill was practically in his backyard.

"Who's here? How many are coming? Tell me everything," she said as he grabbed her canvas duffel and sleeping bag from the backseat.

"Jenn's driving overnight from Denver. Ought to be here by lunchtime tomorrow. She put out the call last night and by this morning had gotten ten solid commitments, all from the upper Midwest. And I picked up three more already from the local university this afternoon. They're inside."

"Great, we'll put them through the training seminar tomorrow night and send them out to recruit their friends."

"Faye should be good at that and Ethan can help with messaging. I'm going to try to hide out here at the lake and I want Ricky with me. You'll see why."

The cozy cabin had a kitchen, living space and bathroom on the ground floor with a ladder leading to the sleeping loft. To Stacie's delight, Faye and Ethan were neatly dressed and rather ordinary looking, just the type of people CLEAN needed to interact with the general public and convey seriousness and maturity. She didn't personally care how people looked or what they wore, but it was a fact that the average citizen was turned off by protestors who wore ragged jeans and T-shirts. Clean-cut kids did well going door-to-door or standing outside public buildings with petitions. The third guy, Ricky, was a slightly built young man of Indian descent whose hobby was electronics—remote controlled flying electronics in particular. That could definitely come in handy so close to the spill site.

"Whose place is this?" Stacie asked.

"Belongs to Matt Stevenson—his father, actually. Matt's an attorney here in Duluth. Jenn found him on the donor list and I met with him this morning. He's also agreed to represent us if we get into trouble."

"You mean when we get into trouble." She looked at the newcomers. "They always find something to hassle us about, so I hope you're ready for it."

Izzy went on, "Turns out Matt's a Democratic Party honcho in St. Louis County and his dad is letting us use this place so we can keep an eye on the cleanup. He also hooked us up with a farmhouse rental where everybody can stay."

Their national network included professionals in every state who could spring into action at a moment's notice. They needed only a handful of dedicated activists to launch a movement, and when this episode finally ended, they'd be even stronger for the next one.

Ricky showed off the pantry's provisions. "We stocked up this afternoon. Izzy figures they'll evacuate this end of the lake soon but we'll lay low till they're gone."

Because oil spills were flammable and their vapors highly toxic, it was legitimately necessary to block public access to an incident, and the energy company usually got the FAA to restrict the airspace overhead, arguing that helicopter blades would scatter the surface oil. Conveniently, that also allowed them to manipulate the news narrative since no one was around to dispute it. They typically made each incident sound minor and always professed to have the cleanup well in hand. If Izzy and Ricky were hiding inside the barriers, they could monitor the veracity of those claims. CLEAN's very own bullshit detector.

"Any more news about the spill?"

"About what you'd expect. The pipeline belongs to Nations Oil. They had a press conference at five o'clock and announced the unintended discharge was now under control, the environmental impact minimal and the cleanup already underway."

Stacie rolled her eyes and addressed the newcomers. "Unintended discharge…no shit. As usual, we've got the foxes guarding the henhouse. They like to make it sound like it's all robins and butterflies so everybody will just go on about their business and act like it's no big deal, and then two years later all the fish have three eyes."

Ethan spoke up. "They're calling it a crude spill. Heavy oil."

Izzy explained, "Ethan writes for *The Statesman*. That's the student newspaper at UM-D, so he went to the press conference."

"Outstanding! Jenn has press credentials too. You guys should coordinate your coverage when she gets here tomorrow. Anyone show up from the community to find out what was happening?"

"Just the guy from the bait shop and a couple of his buddies. They're the ones who discovered the spill," Faye replied. "They got interviewed on TV but didn't seem too upset about how this was going to shut down their business for months."

"The lawyers probably got to them already with their usual song and dance about how too much controversy tends to slow down compensation. We'll need to find some angry locals and get them on the record. Jenn's good at that."

Izzy served up bowls of split pea soup cooked over a portable camp stove. "We'll be cooking all our meals this way now that the power's been cut. One little spark in the wrong place and *boom!*"

After dinner they exchanged contact information and Faye asked Izzy, "How are you guys going to charge your phones and laptops without electricity?"

He smiled wryly. "Ricky rigged up a solar panel on the roof that ought to be enough to charge all of our gadgets as long as it doesn't rain. I doubt they'll shut down the cell towers since they need them as much as we do."

"Plus we have these," Ricky said, opening a cooler to reveal a stash of Sterno canisters and batteries in all shapes and sizes.

Stacie was impressed. "I hear the mosquitoes are pretty bad up here in the summertime."

Faye chuckled. "Like birds, only bigger."

"You forget we're all from Minnesota," Izzy said. "Hardy Midwestern stock. We've got plenty of supplies to hold out for a couple of weeks. That ought to give us enough time to find a drop zone where we can sneak things in and out. These woods are pretty good cover, but I won't be surprised if they hire security to patrol them."

Security likely meant Karl Depew, a ruthless son of a bitch who did everything he could to make their lives miserable. His contacts in the oil industry and willingness to break the rules pretty much guaranteed his presence at every incident. Oil companies preferred to work in secret and they weren't shy about making friends who would help them out. Local law enforcement agencies were happy to "partner" with any company willing to pay for overtime and special equipment. And there was always the possibility Depew would involve the Department of Homeland Security, who considered pipeline threats matters of national concern.

This cabin, Stacie thought, could turn out to be CLEAN's best perch ever to monitor excavation of a ruptured pipeline and cleanup. Now it was up to her to find ears for their information, like someone in Washington or in the mainstream media. There was no guarantee the local regulators or law enforcement would listen, not if Nations Oil managed to buy them off.

After sunset, Faye and Ethan took their leave, the latter driving off in Izzy's rust bucket so the cabin would appear vacant once Stacie left in the morning. According to Izzy, the farmhouse Matt Stevenson arranged for them had four bedrooms and two baths. She always pulled rank and claimed a bedroom for herself and Jenn. Sharing a house with others—some of whom were first-timers on the road and had no idea what to expect—was her least favorite part of every campaign. Privacy was at a premium, and after a few days their time at the house would be rife with petty squabbles over bathroom habits or whose turn it was to do what. It was worth it though. They took pride in knowing they were fighting the good fight, and nothing beat the adrenaline rush from the protests and confrontations.

Still, it was getting harder every year to cope with the nomadic lifestyle of an activist. It wasn't just the no-frills accommodations, or even the lack of privacy. What bothered her more after each campaign was returning home and facing the fact that her activism was the only substantive thing in her life. No one wanted a future with someone who ran off at the drop of a hat and poured her whole heart into a quixotic fight against corporate behemoths.

* * *

Cathryn offered the last slice of a pepperoni pizza to her administrative assistant, Amy Hornbeck, and then crushed the box so it would fit in the garbage can under the sink. Since she was a company director, her per diem was twice as much as both her assistants, but the higher-ups on the corporate jet had a blank check for luxury expenses. While the executives had gone out for steak at a fine dining restaurant and were staying at the North Shore Resort fronting Lake Superior, she and her team were relegated to a residential hotel in Hermantown not far from the spill site. Her envy of their extra perks was mitigated by having a whole apartment, not just a hotel room. Since this was shaping up to be an extended road trip, she was sure to appreciate the extra space and homey feel.

Woody gobbled up his slice and washed it down with his second beer. An entry-level petroleum engineer and only three years out of Texas A&M, he hadn't been her first choice for a technical assistant, or even her second or third. He'd made the cut because his father sat on the university's board of trustees with Hoss, leading Cathryn to think he'd rise quickly in the company—but probably not until he started wearing a big hat like the other men.

Amy lounged on the sofa with her bare feet on the coffee table, clearly tired from their long day. Originally from Shreveport, she'd joined Nations Oil six years ago right out of LSU, where she'd majored in business administration. Unlike Woody, she was Cathryn's first choice as assistant communications director, and focused her efforts on the job at hand instead of always plotting her next advancement. White men in big hats notwithstanding, Cathryn expected to make Vice President of Investor Relations when Clifford Blake retired, and Amy would slide easily into the job of spokesperson, especially given that Hoss found her freckles and curly, reddish-brown hair "perky."

Suddenly Amy shuddered and groaned. "I just had a mental image of Bryce Tucker trying to stick a twenty-dollar bill in some poor girl's underwear. That's going to keep me up all night."

Following their press conference, Cathryn had overheard the men making plans to visit a strip club after dinner. "I probably shouldn't have told you guys about that."

"What do you want to bet they write it off on their expense account?" Woody groused.

"Entertainment expenses are perfectly legal," she said. And it helped explain why there were so few women at the top levels of Nations Oil. It was a boys' club through and through, but she was confident she'd break into their circle one of these days.

Amy shuddered again and smacked Woody on the arm. "But it's creepy. Why do you guys do that?"

"What do you mean, 'you guys'? I'm not at the strip club, in case you didn't notice."

"By the way, Woody—and this goes for you too, Amy—Gregg O'Connor reminded everyone today that we need to be extremely careful about communicating sensitive details concerning the spill, including that email you sent this morning about the pumping station differentials. Bryce's engineers were low-balling the estimate at ninety thousand and your numbers blew them away."

"What's so sensitive about that? I only told them how many gallons went missing. Math is math."

"Yes, but you put it in a document. Now it's part of the paper trail and subject to subpoena. If we clean up ninety thousand gallons and it looks like it's all gone, the EPA could make us keep digging." The fact that he might be correct was not part of the corporate equation. "Gregg wants you to write a corrective memo tomorrow, something about how the alarm failure could have been the result of calibration errors, which would also account for the volume discrepancy. That's possible, isn't it?"

He threw up his hands in resignation. "It's possible aliens came down and scooped it up in their flying saucers."

She crossed her arms and eyed him sternly. "Just get the memo out, preferably by eight o'clock in the morning."

Though Cathryn occasionally joined Woody and Amy after work for a beer, she did not otherwise socialize much with any of her co-workers. A modicum of camaraderie was good for teamwork as long as no one lost sight of who was boss, like Woody had just now. The way to remind him was to snap him back like a rubber band.

The rest of her social life was under the radar at work, thanks to a sexual harassment lawsuit against one of the VPs a couple of years ago, after which conversations of a sexual nature were strictly prohibited for everyone. She'd made no secret of being a lesbian and it was common knowledge around the company, but she welcomed the firewall and never talked with her team about personal matters.

She doubted there would be any opportunities for "personal matters" in Duluth. An Internet search for lesbian dance clubs or bars in the area had come up empty. The lesbian community probably consisted of college students and homesteading couples who got together once a month for potluck. Neither of those segments piqued her interest.

Woody slapped his knees and stood, stretching as though he'd just gotten out of bed. "Guess I'll hit the hay. Long day tomorrow."

"Long month is more like it," Amy replied, yawning for exaggerated effect as she followed him to the door.

They were sleeping together, Cathryn suddenly realized. On the one hand, that pleased her immensely since it meant she'd see less of them after work hours. On the other hand, if they were discovered by any of the higher-ups one of them would be fired—likely Amy, since her father didn't serve on a board with Hoss. As their immediate supervisor it was Cathryn's responsibility to remind them of company policy, but that could wait until they got back to Houston. It might run its course by then anyway.

After dead-bolting the door behind them, she leaned against it and folded her arms, wondering how she'd fill her nights in the Land of 10,000 Lakes. She might as well be at the end of the world.

The moment she left New Mexico for the University of Texas, she discovered she was always meant for a cosmopolitan life. Austin wasn't exactly Manhattan, but it was teeming with women who liked women, and also women who liked politics, business and the arts. Her freshman year proved almost too stimulating, and it took the next three years of straight A's to graduate *cum laude*. That was enough to get her an internship at Nations Oil, after which the dominoes fell perfectly. Just one more rung on the corporate ladder and she'd have it all—professionally, that is.

Personally, not so much. She'd been single for four years, ever since Janice left for Maryland after meeting her soulmate in a cooking forum online. Nine years down the drain. There was no good reason to believe long-term relationships would last, so she'd learned to entertain herself with a series of short-term flings.

Janice had left not long after Cathryn's fortieth birthday, and one of those two events caused her hormones to explode. She'd gone through half a dozen such flings in the last three years, thinking herself modern rather than promiscuous. Most of them she'd met on SappHere, a mobile app for her phone that located lesbians nearby. It was simple to use. She could log in and check out the profiles of lesbians within whatever geographic range she set. If anyone looked interesting, she could send a private message inviting that woman to meet for a drink.

Ten years ago, the prospect of online dating was scary but now it was the status quo. SappHere had built-in safeguards, like allowing her to fix her location to a public place instead of her home so strangers wouldn't know where she lived. She used the name Cate and listed her hometown as Artesia, New Mexico, where she had grown up. Her profile photo showed only part of her face. Rarely did she stay logged in for more than a minute or two, usually just long enough to check out who was around.

Though she'd dated a handful of locals in Houston, her preference was women from out of town, especially those who visited regularly on business. They were usually looking for fun, not marriage, and tended to be career women like her. Best of all, they had hotel rooms, which reinforced her sense of anonymity.

Not that any of that mattered here. SappHere was sophisticated and Duluth was not. To prove her theory, she absently tapped her smartphone and was stunned to actually get a hit, a woman who also used the airport as her default location. And not too shabby if the profile pic was less than ten years old. Short black hair, brown eyes, nice smile, and with a slender neck that suggested an athletic frame. If she'd been any cuter, Cathryn would have written her off immediately. The really gorgeous women on SappHere usually turned out to be men trolling for a threesome.

This cutie was Marlene from Pittsburgh. In the time it took Cathryn to scan the sketchy profile, Marlene was gone. Too bad.

Not that it mattered much—tomorrow would be another busy day. She'd scheduled a press update for eleven o'clock with no intention of showing up before a quarter after. It was vital she set the proper tone and establish early that reporters were at her mercy for information.

After straightening her kitchen, she cleared space in her sitting area for her yoga mat and retreated to the bedroom to change into leggings and a tank top. Yoga was her most important ritual of the day, even if only for fifteen minutes right before bed. It calmed her body and cleared her head for sleep.

Fifteen minutes became thirty as she visualized herself at the front of the pressroom. Ninety percent of her job was poise under pressure, and in a situation such as this one, the pressure grew exponentially with every gallon spilled. Confidence, knowledge, poise.

"Namaste." She exhaled slowly to end her session, ready for rest.

CHAPTER TWO

The predawn air was thick with the smell of oil and death, but Stacie was nonetheless surprised when her paddle struck a blackened waterfowl. She collected its corpse in a large specimen bag and stowed it deep within her kayak. It was morbid but also a visceral display of the consequences of the oil company's recklessness.

According to Izzy's rudimentary map she was still a quarter-mile from the spill. That made the growing frequency of floating fish all the more ominous. She didn't know much about the habits of Lake Bunyan's native species but these poor creatures should have been out of the kill zone.

Using binoculars she could make out the yellow boom that stretched for a couple of hundred yards around the cove. It was designed to stop the spread of oil and there probably was another one inside it containing the worst of the spill. Near the bank were two suction dredges, each connected to a centrifuge truck. They looked like giant cement mixers, with outgoing hoses that led to oil tankers.

She scribbled her approximate distance from the boom on the side of a plastic vial and dipped it in the lake. Then she capped it and added it to her rack of water samples. Jenn would magically track down a local chemist to test the contents and give a more reliable assessment of the damage.

Next she lowered Izzy's homemade "bottom feeder," a weighted vial that worked like a scoop as it scraped along the lakebed eight feet below. She was stowing that specimen when a small motorboat started toward her from the area that had been cordoned off by the boom. In the time it took to close the distance she made sure her samples were secure and out of sight.

The husky, bearded operator of the aluminum skiff wore the uniform of Minnesota's Department of Natural Resources. He greeted her with a tip of his cap. "Good morning. You're out early."

Her cover would be blown sky-high if she told him she was bird watching and he asked what kinds of birds she'd seen. She didn't know a loon from a duck.

"I saw on the news last night there was some kind of oil spill. I couldn't believe it was so close. Thought I'd check it out."

"You live here?" His tone was cordial but businesslike, and it occurred to Stacie this was his regular patrol. He was probably suspicious because he didn't know her.

"Just up for the weekend to stay at my friend's cabin. Needed a little time to myself. You know how that is." She was screwed if this interrogation went much further.

"Well, we're closing down the lake for a few days until they can get this mess cleaned up. They say it's not all that bad but the vapors can make some people sick to their stomach. Better to be safe than sorry."

She pasted on a look of disappointment and spun her kayak toward the cabin. "Guess I'll get on back then."

"I can give you a tow. Now that the sun's up, somebody from the sheriff's department will be coming around to clear out all the stragglers. Mandatory evacuation all the way around the lake."

She had little choice but to comply, since he'd already looped a towrope through the grab handle at the front of her kayak. He then tugged her across the murky lake, cutting her loose a few yards from the shore and watching her paddle to the dock. As she dragged the oily kayak to the cabin, she kept her eye on the back porch, hoping Ricky and Izzy had seen her motorboat escort. If they came outside right now, their cover would be blown.

Izzy was just crawling down from the loft when she came in, but Ricky was apparently still asleep. She related the morning's events, including the fact that there was a dead bird in a sack on the back porch. "Natural Resources is already working with the sheriff's department. He said they're sending deputies around to make sure everyone leaves. It might be a good idea for me to go before they have a chance to run my plates." She'd been arrested many times for trespassing and civil disobedience, a fact that would draw unwanted attention to the cabin.

"Too bad you have to hurry but we knew it was a risk for you to go out there."

"It was worth it though. I don't think we're dealing with ordinary crude, Izzy. It looks like bitumen and it's on the bottom of the lake at least a quarter-mile from the boom."

"You're shitting me."

"I shit you not."

"Ethan sent me a copy of their press release last night before I went to sleep," he said. "That pipeline's over forty years old, so it wasn't built for bitumen. I bet it's only a quarter-inch thick."

"Not only that, this spill is bigger than they say it is—a lot bigger. I got oil all over the kayak, and I didn't go anywhere near the cove."

As she packed her belongings, Izzy forwarded the latest note from Jenn containing directions to the farmhouse. "She'll be there by noon. Oh, and make sure Ethan knows there's another press conference at the North Shore Resort at eleven o'clock."

As Stacie pulled out of the long driveway, a sheriff's patrol car with flashing lights slowed to a stop. "We're evacuating on account of the oil spill," the female deputy said. Her yellow-blond hair was pulled back in a tight bun, and her name badge read *Gustafson*.

"Yeah, I heard. I was out on the lake this morning in my kayak and one of the—I guess he was a ranger of some sort—he told me about it. He said I'd better skedaddle so I packed up."

The deputy pointed to the cabin. "Anyone else down there?"

"Just me. Like I told the guy out on the lake, I came up here to get a little time to myself. Guess it's back to the grind."

Skedaddle was right. Lying to the police was probably a felony in Minnesota.

* * *

Cathryn's stomach growled loudly, prompting smiles from the reporters seated in the front row. "Sorry about that. I've been on the phone all morning and never got a chance to eat." That wasn't just hyperbole. Her voice mail had been stacked with inquiries from all over the country. So much for their hopes this would remain a local story.

A smartly dressed woman, middle-aged with graying hair and slightly overweight, stood and waited to be acknowledged. "Colleen Murray, *Star-Tribune*. The background you provided indicates the pipeline in question, known as Thirteen C, was constructed in 1971, and Nations Oil took ownership eight years ago in its acquisition of Pierce Petroleum. Can you tell us if any of the federally mandated inspections have been conducted on Thirteen C since the transfer?"

"As you know, the transport of petroleum products is governed by the Pipeline and Hazardous Materials Safety Administration, the PHMSA. Federal inspections are required every five years, but only where pipelines cross population centers or sensitive environmental areas, such as state and national parks and sanctuaries. Nations Oil strictly adheres to all PHMSA inspection schedules. This particular segment of Thirteen C did not fall under those inspection mandates."

"So it's possible this segment hasn't been inspected since it was built in 1971?"

Cathryn pretended to check her notes. "I don't have a definitive answer to that at this time"—the answer was probably not—"but it's certainly reasonable to assume Nations Oil did its due diligence at the time of purchase and verified the quality of the infrastructure." She looked for another question but Murray refused to yield the floor.

"Can you tell us then what sections of Thirteen C have been inspected, and share with us the results of those inspections?"

"Yes, of course. The pipeline crosses three State Natural Areas—Big Islands, Kohler-Peet Barrens and Sterling Barrens. As a result of federally mandated inspections in those segments, a total of twenty-seven routine repairs were made, many of which were necessitated by improper digging too close to the pipeline by utility companies and private citizens." What she didn't say was Nations Oil had received multiple extensions from PHMSA on repairs for sixty-one other citations for corrosion, faulty seams and weakened welding where leakage was not deemed imminent. "Further questions about federal inspections should be directed to the PHMSA. What's important here is that Nations Oil values the environment—and yes, it values its infrastructure too—enough to maintain the relevant systems far above what the government requires."

Eager to be finished with that line of questioning, Cathryn scanned the room for another hand. A young man stood and cleared his throat. He'd been taking notes feverishly throughout the press conference, a sign she recognized as inexperience. "Ethan Anders, *The Statesman*. In all of your remarks and background, you've consistently used the term 'heavy crude oil' to describe the product involved in this spill.

Can you describe the difference between heavy crude oil and tar sands?"

There was a collective shuffling of papers as reporters checked their notes and handouts.

The last thing she wanted was for any of them to mention "tar sands" in their stories, as it conjured something so thick and sticky it couldn't be removed. "The difference is in viscosity and specific gravity, which is defined by the American Petroleum Institute. The Provincial Oil Field, where this product originated, is designated as heavy oil."

"Isn't the Provincial Field adjacent to the Cold Lake Oil Sands?"

"Yes, like California is adjacent to the Pacific Ocean. One is water, the other is not." She was walking a thin line with her terse response, since dressing down a neophyte might rankle the other reporters, all of whom once had been cubs. "Heavy oil and oil sands are not the same thing. There are strict API guidelines for classification."

"If I may go further, what I'd really like to know is if this oil spill is actually bitumen, irrespective of its designation?"

"The product is heavy oil," she reiterated insistently, despite her recall of Bryce Tucker's reference to dilbit when he exploded upon hearing Woody's ominous projections. Bitumen, like tar sands, was a loaded term thanks to the disasters in Michigan, Arkansas and Wyoming, to say nothing of the controversy surrounding the Caliber Pipeline, which Nations Oil hoped to build through the middle of the Plains States. She needed to be certain it wasn't mistakenly used in stories about this incident, and no wet-behind-the-ears reporter was going to change that. Her press conference, her message. "Once again, it's heavy oil from the Provincial Oil Field."

The next reporters didn't wait to be acknowledged, simultaneously shouting questions about whether bitumen was more dangerous in a spill or more difficult to clean up. Cathryn provided a brief overview of the cleanup procedure, emphasizing again her use of the term "heavy oil," and explained that it was much easier to manage a spill in a confined area than in a running body of water such as Talmadge Creek or the Kalamazoo River. She made no reference to the sewers of Mayflower, Arkansas, which had caught the spill from Exxon's Pegasus Pipeline and carried it all the way to Lake Conway.

"Will you use dispersants?"

"No, dispersants are used only in a very large body of churning water, such as the ocean or a Great Lake. Nations Oil will completely remove all of the spilled product and restore Lake Bunyan to its natural state."

She saved her last question for Gerry Simmonds, of the *Energy Business Report*. He was a familiar face at many of her press conferences, and also a golfing buddy to several Nations Oil executives. "Do you expect this incident to have any significant impact on your stock price?"

It was a perfect setup. "Honestly, Gerry, that isn't our priority right now. I'm sure our stockholders are paying attention to our bottom line, but our main focus is to do the right thing for the people of Lake Bunyan and Bunyan County. Fiduciary concerns always take a backseat to our environmental responsibilities."

The analysts in New York knew enough to ignore that. Like every other corporation in America, Nations Oil's real priorities were always on Wall Street. Nevertheless, their stock price was impacted by their corporate image, something the analysts also understood, and it was imperative they emphasize their environmental stewardship.

"Thank you all for coming. I'll put out an update at five o'clock, and I suppose if any of you show up at the same time tomorrow, we'll do this again," she added with a chuckle. It was always to her advantage to end a press conference on a light note.

"By the same time, do you mean eleven or eleven fifteen?"

"Touché. Let's say I bring doughnuts. Will that make up for me being late today?"

She ducked out the side door and into a conference room, where Hoss, Bryce and Gregg had watched the press conference on closed-circuit TV.

Bryce's face was beet red. "Who the hell is Ethan Anders, and what does he know about dilbit?"

"He said he was with *The Statesman*," Gregg replied. "The only *Statesman* I know is in Austin, and I can't imagine what they're doing all the way up here."

Cathryn had noticed the young man the day before and searched the Internet for his byline. "Don't worry, it's only the student newspaper at the University of Minnesota-Duluth. And to answer your other question, Bryce, judging from his use of the term 'tar sands,' I don't think he knows much at all about dilbit. You know how college campuses are. He's probably read all that propaganda put out by organizations like Greenpeace and…what's that other band of idiots? The Clean Energy Network, or something like that."

"College campuses are nothing but a cesspool," Bryce hissed. "Ought to put fences around them and call them zoos."

Hoss nodded. "Like deep, dark caves where even the dimmest bulb seems bright. How are we doing, Cathryn?"

"Well, it's still mostly a local story. We had twelve reporters last night and only nine today. If we keep our focus on the cleanup, I think we'll be off the front page within a week."

"You see any threats?"

She shrugged noncommittally. "We always have to worry about the crazies showing up. They may not make a lot of sense but they make a lot of noise, and you know how the press likes conflict."

"We need to get Karl Depew up here before it gets out of hand," Bryce said. "That's what we pay him for."

Cathryn didn't recognize the name, but the others obviously did and nodded their agreement.

"Find out what's taking him so long," Hoss said. He then announced his intention to fly immediately to Washington DC with Bryce to meet with Senator Mike Washburn, a personal friend and the ranking member of the Energy and Natural Resources Committee. Washburn was championing the Caliber Pipeline on their behalf and they needed to assure him this spill was minor and under control.

Bryce listed the teams he wanted to remain. Cleanup and repair were in the hands of Larry Kratke, Cathryn was in charge of communications and Depew would handle security. Gregg and his legal team would work from the downtown resort where they had access to conference rooms and upscale amenities that would impress the people whose property they needed to purchase.

Life would be easier once the rest of the executives left town, she thought. It was hard enough to do her job without adding a layer of direct reporting to the brass.

"Give us a minute," Hoss said to Bryce and Gregg, who then picked up their briefcases and left the room. "You know, Cathryn, if you weren't so daggone good at your job, one of us would have to stay here and call the shots. But you've got a good head on your shoulders and I know you'll handle everything they throw at you. Just make sure you go through Larry for all your updates. If you're not sure about something, run it by him. And I'll call you personally every day for your perspective on how things are going."

They'd been pleased with how she handled Woody's slip-up, and she appreciated hearing from Hoss they were confident in her abilities.

He went on, "We need to make sure we're all on the same page. This security fellow, Karl Depew…he knows how to handle a crisis like this one, and he's coming in here to deal with these lunkheaded tree huggers. He plays hardball, and we pay him big bucks to get his hands dirty so none of us have to. I don't want you sullied by anything that might happen up here because we've got plans for you. I'm talking big plans. Once we get this mess behind us, we're gonna see about getting you a brass nameplate for your office door. That'd be your new office on the East End."

It was all she could do to control the urge to dance around the room. The East End of their building was where the vice presidents worked.

* * *

Jenn rolled up to the farmhouse shortly after noon in a dented white minivan. A new vehicle, Stacie observed, at least new to her. The second thing she noticed was Jenn had cut ten inches off her hair and still it was a mass of violent copper curls.

"New wheels?" she asked as they shared a bear hug.

"My VW finally gave up the ghost. Dad and I buried the steering wheel in the backyard. Had a funeral and everything." Her thirty-two-year-old microbus had been handed down from her father, who bought it the year she was born. "This one has character too though. Half the knobs are gone and I found a half-smoked joint under the driver's seat."

Environmental consciousness was more than driving electric cars and hybrids. It also meant saying no to consumerism, using things until they fell apart instead of dumping them in the landfill at the first sign of wear. That was a regular part of their orientation seminar, the one Jenn would give after dinner tonight once all the volunteers had checked in.

At that moment a shaggy-haired young man emerged from the backseat and stretched his arms skyward, baring his belly. "I guess this means we're here."

Jenn tugged him forward and wrapped an arm around his waist. He towered over her small frame by a foot. "This is Marty Wingate. I think I'll keep him."

Marty wore ragged jeans and a faded Che Guevara T-shirt, and his face sported what Stacie called "fashion stubble," four or five days' worth of beard. Thrusting his hand forward, he said, "I've been hearing about you for the last three months. I halfway expected to see magic bracelets and a lasso."

"If anyone is Wonder Woman, it's Jenn," Stacie said. "Whatever we need she finds a way to get it—and cheap too. I tell you, the woman buys more with a hundred bucks than most of us do with a thousand. Better keep an eye on your stuff or she'll trade it for something."

Stacie had often worried Jenn would meet someone and want to settle down at home in Colorado. Her departure would be a crushing blow to CLEAN, and she tried to head it off every year with a five percent raise from the hodgepodge of grants that helped keep their organization afloat. Marty didn't strike her as much of a threat. From what Jenn had shared in her emails, he was a "true believer" too, and that meant CLEAN was getting two for the price of one.

Jenn handed her a milk crate filled with office supplies and the three of them trudged into the house.

"I don't know how you found this place, Jenn, but you really outdid yourself." It had a large living room and dining room on opposite sides of the entry, and a kitchen, bedroom and bath in back. Upstairs were three large bedrooms and a bath. The furnishings were old but not antique, and Jenn would drill into everyone tonight that they were expected to leave it better than they found it.

"I told Marty he might have to sleep with the guys."

Stacie shrugged. "There's plenty of room for all of us." She and Jenn always bunked together, sometimes with a third girl if the room was big enough, and she appreciated that Jenn wouldn't put her in an awkward position by asking her to share a room with a guy. "I staked out the bedroom on the first floor. It's off the kitchen, which is bad, but it has its own bathroom, which is excellent. If you'll let me leave my stuff in there, I don't mind setting up my cot in the dining room. It'll be like having my own room. Just promise I can have the bedroom to myself for an hour a day."

"Right, your yoga session. No problem."

"How many people are staying here?" Marty asked as he went through the kitchen opening cabinets and drawers.

"Counting the three of us, there should be thirteen by dinnertime. The house can easily sleep that many if people remembered to bring a cot," Stacie said. "Most of these folks will stay at least a couple of weeks to get things rolling, maybe even the whole time. We should have a local team up and running by the end of the week."

Jenn tossed her sleeping bag onto the bed. "We've got about thirty more commitments if we need them. I told them to hold off till we get more space."

Though technically there was plenty of room, thirteen was a crowd in a four-bedroom house. If it got too crazy, Stacie would sneak out to a cheap motel for a few nights.

She caught herself smiling. Or maybe she'd follow up with Cate, the woman who was lurking online last night. Finding someone else on SappHere in Duluth had been a delightful surprise. Cate was forty-four years old and her maturity showed in her interests—reading, art galleries and film. Of course, that was what women listed when they wanted to put out a sophisticated image, when their real interests were lying on the couch watching trashy TV. There was no way of knowing if Cate was sincere, but the tiny part of her face she posted in her profile picture suggested it might be worth finding out. Besides, Stacie was looking for a diversion, not a wife.

"Stacie?"

"I'm sorry. What did you say?"

"I said Marty's dad knows a chemistry professor at the University of Colorado. He gave us the name of somebody at Bemidji State we could work with. Izzy said you got some samples."

She presented the vials and described her reconnaissance in the kayak. "I don't care what Nations Oil says this is. I think it's bitumen. I was scooping it up off the bottom of the lake in clumps as thick as peanut butter."

Marty scowled. "Sounds like the same mess they had in Wyoming. What do you want to bet they're still running it through old pipelines built for conventional oil? It's a wonder we don't read about this happening every day."

That was one of the problems but it wasn't the main issue as far as Stacie was concerned. "All that sand and clay is so corrosive it doesn't really matter what kind of pipeline they use. Does anyone honestly expect all two million seams to be perfect? Any pipe's going to wear down eventually, and they never fix their infrastructure until it breaks. They've done the math. It's cheaper to clean up after a rupture and pay a fine than it is to maintain it. But these people don't live along the pipeline so they don't care if the groundwater is contaminated or the soil is ruined for the next millennium."

Jenn added, "That's why we can't let them build the Caliber Pipeline. They want to run it right through the breadbasket of America, and for what? They'll tell us it's about energy independence, but their real plan is to ship it all to China and make a shitload of money for people who already have a shitload of money."

It took very little to get any of them worked up over the politics of the oil industry, and one of these days Stacie would probably have to take medicine for her blood pressure. For now her outlet was protest, whatever she could do to have an impact on public perception and policy. If they could build a nationwide groundswell of opposition, they could kill the Caliber Pipeline once and for all.

* * *

Cathryn propped open the apartment door with her briefcase and ferried four bags of groceries in from her rental car. Basic provisions—cereal and milk, lots of fruit, an assortment of lean frozen dinners and enough diet soda to float a small boat. Just because she had a kitchen didn't mean she wanted to cook.

As a special gift to herself on this momentous day, she'd also picked up an expensive bottle of chardonnay, but couldn't enjoy it until it chilled. All afternoon she'd been on cloud nine replaying Hoss's words in her head. It was thrilling to get definitive confirmation that her hard work and loyalty would be rewarded soon. Nations Oil had only two women on its corporate slate, the vice presidents for human resources and procurement. A jump to that level would mean a six-figure raise plus stock options worth millions. More important, it would speed up her retirement timetable by eight to ten years.

If she were back in Houston she'd call someone to celebrate. But here in Duluth there was no one.

Scratch that. There was Marlene.

Cathryn had checked in on SappHere a couple of times during the day and was grudgingly pleased not to see Marlene online. Women who stayed logged in all the time struck her as desperate. It was too bad, however, that Marlene wasn't around tonight. It could have been fun to kick back and forget about work for a while.

And then her profile appeared.

CHAPTER THREE

It was a longstanding tradition that Stacie and Jenn made dinner for everyone on their first night together, and they'd also invited the locals who had joined their cause. Curried chickpeas with spinach and tomatoes over basmati rice was always a hit, though Stacie wasn't eating with the group. She had plans for dinner with Cate, who had dropped onto SappHere like manna from heaven.

Also tradition was her welcome speech, which she delivered while everyone ate. Since the dining table wasn't large enough to accommodate everyone, they dragged chairs into the living room and balanced food on their laps while she stood in the center of the room.

"I see a few fresh faces here. It always excites me when new people come on board. And I'm especially glad to welcome back John and Rita. Don't hesitate to ask them for help if you can't find Jenn or me."

John and Rita Mauney were in their fifties, both professors at Michigan State University. They'd gotten involved with

CLEAN during the Enbridge disaster at Talmadge Creek, and were personally responsible for bringing in hundreds of allies. Stacie liked the enthusiasm and energy of young people, but mature couples like the Mauneys could gather support among Baby Boomers, who donated money as well as time.

"In the last fifty years, and particularly since Reagan, we've seen a massive shift in our country toward corporate power. Many of our elected leaders no longer work for us. They answer to the industries that fund their campaigns, and they use their power to do the bidding of their corporate masters. At CLEAN, we don't have that kind of money or nearly as many friends in the halls of government. What we have is the power of people, and it just so happens that people control the right of way where Big Oil wants to drill and build its pipelines. If enough of us say no, the money will have to shift to clean energy. That's what we're about."

The room erupted in a raucous cheer.

"Our objective here is to get the people of northern Minnesota behind us. Nations Oil just ruined one of their pristine lakes, possibly forever. We don't have to yell and scream about that. We don't have to set fire to oil tankers or block people from buying gas for their cars. We just need to make them think, and if we tell them the truth about how ruthless and reckless all these oil companies are, they'll want clean energy too."

At any given time, CLEAN's donor list was 700,000 strong. More important, they could turn out a dedicated team of volunteers like this one anywhere in the country at a moment's notice.

"We have a few hard-and-fast rules for how you should conduct yourself while you're here. In this age of ubiquitous surveillance, environmental activists are often likened to terrorists. Corporations and law enforcement work hand in hand to protect their interests, and they're just itching for an excuse to treat us as a security threat. And you know what? We do threaten their security, and for that they want to shut us up and lock us away. We'll be called ecoterrorists and anarchists. We're hippies who get high all day, we have free-love sex with different people every night, and we never, ever bathe. They'll say we have no respect for authority." She paused and cocked her head. "Come to think of it, they might be right about that last one."

A nervous chuckle rattled through the room. Some of these people had no idea what they were up against. If they survived this baptism of fire, they'd take that resolve and leadership back to their communities and grow the clean energy movement even more.

"There is a high likelihood that sometime over the next few weeks you will be arrested. When that happens, you are to be compliant and respectful. Do not hide, do not run, do not resist. We have an attorney here in Duluth who will handle our cases as they arise, and I've given him a very large retainer in case we need to post bail. That's part of Big Oil's intimidation campaign. They want us to get discouraged and quit. We won't."

"Damn right we won't!" Rita said, pumping her fist.

"A few more rules. No alcohol, no drugs and no weapons of any kind. And no touching anyone without permission. No exceptions. There's nothing they'd like more than to catch us doing something illegal, and we can't give it to them. When you're out meeting with the public, there's to be no cursing and no arguing with people who push back. It is vital to our cause that we always make a good impression. If people don't respect us, they won't respect what we have to say."

John leaned over to his wife and said, "Did you hear what she said? No touching me without permission."

They all laughed at Rita, who jabbed him numerous times with her finger.

Stacie continued, "Several of you are newbies, and I know it can be challenging to share space with a lot of people. If any of you were the selfish type, you wouldn't be here, but that doesn't mean we won't get on each other's nerves. I ask you to remember that everyone's personal belongings are sacred. If it isn't yours, don't eat it, drink it, wear it, read it or use it."

"And speaking of drinking," Jenn said. She held up a red plastic bottle with the CLEAN logo on the side. "No bottled water. I have a couple of boxes of these very attractive, BPA-free bottles out in the van. See me if you need one."

Stacie grinned at Ethan as he surreptitiously kicked an empty plastic water bottle beneath his chair. "That's all the hard-and-fast rules. These last couple of things are just guidelines. You don't have to go out there in dresses and neckties but we do want you to be clean and to wear nice clothing that is appropriately modest. No straps showing or see-through tops please, and no jailing britches with your Batman underwear hanging out the top. That's all part of making a good impression. And the last thing is about our food here at the house. People who are really concerned about their carbon footprint don't eat animal products. Jenn can share some of the science with you if you're interested, but the bottom line is we could cool the planet tomorrow just by shutting down the livestock industry. We promise not to beat you if you've just got to have a hot dog, but please don't bring it here to the house."

As the volunteers finished their dinner, Rita and John collected their dishes and ferried them off to the kitchen.

Jenn passed out hefty stacks of CLEAN brochures. "This talks about CLEAN's mission, which Stacie just covered. Anytime you engage someone who wants to know more, put one of these in their hand and make sure you get their name and email address."

"We have a simple strategy at CLEAN for signing up supporters," Stacie said. "We call it Double Every Day. Starting tomorrow, I want each of you to recruit at least one person who will join our fight. I'm not talking just about somebody who'll sign a petition or swear off buying gas from Nations Oil. I'm asking you to recruit one person every day who will come to our rally, who'll help us gather signatures, who'll stand at an intersection with a sign, and most important, who aren't afraid to ask their friends to do the same. You recruit one person. The next day, you both recruit one person. That's four people. The day after that, you have eight. That's how we build our network."

John laughed. "It's like Amway for the environment."

"Right you are," Stacie said. "The first thing I'm going to do tomorrow is get us some office space so we can set up a phone bank. Then I'm going to plan a rally for next Wednesday. We'll get a local band and some guest speakers. Our goal is to tell everyone how important it is for ordinary people to stand up to Big Oil and stop the destruction of our planet. Since your job is to double every day for the next eight days, my job is to find a place that can hold five thousand people. If we can pull that off, I guarantee it'll be the biggest thing to happen in Duluth all summer. When you get that many people to show up for a cause, the press covers it and that makes government pay attention. You will have accomplished a great, great thing."

A turnout that size was unprecedented but the local media hadn't yet framed its coverage. If CLEAN could get them to use words like "disaster" and "tar sands," it could quickly stir up negative reactions, and their efforts to drum up support could snowball.

Stacie thanked everyone and turned the orientation over to Jenn, who was passing out materials for the next day's assignments. By the time she'd showered and dressed, the training session was finished and Jenn entered their bedroom.

"I can't believe you've been here one day and you have a date already."

"What can I say? I'm a social butterfly. It's just dinner."

"Right. Remember that time we went to Sacramento to testify in front of the legislature? You stayed out all night."

Stacie smiled. "I got lucky." She tucked her pink shirt into gray slacks and fluffed her hair. It was a stroke of luck she'd been at the conference in Chicago when news of the spill broke, so she had several dressy outfits to choose from.

Somehow she doubted Cate would go for her usual faded jeans and workboots. "Besides, do you and Marty actually care whether I come home or not?"

"You got me there. But it's going to get really crowded if you bring her back here with all her stuff."

"How many times do we have to go through this, Jenn? The U-Haul happens on the second date. Tonight we'll profess our undying love."

"Silly me."

"But if you never see me again, tell the police it was somebody named Cate with a C."

She slipped out the back door, counting her lucky stars to have found such a great coordinator for CLEAN. Jenn Kilpatrick could handle most anything, including the executive director job if Stacie could just talk her into it. It was time for Stacie to focus her efforts on lobbying and legislation.

Tonight however was about Cate with a C, and her electronic persona, Marlene.

The best thing about SappHere was its spontaneity. There were no rules or channels, no emails or waiting periods. A lesbian was nearby and she wanted to meet now. Stacie rarely used the app at home in Pittsburgh, preferring to meet women the old-fashioned way through friends and parties. Those were potential relationships after all. Dates like Cate were, for lack of a better word, hookups. Most of the time it was for just a drink or dinner, but she wouldn't rule anything out if the chemistry was right.

The parking lot at Cowboy Grill was packed, and country music emanated from the building like a mournful pulse. A restaurant known for steak and ribs wouldn't have been her first choice, or even in her top hundred, since she was vegan, but it would have been rude to accept the invitation and then insist on a different locale. Cate might very well be the only other lesbian in all of Duluth.

At the bar sat a woman who looked a bit like the fragmented profile photo she'd seen on SappHere—except way better. Long blond hair, an angular face and eyes as green as a cat's. Unfortunately she was cozied up to a man.

On second glance, it was the other way around. The woman pointedly looked past him to wave at Stacie. The man turned and checked her out sullenly, and after a few more words, retreated to the other end of the bar.

As Stacie walked closer, her hopes soared for this to be Cate. Tight black dress with a belt of woven silver chains... and stiletto heels. Anyone who wore shoes like that had calves of steel.

"Marlene?"

"Cate! So nice to meet you." *So very nice.* Stacie suddenly felt like a kid at Christmas.

Cate tipped her head toward the man who had just walked away. "If I had to name the worst thing about meeting someone in a bar, it would be that."

Stacie nonchalantly took the glass of red wine from her hand, sipped it and handed it back. "At least he took 'get lost' for an answer."

That quip earned her a truly charming chuckle, one that lit up a dimple on Cate's left cheek. "Let's get a table and I'll buy us another drink."

They were off to a great start if Cate's visible reaction to seeing her was any indication. It was an unavoidable fact that some women wanted a polished femme while others preferred a stronger, athletic type. Stacie defied labels. Truth be told she could pull off any look she wanted but preferred to be herself... or rather, to be Marlene. If Marlene had a label, it would be laid-back, whether decked out in pumps or boots. There was no point in putting on pretenses when the whole purpose of going out in the first place was to relax.

Though some pretense was necessary. Stacie rarely shared her real name, since the Internet was loaded with news articles about her family's river shipping business, which was worth millions. The first hit would be the *Pittsburgh Post-Gazette*'s profile of how she'd fought against her family's business interests by lobbying river commissions throughout the country to impose expensive and stringent conditions on shipments of petroleum products. As Marlene, she could enjoy a woman's company without the specter of Pilardi Shipping.

Nor did she want to talk about what else someone might find in a Google search—her string of arrests. Some women found her passionate activism difficult to comprehend. She likely would find it difficult too if not for the family wealth that made her advocacy possible. CLEAN was her full-time job, as much a business as running a medical practice, consulting firm or even an oil company.

The hostess seated them in a wooden booth, and their waitress, dressed in a denim miniskirt and cowboy boots, delivered an aluminum bucket of peanuts in the shell and hurried off to fetch another glass of red wine.

Cate said, "I hope you're okay with this restaurant. I've never been here before but it looked popular when I drove by this afternoon. It was the only place I could think of to meet."

That explained the cocktail dress and heels, which were better suited to a fine dining establishment. Even Stacie felt a little overdressed for roasted peanuts. "I take it you're not a local. Your profile said New Mexico."

"That's right. And you…you're from Pittsburgh?"

"Born and raised. I'm here to meet up with a bunch of friends, so I didn't know a good meeting spot either. This is fine though. Lively…the people seem friendly enough."

Cate tipped her head toward the bar. "Especially that guy in there who was so eager to introduce himself. So where are you staying?"

"At a farmhouse in Hermantown. Things get really crazy with so many people in the house, so I needed to get out for a while." She hoped Cate grasped the subtext—they couldn't go back to her place if they hit it off. Hitting it off that well would be a nice surprise but it also was fine if all they did was have dinner and chat. "I'm really glad you popped up on SappHere when you did."

"That's what I like about it. It's so spur-of-the-moment. Makes it easy to find someone who's just looking for company and in the mood to go out."

This was the usual routine to set parameters and expectations. Neither was looking for something with strings attached. Dinner, a bit of conversation. Maybe more if their chemistry was right, but not at all a waste of time if it wasn't.

So far Cate was perfect, and Stacie couldn't resist the temptation to know more, even though SappHere discouraged sharing too much information at the first meeting. "So what brings you to Minnesota? July's not that great for ice fishing."

"I'm here to work on a public relations project."

Stacy raised her eyebrows and nodded, trying to convey that she was impressed. She had strong opinions about public relations but doubted seriously that Cate would appreciate hearing them. The entire profession was geared toward controlling people's thoughts and opinions by doling out certain bits of information and withholding others. In her own way, she was in the same line of work, but fancied herself as the antidote to corporate shills who twisted facts to suit their own vested purposes.

"And what about you? Let me guess. You're a model," Cate said, showing off her dimple again.

"That was pretty smooth, but we both know I'd need eight-inch heels to pull that off. The sad fact is I work for a company that handles freight. Really boring stuff." Her position on Pilardi Shipping's board of directors made that a true statement, though it was arguably spun in the sort of public relations manner she detested. Were she laying the groundwork for a relationship, she'd be more forthcoming. This wasn't that.

"Does it strike you as funny that we were the only two lesbians to show up on SappHere and neither of us is from Duluth?" Cate asked.

"I'm sort of glad you turned out to be from somewhere else. It's kind of sad to think about some poor woman being logged on every night in hopes another lesbian would come to town."

Their vivacious waitress returned to take their order—a six-ounce filet for Cate, medium rare, with a house salad.

Stacie pointed to the menu. "Let's see…I'll have the sautéed mushrooms and a baked sweet potato—hold the butter, please."

By the look on Cate's face when the waitress left, she was supremely annoyed. "If you didn't want a steak, why on earth did you say yes when I suggested the Cowboy Grill?"

This part was always prickly when she met a date at a restaurant. She suspected the annoyance was actually embarrassment, since her failure to order an entrée with meat implied disapproval. Nothing could be further from the truth. "To be honest, I just didn't want to say no. I had no idea what other place to suggest, but I knew I'd be able to find something on the menu no matter where we went."

"So I take it you're a vegetarian."

"Vegan, actually. My stomach is very sensitive to animal products." Indeed, it made her sick to know the livestock industry was responsible for up to half of the world's toxic emissions. "What matters to me is the company, and I'm very glad I came. I intend to enjoy my dinner and I hope you'll enjoy yours."

Their first fight.

"But if she brings us a basket of vegan bread, don't expect me to share."

"Somehow I doubt that will happen in this place," Cate said. "And if it does, I won't fight you for it. I try to stay away from carbs."

"That explains how you stay so slim."

"Yes, along with forty minutes every morning on the stair-climber."

Stair-climbers were famous for producing rock-hard butts, and before Stacie knew it, she was visualizing standing behind Cate as her hips alternated up and down in a pulsing rhythm.

"You don't exactly look like a couch potato yourself," Cate said. "What's your regimen like?"

"Yoga. If I don't get at least an hour a day, I'm miserable. But not nearly as miserable as the people around me. It probably isn't healthy to need something so much, but if I miss two days in a row I get so wound up I can't function. And it isn't just my body that suffers. It's my brain more than anything."

"I know exactly what you mean. I do yoga every night too, usually before bed but sometimes right when I get home from work if I've had a hard day. I feel like I'm putting myself back in order, the same way I straighten my desk before I leave work or clean up my kitchen after dinner."

Stacie nodded. "I like the way you put that. My life gets really out of control sometimes. Maybe that's because I always focus on the big picture instead of noticing all the little pieces that go into it. I'm going to try thinking of it as putting myself back together and see what happens."

"Maybe we should swap techniques. I could use a big picture perspective."

Yoga was a safe topic, one with the potential to reveal what a person was like without all the superficial details about work, family and interests. "How's this for technique? One of my old girlfriends talked me into trying naked yoga once. She found it far more amazing than I did. I realized Gravity was female, and she's a bitch."

Cate laughed and even blushed a little. "I've done Hatha, Iyengar and even hot yoga, but I've never tried any of it naked. The most adventurous I ever got was when I went with my mom to the Painted Desert. She went off on a hiking trail and I rolled out my mat on the roof of her car. It was surreal, like floating on a cloud."

Stacie liked the idea of sharing a yoga routine with Cate as they both let go of their day. Maybe naked yoga wasn't such a bad idea after all.

This wasn't typical of the conversations she usually had with her SappHere dates. More often than not they warmed up by sharing their experiences with blind dating, all the while trying to get a feel for whether this meeting would lead to another or end up in the dud pile. Such a cursory approach didn't lend itself to really getting to know someone, but that wasn't necessarily her objective anyway. Tonight she was Marlene, a woman from Pittsburgh with a sketchy life and no past to speak of.

It was thoroughly against Stacie's rules to probe for personal details, but Cate intrigued her more than most. Throughout dinner they exchanged the particulars of their respective yoga routines, describing the physical and often spiritual sensations they sought. By the time they finished their meal, her sense of kinship with Cate was stronger than what she usually felt on a first date.

Stacie stretched across the table for Cate's hand. "I can't believe we talked all through dinner without either one of us checking our phone or looking at our watch. I don't think that's ever happened before on a SappHere date. You're pretty damned charming."

Cate grinned and lunged for the check. "And you're a pretty cheap date. We should do this again."

"How long are you in town?"

"Depends on how long my project lasts. At least a couple of weeks, maybe as long as a month. You?"

"Same," Stacie replied, flashing her most suggestive look. Nothing ever justified an oil spill but this one had brought her to town at just the right time. If she could manage to stay out of jail, these next few weeks could be a lot of fun.

Cate walked with her across the parking lot, the very picture of poise in those towering heels. She said, "I don't really know my work schedule yet, but I could drop you a note when I get some free time."

"Sounds like a plan. Just do me a favor in the meantime. Stay off SappHere. I don't want some lonely Nordic lesbian snatching you up."

"I will if you will." That dimple again.

Standing next to her Prius, they were shielded from view of the restaurant by a pickup truck sporting monster tires. Stacie tugged her close and snaked an arm around her neck. "I sure hope you like kissing."

Slick lips slid confidently, as though they'd known each other for years. So decadent was their kiss Stacie barely recognized Marlene's persistent announcement. "*Text message from Jenn…text message from Jenn.*"

"Dammit! I thought I turned that off."

"I hope Jenn isn't your girlfriend. That would be bad news."

Stacie silenced her phone and tossed it into the car. "Even worse for Marty, since he's her boyfriend. She probably wants me to pick up something on my way home."

"I should probably be going anyway. Early day tomorrow."

"Me too." She fingered the chain of Cate's silver belt, imagining how easy it would be to slip her out of that dress. "But let's not let early days ruin our fun. Two weeks goes by in the blink of an eye. We can catch up on our sleep later."

Cate kissed her forehead and stepped back until only their fingers touched. "In that case, I'll use tonight to rest up." Then she turned and walked to her car, her calves rippling with every step.

Stacie wanted to feel those legs around her waist, and she had a pretty good idea Cate wanted that too.

She started the car, and as an afterthought, checked the message from Jenn. "*Ethan Anders arrested. War has begun.*"

CHAPTER FOUR

Cathryn stepped out of the shower and took notice of her nude figure in the full-length mirror on the back of the door. High breasts, trim waist and good muscle tone. Not bad for forty-four.

If she could sneak out of the hotel after the morning press conference, perhaps Marlene would meet her for lunch. She'd proven to be more than her profile promised. Her tiny photo had been cropped from an outdoor snapshot, but in normal light her features were much softer. Obviously Italian heritage, with creamy olive skin and wide brown eyes. Long eyelashes and perfectly sculpted brows that stood out without even a hint of makeup.

Such a find was frankly rare on SappHere.

A loud pounding on the door startled her, and grew more insistent as she hurriedly dried off and pulled the flimsy hotel robe around her. If it turned out to be Woody or Amy, the building had better be on fire.

She opened the door to a man of about fifty wearing boots and denim, and enough cheap cologne to choke a horse. His scowl immediately turned to one of the slimiest leers she'd ever seen, and she regretted not taking the time to get dressed.

He tipped his brown leather fedora to reveal sweaty gray hair matted to his head. "Well, well. Hoss sure likes 'em pretty. I'll give him that."

"Who the hell are you?"

He hitched his thumbs in his belt buckle and rocked back on his heels. "Most people call me Mr. Depew, but you can call me Karl."

So this was the man Hoss and Bryce had hired to handle the "dirty work." He certainly looked dirty enough, with his mud-smeared clothes. Clearly he'd been out to the spill site this morning.

"Why are you pounding on my door at seven o'clock in the morning? Is there something that can't wait until I get to the hotel at eight thirty?"

"Why yes, there is," he said, his voice dripping with faux politeness. "In the first place, we aren't meeting at that fancy hotel downtown anymore. And in the second place, if you wait till eight thirty, you'll miss the meeting that starts in fifteen minutes over at the clubhouse."

"The clubhouse?"

He pointed toward the check-in office. "Where they serve that slop they call breakfast. We've bought up all the rooms in this here hotel so it's ours. Fifteen minutes."

Cathryn normally didn't make snap judgments but she was pretty sure she hated this guy. And she also was sure Hoss meant for her to keep her distance from his dealings. "I'm not exactly sure why you're telling me about this meeting, Mr. Depew—"

"Karl."

"My job is to handle the press and to coordinate information with the operations and legal teams. Your job, I presume, is to manage security. Am I right?"

He nodded once. "Among other things."

"To the degree security is relevant to press relations, you may liaise with my technical assistant, Woody McPherson. He's two doors down, and if he has any questions, have him call me."

She then closed the door and flipped the security bolt.

With a shudder, she returned to her bedroom. After that encounter, she needed another shower.

* * *

Ethan appeared on the other side of a secure glass door and shook his personal belongings from an envelope. He looked frazzled, as though he hadn't slept all night.

"Are you okay?" Stacie asked. She and their lawyer, Matt Stevenson, had been waiting since six a.m. for a magistrate to set bail. It was a relatively minor offense—a sheriff's deputy claimed he smelled marijuana during a routine traffic stop—but some jurisdictions were stricter than others.

"I guess. A little freaked out maybe."

"The first time is always tough." It was hard to ask kids barely out of high school to put their futures on the line by taking a stand. "After that you realize it's a badge of honor."

Matt led the way to his car, where Ethan slumped wearily into the backseat. "Ethan, I don't usually ask my clients questions like this but it's very important I know the truth. Were you smoking marijuana?"

"No! I tried it a few times back in high school, but not since I started college. And even if I did, I'm not stupid enough to smoke it in my car."

Stacie had been arrested once for public drunkenness when a cop at a protest site claimed he smelled alcohol, but she shot it down quickly by calling an attorney to the scene who insisted on a Breathalyzer. Fighting a marijuana charge was a little more complicated, but the idea was the same. "They have no proof so it's just your word against his."

Ethan looked ready to burst into tears. "So basically I'm screwed."

"Don't worry. Matt's going to take you to a lab right now for blood and urine samples. If they come back clean the charges will be dropped. Believe me, this kind of crap happens to us all the time. Your questions at the press conference about tar sands must have struck a nerve. This is classic Big Oil and I bet I know who's behind it. His name's Karl Depew, or as I like to call him, Asshole for Hire. He makes a few contacts with the local authorities and gets them to hassle us so we'll feel intimidated and back off."

Ethan choked out a hollow laugh. "It's working. How am I ever supposed to get a job with a drug bust on my record?"

"Once they drop the charges, the arrest record goes away," Matt said calmly. "This'll be over by the end of the week."

"And that's when we push back, Ethan," Stacie said, turning in her seat to face him. "From now on we travel in pairs, and we record everything that happens and upload anything outrageous to the Internet immediately. We need to get this out there in the press so the public will know what these people are up to."

He looked at her incredulously. "You expect me to write about this?"

"Absolutely. We have to compile a public record. Call it something like 'My Bogus Arrest by the Bullies of Big Oil.' You'll be a hero, a crusading journalist. That's not a black mark on your résumé, it's a gold star. And keep going to their press conferences and asking hard questions. Show them what you're made of."

Matt dropped her at his office where she picked up her car. He'd scored her a critical meeting with a county commissioner who could help them navigate the local ordinances and secure permits for their big rally next week. It was getting harder every year to find officials who were willing to cooperate—not because CLEAN's environmental cause or strategy was unpopular, but because Big Oil had spread its largesse up and down the geographical corridors they wanted to control, funding political campaigns for those who would go to bat for them against the public interest.

Americans had somehow slept through the corporate coup and were only now waking up to its aftermath. CLEAN had all the facts on its side but winning the hearts and minds of the public wasn't simply a matter of education. It was convincing them to care at all.

* * *

"Yes, I understand," Cathryn said solemnly, fighting the urge to throw her phone across her apartment. Bryce Tucker's administrative assistant had called to clarify the chain of command at Lake Bunyan. Gregg and his legal team would continue operating independently out of the downtown hotel, but her department was to liaise with Karl Depew.

Don't Make Waves.

Depew was a major horse's ass. He'd already made her dealings with the press more difficult by moving all operations to the command center, a large gravel clearing near the barricades for the road going into Lake Bunyan. It was too difficult to provide security when they were scattered all over the county, he said, so instead of holding her press conferences in a comfortable hotel meeting room, they now would have them outside her portable office building in a parking lot. No microphone, no podium, no water glass.

Already today she'd scratched up her best heels, the ones that looked so great the night before with her black dress.

Making the press drive all the way out to Lake Bunyan would only antagonize them, she'd argued. That was the point, Depew said. If it got to be too much trouble, they'd drop the story and go back to writing about potholes and firemen plucking kittens out of trees.

Even his cantankerous disposition wasn't the worst part of her day. Before her five o'clock press conference, Woody had handed her a revised edition of the press release that included what she believed to be two blatant lies from their operations team. It claimed the spill had been measured as ninety thousand gallons and that cleanup efforts were already forty percent complete.

Woody then explained that "cleaned up" meant different things to different people, to which she'd snapped, "And does 'gallon' mean something else too?" His only response was a sheepish shrug. They both knew the spill was at least three times bigger.

She fully understood the company's need to portray the situation in its most positive light, but anything she said from the podium or put out in a press release that could be refuted would damage their credibility, hers in particular since she stood on the firing line every day. It was why Depew was taking such extraordinary measures to control access to the site. Though the sheriff's department had evacuated cabins around the lake and blockaded the only road in or out, that wasn't enough to satisfy Depew, whose security forces patrolled the woods at all hours to escort trespassers from within the perimeter. The last thing they needed was a curiosity seeker being asphyxiated by noxious fumes. It was bad enough having to take the heat for an oil spill. Cathryn couldn't bear the thought of being responsible for someone's death.

The sound of a fist on her door made her jump, and she knew immediately whose fist it was. Why couldn't Depew knock with his knuckles like normal people?

He'd cleaned himself up, only in that the mud was gone. Different jeans and a white shirt. Same obnoxious cologne and lecherous grin. "I think we may have gotten off on the wrong foot this morning. How about we go grab some dinner? I drove by the Cowboy Grill just down the road. I hear they cook a mean porterhouse."

Surely that was a coincidence. He couldn't possibly have known about her dinner last night, since he and his team arrived by charter jet just before midnight. "I've already eaten."

"Then how about you come along and watch me eat? I'll buy you one of them sassy pink drinks with an umbrella."

As he leaned closer, she caught the unmistakable odor of scotch whiskey, a smell from her childhood that to this day made her want to run away. As coolly as she could, she stepped back and said, "I already have plans for the evening. I didn't pack the right things and I have to do some shopping before tomorrow."

Deciding not to entertain his fantasies a moment longer, she closed the door in his face. It was true she needed new clothes, since a trailer in the woods was no place for silk and heels. If a trip to the mall got her away from that drunken ogre, so much the better.

* * *

Stacie sat outside the curtained dressing room on a bench. "I have to say, this is possibly the most unusual second date I've ever had on SappHere."

Cate stepped out to model skinny jeans in indigo with a slim-fit yellow shirt. "Is this me?"

"Hell, yeah." It pleased her that Cate hadn't gone for the embroidered pockets and floral tops. A woman that pretty didn't need excessive decorations.

They returned to the racks, where Cate selected the same jeans in black, green and faded blue along with several similar shirts in a variety of colors. "I hate shopping, especially when I need something."

"And that begs the question…"

"Don't even get me started. Let's go have a drink." Something was clearly bothering her.

Stacie's day had been trying as well. By late afternoon she'd been back at the sheriff's office filing a report with one of her volunteers, who had discovered four slashed tires and a cracked windshield on her car after collecting signatures against the Caliber Pipeline at a supermarket. Starting tomorrow, they'd do drop-offs and pick-ups instead of leaving their vehicles unguarded. She had rented a car so Marty could drive her Prius to Bemidji with the water samples.

They found two barstools at Boomer's, a bar and grill beside the mall that was decorated with license plates from all over the country. As they sipped coffee with shots of Kahlúa, she expected to see Cate's mood improve, but it didn't.

"You want to talk about it?"

"Just a tough day at work. They brought in this new guy, and besides being an asshole, he's been hitting on me all day."

"Hostile work environment. Look it up. It's against the law."

Cate shook her head dismissively. "I know all that, but he's not an employee. He's a subcontractor and he's been given a lot of authority."

"It's still against the law." That explained her sudden interest in dressing down, though she probably had no idea the jeans made her look even sexier. "Does he know you're gay?"

"My company does, but like I said, he's a subcontractor. I have a feeling that would only make it worse. What I need is a way to shut him down without putting my job in jeopardy."

Stacie felt a wave of righteous anger, the same sort that welled up against polluters and profiteers who took advantage of the powerless. "What you need tonight is to relax. I know that may sound condescending, but it's all I have to offer. If you'll let me help, you can wake up tomorrow feeling like your own boss." She slid two bills under her half-full shot glass. "And you can start tonight by simply saying yes or no."

* * *

Cathryn checked her rearview mirror for the small sedan as she pulled into the hotel complex. Marlene drove on by as planned, intent on returning after several minutes, a precaution by Cathryn to keep her co-workers from knowing she was entertaining a visitor. It was nauseating to imagine Karl Depew salivating over a twisted fantasy with his nasty scotch breath and choking cologne.

There were risks in bringing a virtual stranger to a hotel where she'd be staying for a while, but they had little choice since Marlene was staying with friends. She never brought new dates to her townhouse in Houston, preferring to meet up with women whose profiles indicated they were from out of town. A sterile hotel room severed their connection when they checked out.

SappHere gave its users several avenues for anonymity, but by tapping credit cards every month, it knew its customers' true identities in case there were complaints. Her main concern—and probably everyone else's too—wasn't her personal security. She worried most about hooking up with someone, deciding they weren't a good match and then not being able to shake her. She seriously doubted that would be the case with Marlene, but even if it was, she had the luxury of knowing she wouldn't be in Minnesota for long.

She was pleased to find the parking lot filled with cars but not people. Depew was probably passed out and his security team catching up on their sleep after pulling an all-nighter. Nonetheless she'd already insisted Marlene leave before morning to avoid being seen.

Marlene said she understood. Like Cathryn, she had no trouble sloughing off questions about a late night, but that didn't mean she was an open book. Her friends respected her privacy, she said, and knew not to pry.

Cathryn spent her few minutes alone freshening up. She was calming herself with deep breathing when knuckles rapped softly at her door. "Finally, someone who knows the proper way to knock."

Her eyes hurriedly swept the parking lot as she ushered Marlene inside. With a shudder, she realized her libido had outmaneuvered her common sense. It would be a disaster if Marlene were discovered in her room and gossip traveled up the corporate chain to Hoss Bower or any of the officers. In the wake of their sexual harassment suit, they were hypersensitive and would question her judgment about bringing home a woman she'd just met.

"Look, Marlene…I think I've made a mistake about having you come here."

"Okay, it's no problem. But can I ask why?"

"I just got paranoid all of a sudden about somebody seeing us."

Marlene chuckled and shook her head. "Guess we should have gone to a motel. Oh, wait. We did."

The sound of footsteps on the walkway outside and men laughing heightened Cathryn's fears.

"Looks like I'm going to have to stick around for a while," Marlene said. "If it makes you feel better, I parked around back by the Dumpster and didn't see a soul on my way in here."

That was reassuring. It was clear the guys were still up and around doing who knows what, and there was no way Marlene could leave now.

"As for this being a mistake," Marlene went on, "I distinctly remember that we came here so you could relax. I can see you're wound up and that can't be good for you. Let's just turn out all the lights and sit on the couch."

Cathryn appreciated the concern, not only for her state of agitation but also for her predicament. Another woman might have stormed out in frustration, not caring about the consequences. With Marlene's help, passersby would think she'd gone to bed.

"You want a glass of wine or something? I have some chardonnay in the fridge."

"Nah, half a shot of Kahlúa should do me. I doubt the sheriff's department around here has enough to keep them busy. They probably pull over everybody who's out driving after midnight just out of sheer boredom." She sat at the end of the couch and patted the space next to her. "Come put your head in my lap."

Tentative at first, Cathryn felt the tension start to leave her body the moment Marlene's hands wound through her hair to massage the back of her neck.

"Now here's our cover story if you need it," Marlene said, her voice low and even in keeping with her soothing demeanor. "I'm an old friend. We met in college at..."

"The University of Texas."

"I was in St. Paul visiting friends and learned you were in Duluth on business. Since we don't get many chances to see each other, I drove up so we could spend some time together. Does that work for you?"

"Mmm...perfectly." In fact, it worked so well Cathryn realized she could even pass her off as an old girlfriend, which would dispel the stigma over picking up a stranger. "I like that scenario quite a bit."

While one of Marlene's hands kneaded the knotted mass of muscles at the base of her skull, the other trailed slowly across her collarbone and down to her chest.

"And I like what you're doing too."

"Shush and let me relax you."

She concentrated on Marlene's fingertip massage, paying special attention to those moments her fingers wandered into the hollow of her breasts.

"If I do anything that makes you tense, just put your hand on mine and I'll stop. It's all about making you feel good."

Marlene released her buttons one by one and slid her hand across every inch of her torso except her breasts. They absolutely ached for attention, so much that Cathryn reached beneath herself and unhooked her bra.

"Very soft," Marlene murmured, tenderly stroking the outside of her breasts with the back of her fingers. "I bet you could relax even more if we got some of these clothes out of the way."

Cathryn discarded her shirt and bra, and returned to Marlene's lap. The comfort of darkness emboldened her to offer up her body.

Marlene took her sweet time, stroking and kneading, pinching and tugging, until Cathryn was ready to scream.

"Try to relax. Let it come to you. I promise I won't leave you like this."

She stilled her rolling body and focused again on Marlene's fingertips as they methodically painted a trail of goose bumps, which she then calmed with a warm, flattened palm. It was only when Cathryn completely stilled that she felt those fingers work the snap and zipper on her pants, and then slide inside to cup her warmth through her satin thong. For a moment she was self-conscious of how wet she was but then Marlene moaned her approval. It was all she could do not to thrust herself upward.

At Marlene's urging, she kicked off the rest of her clothes and relaxed again under the tantalizing onslaught, opening her legs to signal her want.

Marlene soon finished her scintillating ritual, apparently satisfied she was ready. Her hand swept through the slickness, catching her hypersensitive pearl with each upward stroke.

Cathryn fought the instinct to tighten her hips and force herself to come, placing all her faith in Marlene's promise not to leave her there. But when her climax started deep inside, she feared it might flee without help and arched upward to prolong the sensation.

"That's it. You can let it go now."

Reading perfectly the instant she peaked, Marlene lowered her fingers to a less sensitive spot, but continued applying pressure until Cathryn could stand it no more and covered her hand.

After a minute of rest to catch her breath and allow the pulsing to wane, she stood and pulled Marlene toward the bedroom. "I've just noticed only one of us is naked."

CHAPTER FIVE

The storefront had display windows on each side of the front door, perfect for posters and photos that would catch the eye of passersby. CLEAN had plenty of visual proof the spills in Michigan, Arkansas and Wyoming were devastating, but none yet on Lake Bunyan. Not that they'd post them, since photos of the spoiled lake would alert Nations Oil about how close they were to the spill. It was too soon to do that.

A telephone company technician had already wired their new office space for a dozen landlines, and carpenters worked to assemble the last row of phone carrels where the activists could work. Both the store and equipment were rented at premium rates for thirty days with an option for thirty more.

"Great space, Stacie," Jenn said. "And a break room in the back. Think we can afford a refrigerator too? It saves us a lot on eating out."

"Sure. Find one and have it delivered. And a coffeemaker too." It was vital they get their phone campaign up and running. Matt Stevenson had shared his list of Democratic voters in the district, since after the local college students, Democrats and members of the Green Party were CLEAN's most likely supporters, and there were lots of them around Duluth and Bunyan County. "How are we doing on numbers?"

"Not bad for just four days. Matt was right about the people. Everyone's really friendly, and they're responding well to our information. I already had to order more brochures."

Volunteers were claiming the carrels as soon as the carpenters got them assembled, and within minutes they started dialing through their lists to invite people to CLEAN's rally next week in Chester Park. Thanks to news coverage of the spill, most people were aware of the incident.

John Mauney waved her over to his corner. "Hey, Stacie, I just talked to a guy who said he read Ethan's story this morning about all the harassment, and it made him really mad. He runs an auto-body shop and offered to fix Heather's broken windshield for free."

"Awesome! Tell him we're saving his whole family front row seats for the band next week." That was exactly the reaction she was hoping for from Ethan's story, which had been picked up on the wire last night by the state's major newspapers. People needed to see how far Big Oil was willing to go to get its way.

Jenn worked with one of the volunteers to erect a pair of partitions that effectively walled off an area for a private office. Extra brochures and sign-making materials were stacked in one corner behind a worktable that would serve as her desk. She handed Stacie a key. "No doors on our office, but here's the other key to the file cabinet. I'll keep our petitions and local volunteer lists locked up, and if we have to run out during the day we can keep our laptops in here too."

Their electronics were password-protected, but for added security they kept their donor list in a secure cloud file. No one but she and Jenn had access.

"Where's Marty?"

"Cleaning out the break room. I like being tough and independent, but it's really nice to have a guy around who'll pick up dead bugs."

"Good to know he's making himself useful." Though she said it tongue-in-cheek, she'd noticed Marty hanging back the day before when they were gathering signatures at the mall for their petition to stop the Caliber Pipeline, and it also was apparent he had no interest in working the phones. He was helpful when it came to heavy lifting and running errands, but Stacie now considered him only a tepid activist for their cause.

His lack of enthusiasm for CLEAN worried her for other reasons. If his heart wasn't in what they were doing, he might someday grow impatient at having Jenn run off every time they had an oil spill or protest. As much as Stacie needed Jenn—and that would be even more if they ramped up their activities—she couldn't ask her to give up a life with someone she loved.

* * *

Cathryn pulled into the gravel lot by the press trailer, pleased to note Woody and Amy were already inside. For everyone on the communications team, the day was already off to an inauspicious start.

As she locked her car, she checked her reflection in the window. In three short days, she'd grown accustomed to dressing down for work, though the ankle boots and blazer made her look more like a TV street detective than a corporate spokesperson. At least she wouldn't ruin any more heels. Since the cameras usually focused only above the waist, she could dress up her look with scarves and jewelry without worrying about her jeans. For today's press conference, she might also need a whip and a chair.

Amy leapt from her desk the moment she walked in. "Cathryn, we have a situation."

"I know all about it. As far as I can tell, it's only in the local papers and the papers in Minneapolis and St. Paul, but it's juicy enough to get picked up on the wires."

The original story had broken last night from Ethan Anders, the young reporter from the local college. Though Cathryn wanted to believe there was nothing linking Nations Oil to accusations of harassment and intimidation, the claims were piling up at an alarming rate that couldn't be a coincidence, especially given Hoss's characterization of Depew as someone willing to get his hands dirty. A bogus marijuana arrest, slashed tires, a broken windshield and loitering citations for those who were gathering signatures on their petitions to block the Caliber Pipeline.

She asked Woody point-blank, "Is Depew doing this? Don't lie to me."

He too had taken to wearing jeans to work, but still managed to look crisp in his buttoned-down shirt and tie. "He doesn't share a lot of details at the briefings, just reminds all of us to keep up with our cell phones and laptops, and not to leave any documents lying around. What's really creepy is how his security team stands around us in a circle in those tight black T-shirts that show off their muscles. They look like those phony wrestlers on TV. Oh, and they wear sunglasses inside. Cool, huh? It wouldn't surprise me at all if they were out there roughing people up."

"To what end?" This could only mean the corporate brass didn't have confidence in her ability to handle a hostile press. "It's just going to make our job that much harder. Please tell me there's good news in the operations briefing."

"Not too bad, actually." Amy handed her a document. "Cleanup continues…pipeline repairs expected to be complete by the first of next week. You might get some grief over why it isn't the other way around."

It was their job to anticipate such questions and prepare the answers in advance. The straight fact was Nations Oil was losing eight million dollars every day the pipeline was down because they didn't have enough trucks to transport the oil overland from the main pumping station in International Falls to the port in Illinois. Fixing the pipeline would stop the bleeding, whereas the oil in Lake Bunyan wasn't going anywhere.

Cathryn slid into her chair and launched immediately into preparing her notes for the midday press conference. One of the skills that made her indispensable to Nations Oil was her ability to sort out solutions quickly. She spoke her words as she typed, "Our number one priority is to make absolutely certain no more product is released. To do that our engineers must excavate and redirect that which is sitting in sections of the pipeline already compromised. It would be irresponsible to divert our resources from this imperative."

As a team, they hammered out her talking points, leaving until last the accusations reported in the newspaper.

"I had a beer the other night with one of Depew's guys," Woody said. "You want me to chat him up and see if I can find out anything?"

The idea that Nations Oil might be behind these incidents—and perhaps even working in cahoots with local law enforcement to harass reporters and activists—was disturbing. Hoss would never approve something so outrageous but she couldn't say the same for Depew, who seemed capable of anything. Whatever he was up to, Hoss wanted her clean and she intended to stay that way.

"No. If Depew's behind this, I don't want to know—and I don't want you to know either. Stay as far away from it as you can get." It was hard enough to stand in front of a room and spin away unfavorable facts. She didn't want to be forced to lie about unethical—or worse, criminal—actions. Hoss had given her plausible deniability and she was going to take it.

* * *

Stacie peered over Jenn's shoulder at the images on her laptop while holding the phone to her ear. "This is phenomenal, Izzy. You've outdone yourself this time."

"Don't thank me. That's Ricky's drone. We noticed all week there weren't many guards around early in the morning, like between six thirty and eight. We figured they must have a daily meeting at that time or something, so that's usually when we try to slip out and take a look around. When we heard them out on the lake this morning we knew they were up to something."

There was barely enough daylight for video but the images were unmistakable. Hundreds of dead fish and birds were floating atop the lake, and a dozen motorboats were working in teams to drag nets across the surface.

"I can't believe you got the drone this close without anyone seeing you."

"It flies pretty high up and you can see how they're all staring down at the water. The boat motors must have covered up the sound. It was perfect. Have you gotten to the end yet? You're not going to believe what happens."

They watched with revulsion as the carcasses were offloaded into a dump truck and then carted to a deep hole near the excavation site, where they were promptly covered with dirt. A small portion—hardly enough to fill a bushel basket—was placed in the bed of a pickup truck belonging to the Department of Natural Resources. Stacie was willing to bet that would be the "official count" of wildlife lost to the spill.

"Bastards," Jenn muttered. "That lake is dead."

"You guys did good," Stacie said. "Have you found a drop zone yet?"

Izzy described a culvert on Lake Bunyan Road, the road that encircled the lake. It marked the perimeter of the area the guards were patrolling. "If you look on the map, there's access through the woods from State Road 194. Just don't come at night. These guys use night vision goggles, which means they can see you but you can't see them."

She made a list of things they needed—fresh fruit and vegetables, bread and nuts, more Sterno. Otherwise they were fine. When she hung up the phone, she twirled one of the DVDs Jenn had burned with the incriminating video. "We need to get this on the six o'clock news."

"Not so fast," Jenn said. "It's Friday. The news cycle all but shuts down for the weekend, and it won't get much play. We need to save it until Monday, and between now and then we'll get their spokesperson and the Department of Natural

Resources on record describing the impact on fish and birds. I can't wait to catch them in that lie."

"Brilliant. Let's hope it goes viral." It was classic "gotcha" journalism, exposing the company's outrageous lies in dramatic fashion so the news audience would treat all their subsequent pronouncements with skepticism.

"This'll be good for our rally. It'll be fresh in people's minds and we can use the news story to boost turnout."

"Good idea. I'm going over to the commissioners' office this afternoon to add another thousand people to our permit for Chester Park. I had no idea response would be this good."

There was another reason to wait until Monday, Stacie noted. She had plans for the weekend with Cate—a two-night reservation at the waterfront Weller Regent, with no plans to see anyone other than the room service staff.

"By the way, Stace, you remember Faye?"

"Sure, Ethan's friend. I met her at the cabin the first night I got here."

"She dropped out last night. Apparently her father put a lot of pressure on her after she told him what happened to Ethan."

"Damn." That was exactly how intimidation was supposed to work, especially with new recruits who weren't thoroughly committed to the cause. Minor threats to property or reputation usually did the trick. The oil companies counted on that, and they hired thugs like Karl Depew to make it happen.

"Her dad wrote us a nice check though. I think he felt guilty."

"Better than nothing, I guess." At least Faye and her father were on the right side of the issue. Maybe they'd even show up at Wednesday's protest.

CLEAN desperately needed the media on their side too—no easy task, since most TV stations and newspapers were owned by corporations whose officials also sat on the boards of Big Oil, Big Pharma, big banks, defense contractors and agribusiness, none of which could be trusted to act in the public's interest. Their unholy coalition funded candidates and legislation to consolidate their power and perpetuate the status quo. Some days it seemed as if nothing short of a mass citizen uprising could break their grip.

Marty joined them in the office and tossed the Prius keys on the desk. He'd gone back to Bemidji to pick up the results of the water analysis from the guy his father had recommended. "I got the results. It's clay sediment. No trace of oil or hydrocarbons."

"How is that possible? My kayak was covered with oil. And what about that bird? You can't tell me that wasn't bitumen."

"Nope, conventional oil. It must have flown into the contaminated area. I don't know about your kayak. Maybe it was just sludge."

She knew oil when she saw it, and there was no way the gunk she'd picked up off the lake bottom was clay sediment. Something must have gone wrong with the tests, but she didn't want to disparage the scientist because he was a friend of Marty's father.

"That's good news, isn't it?" Marty asked. "Maybe the lake isn't as bad off as we thought."

"Except it is." She shook her head and sighed, frustrated that her perfectly executed reconnaissance mission had been for naught. "I don't understand what happened. It was even on my hands after I dipped them in the water. I must have mishandled the samples or something."

Jenn looked equally distraught. "We could ask Izzy to try again."

"It's too risky. If he gets caught, they'll lock him up for trespassing."

"How far away is the cabin in relation to the spill site?" Marty asked. "Maybe they could slip out at night and try to get closer."

"Izzy thinks they're using night vision goggles. Like I said, too risky." That didn't mean she wouldn't ask him to try. Izzy wasn't afraid of risks, and Ricky was smart enough to figure out how to do it without getting caught. One thing she knew for sure—if she could get her hands on more samples, she'd find another chemist to check them out, perhaps someone at the Department of Health in St. Paul.

* * *

Cathryn raised her eyebrows as Marlene fanned four fifty-dollar bills on the dresser. "Have I misunderstood the nature of our relationship?"

"I went online and saw how much the room was. I figured if I paid half you'd be less inclined to kick me out."

"I don't think you have anything to worry about."

Since they'd agreed in advance to hole up in the room, both had shown up in yoga wear and kicked off their two-night date with an hour of posing, stretching and meditation. Cathryn found it strangely arousing to share the routine over Marlene's lavender candle, which they used as a focal point. And now that she was aroused...

Marlene peeled out of her clothes and stretched nude across the bed. "I have to warn you. My period is due tomorrow so I plan to make the most of tonight."

"And I should warn you I don't care if you're on your period or not. Unless you've brought a garlic necklace, you won't be safe from me." Janice had been prickly about "red sex," crossing two weeks of every month off their intimate calendar.

"Fine, but let's at least pretend tonight's our only shot. I've been looking forward to this all week and I want my money's worth."

Cathryn pointed to the bills on the dresser. "I thought you said...oh, never mind." She discarded her clothes and crawled onto the bed, wedging her knee between Marlene's legs.

Already they knew each other's rhythm, contracting and stretching to meld their bodies from shoulder to toe. Her hands held Marlene's face as they kissed with passion that was almost emotional. There was no love between them to express, but that didn't stop her desire for the deep, physical pleasure of deep, physical kissing.

Marlene began to writhe beneath her, gripping her buttocks to grind their hips together. Between her heavy breathing and driving thrusts, it was clear their friction alone might cause her to climax. Cathryn tightened the muscles in her thigh and ground harder, aware that she too was breathing heavily.

With a low moan that steadily grew more desperate, Marlene lurched upward, rolling both of them onto their sides, and grasped the back of Cathryn's thigh to pull it firmly against her. Then after a long moment during which both of them held their breath, she finally exhaled with great force and went limp.

Cathryn had never seen anyone come without at least a little direct stimulation. She tickled the hair on the back of Marlene's neck. "That's a nice trick."

"Mind over body. I actually started feeling it when we were meditating. I could teach you how to channel that if you want."

"Hmm…that almost makes it sound like you did it by yourself."

Marlene touched her cheek and looked at her seriously. "No, it wasn't like that at all. It helps me focus on all of you and not just what your hand or your mouth are doing. The big picture. Trust me, it's a good thing. Not that I mind the little pictures. Those are good too."

She was touched at how quickly Marlene responded to her feelings of insignificance. "Forget teaching me then. I was hoping it was something I could use to get off while humping my favorite pillow. The cute one with the sweet personality, of course."

"I never would have guessed you had trouble getting off." She slid two fingers between Cathryn's legs. "You certainly don't have any trouble getting wet."

Cathryn hissed with excitement as a jolt of pure pleasure traveled from Marlene's fingertips to the base of her skull. Two hundred dollars never felt so good.

* * *

Stacie awakened first and tiptoed to the door to retrieve the newspaper. Careful not to wake Cate, she slipped into the bathroom to read the coverage of the oil spill, which was still playing on the front page. It was no surprise Nations Oil was categorically denying an intimidation campaign against the activists. Their spokesperson even went so far as to suggest CLEAN was fabricating events to garner public sympathy.

Ethan's arrest and toxicology report were hardly fabricated, but PR professionals like this Cathryn Mack person weren't interested in evidence. If they couldn't twist the truth in their favor, they smeared their adversaries with accusations and innuendo—an age-old strategy that worked all too often. It was no accident the public thought most environmental activists were radicals who sometimes killed people for their cause.

At the end of the article was a quote she'd given as head of CLEAN.

"Environmental disasters like the one at Lake Bunyan happen all too often, and so do these harassment campaigns. Oil companies don't want the public to know how reckless they are, how they put profits ahead of people, and how they leave their oily footprint around the beautiful lakes and rivers where we raise our children. Our mission at the Clean Energy Action Network is to help communities hold them responsible for the damage they've done and make it harder for them to do it again. We're holding a rally at Chester Park on Wednesday at five o'clock, and we hope folks will come out and show Nations Oil how much Lake Bunyan means to the people of Bunyan County."

Cate called from the other room, "Did you fall in?"

She folded the paper and walked out, toying briefly with the notion of outing herself as Stacie Pilardi, executive director of CLEAN, and to show off her importance with the front-page quote. There were too many reasons to keep that under wraps. It might screw up their chemistry if she suddenly became a real person. That would be a shame, since Cate was the best match she'd ever found on SappHere. An even greater risk would be learning Cate didn't care at all about the environment, or even worse, that she was one of those global warming skeptics who didn't believe the science. That wasn't likely, since she seemed too smart to have her head in the sand, but why take a chance?

"Oh, we got a newspaper," Cate said. "Anything in it?"

"Nah, I was just killing time until you woke up." She crawled back into bed and snuggled up to Cate. "Are you as hungry as I am? I bet I burned five thousand calories last night."

"I suppose I could eat again…breakfast, that is. What did you have in mind?"

"Coffee mostly, and some toast. And then maybe I'll put blueberries all over your belly and roll them around with my tongue. How does that sound?"

Cate chuckled and snaked her arm around Stacie's shoulder to pull her close. "I don't suppose you'd let me do the same to you with bacon and eggs."

"That wouldn't go well."

"Then maybe we should order pancakes and take turns feeding each other."

"Oooh, syrup could be fun."

"I would say you're already sweet enough," Cate said, "but you'd probably accuse me of shooting you a line just to get you in bed."

"Save your sweet nothings. I'm already in bed." She ran her hand from Cate's hip to the soft mound of flesh below her navel.

"Better not touch me there. I have to pee."

"So get up and pee. I don't think I can hold off much longer."

Cate threw back the comforter and shivered, hugging her body as she hurried into the bathroom, where she left the door slightly ajar. "Did you start your period?"

"Not yet. I've been having so much sex lately, my body probably thinks I'm someone else."

"I think this situation calls for a very close inspection." Cate retrieved her reading glasses from the dresser, yanked the covers to the foot of the bed and positioned her head squarely between Stacie's legs. "Let's see if everything is in order."

"Oh, dear. If I don't pass on the first try, will you let me take the test again?"

Cate used her thumbs to part the folds. "Well, hello. Someone's glad to see me."

Trips to her gynecologist would never be the same.

"Are you sure you didn't put syrup on this already? It's awfully wet."

"I can't remember. You'll have to taste it to find out."

"Oh, I intend to. But first I'm going to suck on this ripe red raspberry."

Stacie closed her eyes as the warm lips took her in. She'd had lots of lovers but there was something special about women in their forties. They understood sex was more than having a climax or even expressing undying love. It was a celebration of the female body and the many ways it came to life under a nuanced touch.

The temptation to watch Cate work was irresistible, but then she stifled a laugh to see the reading glasses were still in place and completely fogged over. Proper inspections were very serious business.

* * *

"I don't understand movies anymore," Cate said gloomily. "It's like the whole purpose is to make you feel hopeless."

While sharing pasta with marinara sauce and a fruit plate, they'd watched two films on the hotel's pay-per-view. The last one, an acclaimed story about debauchery among hucksters on Wall Street, was as depressing as any Stacie had ever seen.

"You realize most of the writers and directors in Hollywood are men, and their fantasies are making a lot of money and screwing a lot of women," Stacie said.

"Teenage boys and young men are going to watch that and think they're entitled to trick everyone out of their money and treat women however they want. There's no punishment at all and the worst part is that it's based on a true story."

Needing a dose of silliness, Stacie flipped over to the cartoon channel. "This will be better. It's just talking animals that blow each other up."

"I almost asked you to turn off that movie before it got to the end. I had a feeling he was going to get away with it and I wanted to pretend he didn't." Cate's voice was genuinely bitter, as though she were talking about more than a film.

"That bothered you a lot, didn't it?"

She thinned her lips, obviously taking pains to decide whether or not to talk about what was really on her mind. Finally she sighed. "It hit a little close to home. My father was one of the worst people who ever lived…still is, if he's even still alive. He'd get drunk a lot, always scotch, and then he'd beat on us, my mother and me. She divorced him when I was twelve and I only saw him a couple of times after that. He had this girlfriend, a woman who worked at the bar where he hung out. One day she told a friend of hers she was pregnant and then all of a sudden she went missing. No one ever saw her again. I know the son of a bitch killed her and so does everyone else in town, but the police couldn't prove it. I'm not even sure they tried. If they were anything like those guys in the movie, they probably thought he was justified to save his skin."

"God, that's awful. And to think, that could have been you or your mother. Must have scared you both to death. I bet it made you the toughest kid on the block."

"I was. To this day I can't stand the smell of scotch, and there's this guy I work with—also an asshole—who drinks it all the time. Makes me want to throw up every time he comes around."

Stacie's life hadn't been easy either, losing her mother to bone cancer when she was barely out of elementary school. Unlike Cate, she'd had her father's love and support until he died three years ago, and their family was well respected in the community. "I think there's truth to the saying that what doesn't kill us makes us stronger. Looks like you've done pretty well for yourself."

"So has my mom. She married a really nice man on the next go-around. He has a huge ranch with lots of horses, and they go riding practically every day. There's that other saying about living well being the best revenge."

She propped up against the pillows and tucked Cate's head to her chest. Then she grabbed the remote and scrolled back to the movie menu. "Screw these bastards and their misogynist crap. I'll take a chick flick any day of the week."

CHAPTER SIX

From her desk by the window, Cathryn watched as the parking lot filled. There were more cars than usual, including several satellite trucks, which made her uneasy. An oil spill wasn't sexy enough for television news, not since the initial excitement right after it was discovered over a week ago. The accusations that Nations Oil was interfering with reporters and activists had gotten more play in the papers on Saturday, and there was an ad in Sunday's paper about a rally on Wednesday, but there was nothing to explain this sudden turnout. Unless…

"Did somebody schedule a press tour for today? I've got nothing on my calendar."

Woody walked to the window and peered through the blinds. "Wow, you don't think operations would have arranged something without letting us know?"

Operations wouldn't but Cathryn couldn't say the same about Depew. She wouldn't put anything past that SOB, least of all an opportunity to jerk her around. "Go see if you can find out." She was all in favor of letting the press inside the barricades once in a while to verify their progress, but she didn't appreciate being blindsided by Depew.

There was quite a bit of progress to report, and she'd included it in her press release, which had gone out over the wire an hour ago. Repair crews had made significant headway over the weekend, putting them ahead of schedule for getting the pipeline up and running again. Even better, two grab dredgers had arrived at the spill site on Sunday afternoon, which meant they were in the final phase of cleanup. The only bad news was the report she'd gotten from the Department of Natural Resources—thirty-seven fish and four birds had been killed by the spill. By disaster standards that wasn't horrific, but the animal rights advocates would be outraged. Nations Oil had already promised to restock the lake and give a grant to local biologists to monitor the wildlife populations going forward. All part of their plan to leave Lake Bunyan even better than they found it.

She'd committed the talking points to memory. If in fact Depew had arranged a press tour today, it would allow her to reinforce her message. Still, he was a first-class jerk for not letting her know about it in advance.

Amy finished collating the handouts for the press release. "I made a few extra copies. We've never had this many people before. Anything else you can think of?"

Cathryn peeked out the window at the refreshment table they set up each day for the press. "All the cookies are gone. Do we have another bag?"

Woody bustled back into the trailer, out of breath from running across the compound. "Depew isn't in his office, but they told me he didn't schedule anything for the press today. Something's definitely up, though. There must be twenty reporters out there."

The sight of such a large press contingent was unnerving but her only option was to walk out there and find out what was going on. Business as usual. Maybe this was just a show of force because one of their own, that kid from the school newspaper, had reported being intimidated. She could hardly blame them for that, and if Depew had anything to do with it, she secretly hoped they could prove it. He was a public relations nightmare and nothing would please her more than to see him sent packing.

No, that wasn't true. She'd be even happier to see him arrested.

She touched up her lipstick on the off chance of ending up on the evening newscast, and went out to face the media.

"Good morning, everyone. I thought we'd break tradition and start on time for a change. Did you all get coffee?"

Amy passed out copies of the update while Cathryn ran down her list of bullet points. Response was muted until she reached the wildlife report. That set off a surprising din of paper shuffling, and also a bustle in the crowd as those with cameras and microphones jostled to get closer. Apparently Minnesotans cared a great deal about their fish and birds, and she wasted no time detailing their plans for replenishing the stock once the lake was returned to its pristine state.

"And that's all I have for the briefing. I can take a few questions." She made it a point to call on the young man from the college newspaper as if to prove Nations Oil wasn't out to get him.

"Ethan Anders, *The Statesman*. How would you describe this fish and bird kill relative to other environmental disasters involving oil pipeline ruptures?"

Though she took issue with his use of the phrase "environmental disaster," she didn't dare call him out, not after his arrest accusation. "That's a very good question, and I happen to have that information handy. It's comparable to the Talmadge Creek spill, but it's important to remember that was flowing water, which meant the fish weren't contained within the spill area the way they are in a lake. However, the booms we put in place within a few hours after discovering the spill are specially designed to prevent fish from swimming into the containment area, and we made every effort to rescue all the wildlife—I'm referring to fish, turtles, muskrats, birds—

whatever might have been nesting inside. Those animals were relocated to other parts of the lake, and in some cases, to other lakes in the area. Even now we keep a guard in place at all hours to sound a horn when birds or other animals stray into the containment area."

"Colleen Murray, *Star-Tribune*. How many people are actively involved in wildlife rescue and who is taking the lead in directing these efforts?"

"I don't have an exact number for you. We're working closely with the Department of Natural Resources. They're spearheading the effort because they're the experts, but Nations Oil is assuming all financial responsibility."

Gerry Simmonds, her ace-in-the-hole financial reporter, had skipped today's briefing, leaving her no choice but to end with a query that might be less than friendly. Only one hand was up, that of a woman from one of the environmental blogs whose pointed questions were barely shy of being rude.

"Jennifer Kilpatrick, Clean Energy Action Network. Two questions. Did you personally witness the collection of any of these wildlife that were killed in this environmental disaster, and what can you tell us about the process?"

Again with the loaded words. At least her question wasn't as churlish as usual. "I did not personally witness it, and therefore I'm afraid I cannot describe the process. I would direct those questions to Natural Resources."

"Are you confident the numbers you're reporting are accurate?"

A ridiculous follow-up that tested her patience. Did anyone actually think she'd stand up here and lie? "I can't tell you the exact species, but I'm confident of the count—thirty-seven fish and four birds."

As the reporters dispersed, she began planning her afternoon call with Hoss. She'd greatly underestimated the press's interest in the loss of wildlife, but now that she knew it was a critical issue, she could suggest ways to address it. Locals would probably appreciate extra funds for education or sporting and nature clubs, programs that would win back public confidence. If she could get Hoss on board, tomorrow would be a great day.

* * *

The farmhouse was teeming with nearly three dozen volunteers, most of them seated on the floor in front of the television. The anticipation was palpable. Catching oil companies in their brazen lies was as common as ants at a picnic, but today's takedown would be one for the ages. According to Jenn, the press had played its part perfectly, following their tip to document the wildlife report with the promise of a major breaking news story later in the day.

Most of the mainstream news outlets had lost their drive for investigative stories. It was far easier to send a reporter to a press conference, have them write down what was said and report it as the "news." God forbid they check out the information to see if it actually was true, or ask around in case there was a countering point of view. When the press failed to hold corporate or government feet to the fire, the public got only one side of the story—the powerful side. It was up to groups like CLEAN to speak for the little people.

Stacie squeezed onto the couch next to Jenn. "Did you get any grief over whether or not the video was authentic?"

"It was geocoded and time stamped. I also sent a copy to Nancy Collier at the EPA in Washington, and I bet she's sent someone out there to dig up that dump site by now."

Today's video was certain to go viral, shared at least a million times around the world by citizens fed up with companies covering up their crimes and irresponsible exploitation. By the end of the week, Nations Oil would be a laughingstock, the corporate symbol of greed for oil profits at the expense of the planet.

"Did Nations Oil get caught telling fish stories? Details next on News at Six."

Marty rolled his eyes. "Fish stories. Who writes this stuff?"

Jenn jabbed him with her elbow. "You should talk. Your jokes are a lot worse."

"Both of you hush," Stacie snapped. "I don't want to miss this."

"Don't worry. I'm recording it, and the other local channels too."

"We have breaking news tonight from Lake Bunyan, where Nations Oil reported today on wildlife killed as a result of last week's devastating pipeline rupture, which we've been following here on News at Six. We go live to Peter Coleman, who's reporting from the spill site. What can you tell us, Pete?"

"Don't you love it?" Stacie asked. "Yesterday it was barely on their radar but today it's devastating."

The reporter, dressed in a plaid shirt and Windbreaker, had one finger to his ear while his other hand held a microphone. In the background was the barricade on Lake Bunyan Road, and an overlaid seal of the EPA.

"We've got a real mess here, Chris. Hundreds—maybe even thousands—of oil-covered fish and birds were discovered buried in a massive hole near the site of the Lake Bunyan pipeline break, and personnel from Nations Oil and Minnesota's Department of Natural Resources are pointing fingers at each other. A statement released by Nations Oil this morning reported wildlife casualties as three dozen fish and only a handful of birds, but as we're finding out, the damage is far worse. Here's company spokesperson Cathryn Mack talking to reporters today."

"That's me!" Jenn exclaimed. "That's my question. Now just listen to this bald-faced lie. Priceless!"

"I can't tell you the exact species, but I'm confident of the count—thirty-seven fish and four birds."

Stacie felt as if she'd been whacked with a side of beef. "Ohhhhh, my God." Cathryn Mack was her Cate. In town for a couple of weeks working on a public relations project. How had she missed something practically staring her in the face?

"I know, unbelievable," Jenn said, giddy with excitement. "They're probably talking that woman off the ledge right now. Can you imagine anything more humiliating? She's in 'Heckuva job, Brownie' territory."

This was the same woman with whom Stacie had spent the past two days in intimate pursuits, whose touching story of a difficult childhood had triggered sensitivities that bordered on genuine attraction, not just the lustful cravings she usually felt for women she met on SappHere. "She was probably lying the whole time," she mumbled.

Jenn sat up straight and looked at her quizzically. "Of course she was lying. That was the whole point."

Stacie shook her head and pushed herself off the couch. "I'm feeling claustrophobic all of a sudden. I'm going to watch the rest from the back of the room." Where no one could see her growing pale and sweaty.

"Not long after that statement, News at Six received this video, taken early this morning by a spy drone operated by a hobbyist near Lake Bunyan. The Clean Energy Action Network, a national environmental group, is taking credit for the film. I want to warn viewers, what you're about to see is graphic."

The station had sharpened the video and spliced it to show the key elements—workers wearing camouflage fatigues skimming the lake, harvesting a small sample for the official count and burying the others. The shortened version was even more impactful than the original.

"We tried to reach Nations Oil for comment. Their spokesperson refused to appear on camera again but did release this statement: Disposal of wildlife losses is the joint responsibility of Nations Oil and the Department of Natural Resources. In our earlier report, we inadvertently failed to combine figures from both disposal teams. We regret any confusion this error has caused and will issue a new report when it becomes available."

"Epic!" Jenn shouted, and the volunteers erupted in congratulatory cheers. "When Ricky comes out of hiding, we need to give him a medal."

Stacie's head was reeling. How on earth had she gotten herself into this mess? She was sleeping with the enemy, for God's sake. Of all the quirky risks associated with anonymous dating—she could have ended up with a cattle rancher or a Republican governor—this one took the cake. Could anything be more ironic?

Marlene dinged in her pocket, the sound she made when Cate contacted her through the SappHere app. Not only were they still using fake names, they hadn't even traded phone numbers.

"*Worst. Day. Ever.*"

Stacie stepped out on the porch and tapped out her reply. "*Same here. Need 2 see u.*"

"*Busy tonite.*"

"*Pleaz.*"

Several minutes passed before Cate answered, agreeing to meet at Boomer's at the mall at ten thirty. That gave Stacie four hours to plan her coming out party, whether she wanted one or not. She was the public face of CLEAN and would be leading the rally on Wednesday night, giving interviews to every news organization that came to cover it. If she didn't reveal herself in the next two days, Cate would meet Stacie Pilardi the same way she'd met Cathryn Mack.

It was just her luck the best match she'd ever found on SappHere turned out to be her worst enemy.

* * *

Cathryn parked outside Boomer's but stayed in the car to calm herself. On the drive over she'd grown increasingly annoyed at Marlene's insistence on seeing her tonight, despite her message that she'd had a terrible day. The last thing she needed in her life was a drama queen who went off the rails whenever she wasn't getting enough attention. Until now Marlene hadn't struck her as the needy type. Quite the opposite in fact, and it worried her that something very bad might have happened. Something even worse than being humiliated in front of millions of people for all time.

Marlene sat at a tall bar table sipping what looked to be an iced tea.

After a quick kiss on the cheek, she slid onto the other stool. "I can't stay long. All hell broke loose at work today."

"I saw you on the news."

If Marlene had called her here to add her voice to the chorus of critics, she was going to be extremely pissed. "It wasn't what it looked like."

"That's good, I guess, because it looked like you were caught lying through your teeth." She sounded more disappointed than angry.

Cathryn slung her purse back on her shoulder and stood. "If I'd wanted to listen to this crap, I could have stayed at my desk and answered the phone."

"Don't go, please. I have something important to tell you." She placed her smartphone in the center of the table. "I'd like you to meet Marlene. She's my cell phone, my navigation system, my search engine…and also my SappHere app. My real name is Stacie Pilardi."

"Stacie Pilardi." The name sounded vaguely familiar but she couldn't place it. Easing back into her seat, Cathryn studied Marlene's—er, Stacie's expression. It was stern, and even a little timid, sparking the ominous feeling another shoe was about to drop. "And that's important because…"

"You know how it is on SappHere. You never know what sort of person you're going to meet, so you don't want to tell them everything up front in case they turn out to be nuts. You didn't share a whole lot of personal information either, so I figured you felt the same way, and that was okay with me. But then I found out today who you were."

"And since I'm a sleazy corporate liar, you want to what? Trade business cards?"

"If you Google my name—and I assume you'll do that as soon as you get home—you'll discover that I'm the executive director of something called the Clean Energy Action Network.

We're in town to protest your oil spill and to make sure you clean it up without taking any shortcuts."

Clean Energy Action Network...the environmental crazies.

"Please tell me you're kidding." Her worst nightmares weren't this bad. "Oh, God, you're not. Holy shit."

"I said the same thing."

"I've been sleeping with the enemy."

"I said that too."

Cathryn fought back a wave of nausea, trying her best not to entertain the what-ifs. What if one of Depew's thugs had spotted Stacie at the hotel and run her license plate? What if she'd left her laptop out and Stacie had downloaded sensitive company documents? What if someone was watching them right now?

"I need to go. I could get fired for even being here with you."

"I'm surprised you still have a job to lose. Nations Oil needs a scapegoat and you were the one who got caught lying to the press."

Fired? The notion hadn't even occurred to her, but Stacie was right.

"I didn't lie...but it was my fault for not making sure I had all the information. It's my job to know all the procedures and I screwed up."

"Seriously, Cate...or Cathryn. Whatever you call yourself. Do you actually think anyone believes there were two reports and you only got one? Either you were duped, or you knew there'd been a massive kill and you lied to cover it up."

"There's a third option. I could be telling the truth. Did you even consider that?"

"Oh, come on. If it was proper procedure, why is the EPA out there digging up your dump site?"

Sometimes it seemed half her job was dealing with environmental whackos and their slanderous accusations, and while there were dozens of talking points to refute anyone's charges of apathy or malice, she doubted she could budge

Stacie off her high horse. Logic and reason were useless when it came to extremists.

"Look, you probably think you have all the answers but you don't. I've worked at Nations Oil for twenty-two years. I know the people who run the company, and they're kind, decent human beings who get vilified on a daily basis for giving people exactly what they want. And why? Because they make money doing it. If the world wants us to stop pumping oil, why don't they just stop using it? Park your little hybrid and get on a bicycle. Is that what you want?"

Stacie blew out a breath and shook her head. "Calling me a hypocrite doesn't change the facts about what your company is doing. If you manage to keep your job, let me save you from another embarrassment. Those kind, decent people you work with are also lying about this spill being heavy oil. I was at the lake last weekend before it was evacuated, and I got some samples from the sediment. I saw it with my own eyes and I know it's bitumen. Not only that, I took those samples in the middle of the lake, which means this isn't some minor spill that's contained behind those booms in the cove. It's enormous."

Cathryn could feel her face burning, and she hated Stacie's smug, satisfied look. She'd known in her gut Woody's estimate was correct, and it was no accident Bryce Tucker had referred to the spill as dilbit on the plane. Nations Oil was having her put out bogus information and the reasons were obvious. Their pipeline wasn't approved for dilbit. It was too frail for such an abrasive mixture, and transporting it without a permit made them civilly and criminally liable. Since it was their second offense, the fines would be unprecedented. If that weren't enough, a large-scale accident would torpedo their stock price and damage their efforts to secure approval for the Caliber Pipeline. That was the real reason corporate was scrambling to buy up all the lake properties—to keep the truth from ever coming out.

She remembered the young reporter's question about bitumen. "Is Ethan Anders working with you?"

"Yes. Is Karl Depew working with you?"

Her nausea surged again. There was probably no point in playing dumb since Stacie had an obvious knack for getting information. Still, Cathryn owed it to Hoss to protect the company's image as best she could. "He's that drunk I told you about who keeps hitting on me. He's not one of us though. He was hired to handle security, and I can't imagine he'll be on the payroll after today if he had anything to do with this. We have nothing to gain from his kind of publicity."

"Don't kid yourself. I've tangled with Depew before. He's there to keep the corporate honchos from having to get their hands dirty, and I bet he has a blank check to pay off the local authorities so they'll rough up people like Ethan or lie about the fish kill. Don't be surprised when somebody magically produces a backdated permit for that landfill, or even when the EPA puts out its report and calls this heavy oil. That's what we're up against with people like Depew, and your kind, decent bosses are the ones who hired him to pull all these strings."

It was unnerving to hear Stacie repeating practically the same words Hoss had used to describe Depew—he was there to handle the dirty work so she wouldn't be sullied—and Cathryn had chosen to be willfully ignorant of what his dirty work entailed. Up to now, knowing it was in Depew's hands had been enough to make her feel she was above the fray, but Stacie's indictment stung. All of them were guilty because they blindly authorized his actions and reaped the benefits.

"Why are you even telling me all this?" she asked. "It's obvious you'd rather spring a trap and make a big splash on the news like you did today. And don't even try to pretend that wasn't a setup. Somebody tipped off those reporters to come out there and ask all about the fish kill."

"Of course it was a setup. But I didn't know it was you, and the reason I'm telling you about the rest of our evidence is so you won't make a fool of yourself again."

If that was supposed to make her feel better…it actually did. There was no question Stacie could have hurt her if she'd wanted to.

"I'm sorry this happened to you, Cathryn. You didn't deserve it, but I'm not the one who hung you out to dry. Your bosses did that."

Cathryn had to admit that was true. "I realize that. In fact you're probably the nicest environmental whacko I've ever met…but you're still an environmental whacko."

Stacie chuckled. "It's good sometimes to see a human face on the other side. I like to think it helps us treat each other better."

"Under the circumstances though, we can't see each other anymore."

"I know, and that's really a shame because you're an awesome kisser."

"You're not so bad yourself." Although their relationship was never meant to be more than a fling, she was genuinely sorry to see it end. But now that she knew Stacie was her arch enemy, there was nothing else they could do.

CHAPTER SEVEN

Stacie tiptoed back to her cot in the dining room, already dressed for the day in jeans and her favorite shirt, red and black flannel, laundered hundreds of times until it was downy soft. She was being careful not to wake any of her twelve housemates, the closest of which was asleep on the couch in the next room. At a quarter to five, it was too early to rummage in the kitchen for coffee, but she had little hope of going back to sleep. The confrontation with Cathryn had bothered her all night, not because either of them had done anything wrong but because the relationship they'd both cultivated so carefully to brighten their time in Duluth was now moot. Her principles defined her and she couldn't compromise them for something as trivial as good sex.

Or even great sex.

And there was more to Cathryn than that. Even though she'd defended her company's actions, it was obvious she was troubled by the allegations. She hadn't pushed back at all over the bitumen nor the size of the spill, not even in corporate speak of nondenial denial.

From the corner of her eye, Stacie thought she saw something move on the porch but after looking closer decided it was only the shadow of a tree swaying in the breeze. The moon was nearly full and that made her want to slip outside and watch it fade in the coming dawn. It wasn't exactly privacy she craved. It was solitude. If she could get to her yoga mat—

Exploding glass sprayed the room and a stream of firecrackers began popping only a few feet away. On pure instinct Stacie rolled off her cot and crawled beneath the dining room table in time to hear the wood splinter as the front door gave way. Shadowy figures armed with rifles filed into the house, their penlights giving off an eerie glow in the acrid smoke from the firecrackers.

"Nobody move!"

Several men stormed up the stairs while two others charged toward the back bedroom where Jenn and Marty slept. All were shouting different commands.

"*Stand up!*"

"*Face down on the floor!*"

"*Hands in the air!*"

"*Freeze!*"

It would be a miracle if no one got shot for defying orders. Stacie lay perfectly still, knowing they'd find her eventually but not wanting to get her head blown off by some jacked-up, trigger-happy cop. Of all the times she and her team had been roughed up, this was by far the worst. How could anyone possibly have thought they needed a SWAT team when a simple knock on the door and a warrant would have gotten them permission to search the premises?

There was little doubt Depew was behind this. He'd done something similar at a nuclear energy protest in California last year, taking advantage of the fact that, post-9/11, law enforcement agencies all across the country had gotten grants to upgrade their force under the auspices of fighting terrorism. It was only natural they'd be bursting with excitement to put their new firepower and training to use, and terrorism was whatever they said it was.

Lights came on throughout the house, and one by one her friends, all of them barely dressed and in plastic handcuffs, were marched outside. Jenn was demanding to see a warrant and yelling that their attorney was already on his way.

On the outside chance Jenn was blowing smoke, Stacie quietly retrieved her phone from where it had fallen and sent a text message to Matt Stevenson. "*SWAT team at house.*" Then she set it to silent and tucked it inside the sagging cloth that underpinned one of the dining chairs.

It took a lot of balls for Depew to pull something like this when Nations Oil was already under scrutiny by the press for intimidating activists. That guy had more connections than a Colombian drug lord.

Black boots stopped only inches from her head. "We've got another one in here!"

"I'm not armed," she said calmly.

"Well, I am so you'd better not move a muscle."

Another pair of boots appeared. "Come out of there nice and slow."

Trying her best not to sound sarcastic, she asked, "Don't move a muscle or come out nice and slow. Which is it? I'd rather not get shot."

"Just drag her ass out of there," the first one barked. He was dressed in fatigues with a black T-shirt beneath his tactical vest.

She went limp as the second man, wearing a deputy's uniform and a flak jacket, hauled her out from under the table by her feet. He then rolled her over, and with his boot on her back, pinned her wrists with plastic cuffs. After all the times she'd been arrested, Stacie knew to twist her arms so the cuffs wouldn't be tight once she relaxed. She also knew these guys were on a power trip and that antagonizing them would only make the situation worse. Her physical comfort was the least of their concerns.

No sooner had she struggled to her feet than he shoved her forward and into the doorjamb. For a moment she saw stars, the pain above her eye so sharp she thought she might cry.

"I found this in the kitchen," one of the commandos yelled, waving what looked like a bag of marijuana.

"Because you put it there," she answered before she was pushed outside.

On the front porch were several plastic bins containing laptops, cell phones, notebooks, papers and miscellaneous electronics and data storage devices. These guys were idiots if they thought they'd find anything useful. Everything of importance required a password to access and their sensitive files were heavily encrypted.

Amid dozens of flashing blue lights, some emanating from black SUVs with ordinary Minnesota plates, the men escorted her to a waiting paddy wagon. Before she stepped in, she looked back at the SWAT team and noted that only two were wearing deputy patches on their shoulders. The others were dressed in camouflage pants and black T-shirts—Depew's men.

Inside the wagon, she squeezed in next to Jenn at the end of the bench. "Is everyone all right?"

"My arm is bleeding," said Alex, a recent college grad from Des Moines. "I think there's a piece of glass in it."

"Make sure you show that to Matt when he gets to the jail. With any luck, he'll get you a few thousand dollars for it." She asked Jenn, "Did you get a look at the warrant?"

"I saw it on the table by the front door but they wouldn't let me read it. You think this is Depew?"

"I know it is. He's never gone this far against us before but we've never had a takedown quite like that one yesterday. We must have really kicked the hornet's nest."

Or maybe Depew had gotten wind of their discoveries and was coming to collect whatever evidence they had, which was none, thanks to her careless handling of the water samples. Until that moment, it hadn't occurred to her Cathryn might rat her out.

Marty was the last to arrive at the wagon, and in response to a shove, spat in the direction of a deputy. "You fucking pig!"

"Marty, stop it!" Jenn yelled.

It was too late. He took a blow to the jaw and went down.

The deputy wiped his face with the back of his sleeve. "Throw this son of a bitch in the back of my car. If he knows what's good for him, he'll shut that pretty mouth before I bust it again."

Stacie had little doubt he was in for a beating no matter what, but she selfishly worried more about CLEAN's reputation than Marty's well-being. He couldn't spit in a man's face and not expect retaliation, whether it was legal or not. It was just a plain fact that some people weren't suited for peaceful activism, but she'd leave it up to Jenn to handle him. If he couldn't adapt to their methods, he'd have to stay home, no matter whose boyfriend he was.

* * *

"There's no question our credibility took a hit," Cathryn said, twirling in her chair to face the wall. How was she supposed to have confidential briefings with Hoss while sharing office space with her staff? "I'd like to schedule a press tour of the cleanup site. They need to see us doing what we promised. Not all of them—especially not the bloggers or that kid from the college paper—just a handpicked few."

"I like the way you think, Cathryn. Always have. Sort it out with Larry if you think that's what we need."

"Hoss, there's something else I need to talk to you about… Karl Depew. I think he's being a little overexuberant and I'm worried there's going to be blowback."

"That's the thing, honey. He's up against a bunch of hooligans. Heck, they killed people out in Oregon driving spikes through that lumber, and they burnt down a building once with some poor fellow still inside it. We're the ones dishing out blowback because that's what it takes to shut these vandals down."

There had been a handful of ecoterrorist incidents several years ago, but their tactics had been denounced by all but the environmental fringe. Cathryn had stayed up half the night reading about Stacie and CLEAN, and their approach was community activism, educational campaigns and lobbying for environmental regulations and clean energy investment. According to her profile in the *Post-Gazette*, she'd been arrested twenty-one times for civil disobedience, mostly trespassing and failure to disperse. There were other more nefarious incidents, she'd said, like when she was stopped for driving with a broken taillight, one that was *"broken when struck by a billy club."* After two arrests for driving under the influence—both of which were dismissed for a lack of evidence—Stacie never drank more than half a glass of anything. *"I can't give them any ammunition."*

"I just don't want anyone hurt, Hoss," Cathryn said. "That would put us in a difficult position."

"Now don't worry your pretty little head about it, sweet thing. Karl knows where the line is."

As she hung up, Woody came in waving the morning update. "Good news, sort of. Turns out there was a mix-up down at the courthouse and our permit for the landfill didn't get filed. That's why it looked like we were trying to hide something. It doesn't get us off the hook for not reporting the other set of numbers on the fish and bird kill, but at least it shows we had permission to bury all them."

Stacie had predicted something similar, that someone would miraculously produce a backdated permit to legitimize their wrongdoing.

Amy looked up from her desk, where she'd spent the last twenty minutes repairing a broken fingernail. "I can't believe it. After all they put us through yesterday, and it turns out to be some stupid clerical error. Bet you anything they barely mention it on the news because that would be like admitting a mistake."

Cathryn's disbelief was more literal than figurative. Depew had obviously greased a palm or two in the county clerk's office, someone willing to admit a mistake he never made in return for a few thousand bucks. The new figures were still damning—over three hundred fish and thirty-one birds. That probably wasn't even half the actual number.

She passed the document to Amy. "Write up the first draft of today's press release. I want to be sure we start on time, but I need to go talk to operations."

The command centers for operations and security were two adjoining trailers twice the size of hers that were carved up into several private offices. Larry Kratke was handling operations, which consisted of cleanup and repair. His hardhat and filtration mask sat on the corner of his desk, and if the look on his face was any indication, he was as miserable as she about being stuck in Duluth.

"Larry, I just got off the phone with Hoss. I want to set up a press tour out to the cleanup site, just a few friendlies who can go out and document our progress."

He shook his head. "I don't think Depew will go for that. He's got things locked down out there."

"It's not his call. Thanks to that debacle"—she wanted to say cluster fuck—"with the landfill, the press doesn't trust us right now. We need to get them back on our side."

"It's not me you have to convince." He looked up as Depew stomped into the trailer, cursing at someone on his cell phone. "Speak of the devil."

"I'll talk to him. Think we can be ready by Wednesday?" A positive story about the cleanup could offset the impact of Stacie's community rally.

"I'll see what I can do. Just get the Dark Lord to sign off on it." His voice held so much misery that she felt lucky to have a separate tiny trailer, even if she had to share it.

Since she already had Hoss's blessing for a press tour, she wasn't going to suck up to Depew. The moment he ended his call she stepped into his doorway, drawing power from the fact that she was standing while he was now seated at his desk. "We're doing a press tour out to the cleanup site on Wednesday. I already cleared it with Hoss."

"You did, did you? And what if I don't think that's a good idea?"

"You may not have noticed on your end of things, but we took a beating yesterday in the press. It's my job to fix it and I need a press tour on Wednesday because there's supposed to be some big protest rally at the park and I want to steal their thunder."

He looked at her through squinting eyes and then laughed. "You can have your little press party, missy. I'll make sure we're ready for company. But I wouldn't worry too much about that protest rally. Those ass-clowns might not be able to make it."

"What are you talking about?"

"Just something I heard from a little birdie down at the jail." He leaned back and propped his feet on his desk. "Can't have people flaunting occupancy codes, now can we?"

She had no idea what he meant by his cryptic remark, but it sounded like more harassment. Her job was hard enough without having to clean up after his boorish bullying. Stacie was absolutely right that he—

Stacie! Was Depew saying she and her friends had been arrested?

Cathryn walked back into the trailer to find Amy leaning provocatively across Woody's desk. "Is that press release finished?" she snapped.

"Give me a few more minutes," Amy said, lunging back toward her desk.

She retrieved her cell phone from her purse and sent a text to Stacie through SappHere. "*R u okay?*"

When there was no response after an hour, she considered two possibilities—either Stacie was no longer speaking to her or she was in fact in jail. Or maybe she was just out of pocket planning her big rally.

"Cathryn?" Woody was standing at the window looking out. "I was just saying the press is ready. You said something earlier about wanting to start on time."

The crowd was noticeably smaller today, only six reporters and no TV cameras. She kicked off her statement with a self-deprecating apology for the fiasco on the wildlife kill and followed with a solemn update on the revised numbers. "We truly regret these losses, and Nations Oil will spare no expense to return this beautiful lake to its prior state. That's all I have today. I'll take your questions."

She started off with Colleen Murray, who was mild-mannered and asked smart questions but without an obvious agenda. Colleen would definitely get an invitation for the press tour.

"The drone video given to the press yesterday seemed to show a wide area of impact for fish and birds. Can you speculate on how that happened given that you've reported the spill as one hundred percent contained in a small area of the lake?"

"I've been told the marsh area near the shoreline is a nesting area, and that these creatures likely ingested oil toxins soon after the spill before we even knew it was there. Obviously it took several days to take effect, and that's why we saw a sudden mass phenomenon."

"But you're confident the spill is in fact contained."

That was exactly the type of question that had gotten her in trouble the day before, and after hearing Stacie's report on the water and sediment samples, Cathryn wasn't confident of anything. "We got the booms in place immediately and they're specially designed to limit the flow of water. I'm confident we've seen the worst of it."

"Mark Freeman, *News Tribune*." Another professional she'd invite. "There have been reports that, in the wake of this environmental disaster, Nations Oil is aggressively—"

"For the record, this was only a minor to moderate spill relative to others, such as Deep Horizon and Talmadge Creek." She'd let the young college reporter get away with calling it an environmental disaster last time but it wasn't tenable to allow all of them to frame the issue with such inflammatory language. "It was quickly contained, and the cleanup and restoration is nearly complete, so I take issue with your characterization of this incident as an environmental disaster."

"I suspect the fish and birds would disagree," he said, prompting a round of snide chuckles from the others. "There are reports that Nations Oil is aggressively purchasing the lakefront properties at Lake Bunyan."

It was curious that Ethan Anders wasn't in attendance. Until today he'd been at every briefing.

"...If all the properties in the affected area come under the ownership of your company, can the residents of Bunyan County continue to expect a timely resolution to this spill, or will it lose urgency?"

"The offers of purchase have been extended in order to alleviate concerns about how the spill will affect market values. It will not impact our timetable or our sense of obligation to restore the lake to its prior state." Though it was a fair assumption if they were able to acquire all the properties, there would be no reason to restore or restock, since access to the lake would become privately controlled. No need to share that.

Someone else was missing—Jennifer Kilpatrick, CLEAN's blogger, and it lent an uneasy credence to Depew's sinister claim. If Anders and Kilpatrick were locked up, then so was Stacie.

* * *

All six of the women were crammed into a small cell, and Stacie assumed the same for the men in their group. Though her watch had been confiscated, her stomach told her it was early afternoon. Hunger was the least of her worries, since her eye was swollen shut from where they'd rammed her into the door.

Alex, who had been cut by flying glass, slumped against the wall to the floor. "How much longer do you think they'll keep us here?"

"We should get out soon," Jenn said, "because I doubt they plan on feeding us. The longest I've ever been held without food was twelve hours, and that was overnight because they couldn't find a magistrate."

Stacie wondered if in fact they were going to be arraigned. Matt was probably negotiating for their release without charges, and the sheriff was dragging his feet so they could pick through the contents of their laptops and smartphones.

The drugs, however, were a problem. Possession of more than an ounce was a felony, and it was possible the sheriff wanted someone to claim them before he'd let anyone go. That wouldn't happen, of course, because they didn't belong to anyone in the house. Part of the reason they were planted in the kitchen instead of one of the bedrooms was so they could accuse everyone.

A female deputy, stout and fair-skinned, opened their cell door. Stacie recognized her as the one she'd encountered the morning she left the lake, and lowered her face to keep from being recognized. "You're all free to go. Sign for your belongings on the way out."

When the others filed out, Jenn stiffly addressed the guard, Officer Gustafson. "Did you guys finally figure out you had the wrong house?"

Gustafson laughed and shook her head. "They don't tell me anything, but it must have been something like that because they aren't charging anybody with anything. Just promise you won't sue us for false arrest."

Assault and battery was more like it.

Their personal effects had been saved in individual envelopes and their electronics were displayed in the two bins she'd seen on the porch. All of the cell phones had been crushed, from the looks of it with heavy-duty pliers, and the laptops and tablet computers were in pieces.

Marty was brought out last from a separate cell. His upper lip was split and swollen from the first blow, but he was otherwise unharmed. Apparently he'd learned to control himself.

As they were huddled near the door, Matt said, "The officer who transported your electronics sends his apologies.

He claims he swerved to miss a deer and the crates accidentally spilled, miraculously breaking every single device in exactly the same way."

They were used to this sort of harassment. Twenty thousand dollars' worth of personal electronics ruined and no one held to account.

"You got his statement, right? We'll wait a couple of days and submit a claim to their insurance company."

"Of course we will, but let's walk out the door first. I don't want them to come up with another reason to detain you."

"What about the drugs?"

"I demanded they take urine samples from all of you, but they said they didn't have the resources to authenticate the results." Drug testing was a risky strategy, since marijuana traces stayed in the system up to a month. Even Jenn could have been caught in that trap, and probably Marty too. Fortunately, the sheriff was worried about looking foolish again and hedged.

"I then asked to examine the drugs, and lo and behold, they never made it to the station. So there won't be any drug charges."

"Color me shocked," she deadpanned.

Outside Stacie opened her wallet and passed out a handful of bills. "You guys go get something to eat. We'll ride with Matt out to the farmhouse and check things out. Then we'll come back and pick you up."

As soon as they reached Matt's car, Jenn whirled on Marty and got in his face. "I can't believe you went off on the cops like that. If he hadn't hit you, I would have."

"I know," he answered sheepishly. "I just got pissed off because he kept shoving me every step like I didn't know how to walk. Trust me, I was a very good boy after that, and I'll never do it again."

She hugged him tenderly. "Good. I wouldn't really have hit you. I just said that because I was mad."

"Which only proves how easy it is to lose our temper," Stacie said. "Matt, did you find out what this was all about? What was in the warrant?"

He rolled his eyes dramatically. "Oh, it was a beauty. They were looking for guns, knives, explosives, chemicals, flammables, evidence of espionage...basically your run-of-the-mill terrorist tool kit. That's how they justified the show of force. I should warn you, the house is a wreck."

That proved to be an understatement. The SWAT team had ransacked every room, dumping the contents of drawers, cabinets and closets, and stripping all the linens. Mattresses and seat cushions were slit, though Stacie found her phone exactly where she left it.

In the kitchen, all of their food—rice, beans, even canned goods—had been emptied into the sink and doused with dishwashing soap.

"Bastards," Jenn hissed.

Matt grimaced. "Oh, and I have a little more bad news. The fire marshal says you can't have this many people renting one house unless it has a hotel license. Personally, I think he made that up. He set the limit at eight and he wants smoke detectors and fire extinguishers installed today."

Marty raised his hand. "I'm on it."

"We'll have to move five of our people in with some of the locals. I can look for another rental if you want, but first I have to get a new laptop."

"Use the credit card," Stacie said. "And take the others with you so they can replace their stuff too. I'll cover it until the insurance company settles. I need to call in some favors, so I'm going to check in to the Weller Regent downtown and work the phones. Let me know when you're back up and running."

"One other thing," Matt said as Jenn and Marty walked to their car. "They called me again about Dad's cabin. I'm telling you, they're offering him a ridiculous amount of money, about three times what it's worth. He'd be stupid not to take it, but we can drag our feet a little while longer and let your guys finish up."

That made Stacie's mission to get another set of water samples more urgent.

After he left, she walked through the house narrating a video of the destruction. CLEAN's big donors would be outraged and would use their money and connections to get her some attention from the legislature. What she really needed was someone she could trust inside the EPA and local law enforcement, but Nations Oil's tentacles ran deep.

CHAPTER EIGHT

Before driving into the parking garage of the Weller Regent, Cathryn pulled to the curb and waited to make sure she wasn't followed. A hotel tryst wasn't exactly at the top of her critical list tonight but she needed to see for herself that Stacie was all right.

She'd flipped around on all the TV channels to see if anyone was reporting an early morning police raid, but there hadn't been a peep. It was hard to believe something like what Depew had implied could happen under the radar, but the absence of CLEAN's reporters suggested otherwise.

All day she'd worried about Stacie, until finally she got a reply to her text message—an invitation to meet here at the hotel—and it had come as a huge relief. It was still a mystery why Stacie had taken so long to answer, and Cathryn rapped gently on the door of her hotel room, half expecting to be treated with indifference.

"Oh, my God! What happened to you?" Stacie's left eye was swollen and dark blue.

"Head, meet door."

She gently took Stacie's face in her hands, tipping it toward the light to get a better look. For a fleeting moment she saw her mother, battered and ashamed, and it filled her with rage. "Who did this?"

"You haven't heard? Depew's friends paid us a visit this morning, and they're definitely working with the sheriff's department and the county code enforcer. Apparently having too many people sleep under the same roof calls for a SWAT team. So my day started off with a bang, followed by a boot in my back and a couple of guns in my face." She pointed to her eye. "Oh, and then I *tripped* on my way out the door in handcuffs."

Though Cathryn couldn't bring herself to believe Hoss had signed off on something so brutal, it was clear Depew believed he had the authority to turn his goons loose on whomever he pleased. It was one thing to harass protestors by laying obstacles in their path or even with nuisance citations, but quite another to beat them up.

"If I find out Depew's behind this, I'll make sure my people rein him in. This isn't who we are. You have to believe that." She gently brushed Stacie's cheek. "You should put ice on this. Have you seen a doctor?"

"It's just a black eye. Ice might have helped at first but I was locked up for eight hours and couldn't get to my fridge."

She listened in horror as Stacie described the day's events. A week ago she might have dismissed the allegations against Depew as paranoia, but her general impression of him left little doubt he was capable of both malice and violence. He danced on the edge of lawlessness without stepping over, or at least without leaving an incriminating trail. Stopping him would be no easy task, especially if Nations Oil executives got the results they wanted while holding on to credible deniability. That's what dirty work was.

Climbing into bed with Stacie hadn't been on her agenda tonight but there was no place else to sit. The chairs and table were stacked with computer equipment and the boxes they came in. A new computer to replace one that was destroyed, Stacie explained. It certainly wasn't paranoia when it actually happened.

She kicked off her boots and leaned against the headboard, stretching her legs alongside Stacie's. In another wave of traumatic memories, she recalled sitting this way beside her mother in the bathroom as they braced the door so her father couldn't get in.

"I'm sorry this happened to you."

"Funny, but I'm not. The more success we have getting people behind us, the harder the pushback. These guys wouldn't have done something so drastic if we hadn't hit them where it hurts. I saw your press release from this morning. Do you even believe the things you say? I told you they'd doctor the documents."

"All I have to work with is the information I'm given. I may leave out a few disparaging details, and I'm very careful in my choice of words, but I don't stand there and knowingly lie. It's my job to project my company's image, and to cast them in the best possible light. Why would anyone expect anything else?"

"So if a kid shows up covered with bruises and his dad says he fell, you're just going to take his word for it?"

After she'd been grappling with her unpleasant memories of her mother, the question was like a slap in the face. "You're comparing this to beating up a child?" She scooted off the bed only to be tugged back down by her elbow.

"Oh, my God. I'm so sorry. What a stupid thing to say to somebody who's actually been there."

"For what it's worth, Stacie, I'm sure you're telling the truth about everything that happened to you. Like I said, I'll talk to the higher-ups, and not just because I think what's Depew's doing is morally wrong. It doesn't make good business sense to be associated with someone like that. I don't know exactly what you expect me to do, but I'm a whole lot more effective at making a difference from the inside. And I'm only talking about Depew, not everything we do at Nations Oil. You just have to accept there's another side to the oil business. It isn't as black and white as you seem to think it is, and the people who work there are no more evil than people anywhere else."

"I don't think you're evil, Cathryn. What I don't get, though, is how all of us can look at the same science, and you guys and all your powerful friends come to a different conclusion."

"That's an exaggeration. It's obvious the earth is warming, but whether or not it's caused by fossil fuel consumption isn't settled science. Do you think scientists would have shouted about global warming when we came out of the Ice Age? It's a natural process of the earth."

"Over hundreds of thousands of years, yes, but not forty. Natural warming happens from volcanoes and fissures in the earth, or when a herd of zebras break wind. Fuel consumption by humans is not natural. I know you've seen the charts. Answer me honestly. If you weren't in the oil business, would you believe the research?"

"But I am in the oil business, and I think that gives me more knowledge about it than the average person who just defers to the so-called experts."

"I'm in the oil business too, Cathryn, and I know these scientists you so easily dismiss don't just make up their data in a vacuum."

"Did you ever hear of the herd effect? That's when people all start saying the same thing because they're afraid to go against the grain. Science journals won't publish articles that aren't part of the conventional wisdom, so why bother writing them in the first place? Especially if you want tenure or government funding." Cathryn was tired of the conflict. She relaxed against the pillows again and laid her head on Stacie's shoulder, taking care not to bump her eye. "Let's just drop it. Why did you ask me here if you hate me so much?"

"I don't hate you. I just wanted to prove to you what those assholes had done. And maybe I wanted a little sympathy…

somebody to baby me over my boo-boo. Think you could do that? I've had a really bad day."

She couldn't help but laugh at Stacie's sudden child-like plea for comfort. "You want me to kiss it and make it better?"

"I'm not sure I could handle that. It's pretty tender."

"How about butterfly kisses?" She carefully flicked her eyelashes against the swollen brow. "Can you feel that?"

"I can feel your hand in my crotch."

It was only then she noticed she'd braced herself on one arm, which was wedged between Stacie's legs. "We're going to have sex again, aren't we?"

"I sure hope so, but if I lie down my head will explode."

"We can't have that." Cathryn loosened the buttons on Stacie's plaid shirt. "I like this. It's soft."

"It's my favorite. Somctimes I prefer it to nothing at all."

"And you aren't wearing a bra. I like that too." She left the last two buttons intact and switched her attention to the jeans, standing up to tug them off along with the panties. Sitting there only in her shirt made Stacie sexy as hell. "I don't suppose you have a nice, fat dildo in that bag over there? Because I'd really like to watch it slide in and out of you."

"I don't…and believe me, no one is sorrier about that than I am. But it would have run into a little resistance, if you catch my drift."

"You got your period. No babies for another month."

Stacie shooed her away and motioned for her to undress. "I bet if you laid here in my lap and closed your eyes, I could make you forget all about dildos."

Cathryn left her clothes in a rumpled pile on the floor and returned to the bed. It took several tries to situate herself diagonally across Stacie's lap so all the relevant hot spots were within reach for both of them. She liked the feel of the soft material on her skin. "I'm closing my eyes now."

"Me too, but I'm picturing what this looks like." Stacie tickled her folds and spread the wetness all around. "I studied you the other night. You have the most lovely labia…brown like cinnamon on the outside, and then underneath it's bright pink. This part right…here."

A finger slid around her opening, sending a jolt deep inside her. "My imagination is wondering where that dildo is."

"I'm sure you can beg better than that."

As a matter of principle, she held off a bit longer, visualizing the pulsing waves that reached out to pull the fingers inside. Stacie was in charge though. If it was begging she wanted, then begging she'd get. "I need to feel you inside."

Stacie entered her with what felt like two fingers, pressing down against the bottom of her canal. The elusive G-spot, where the right amount of pressure drew the hood across her clitoris. In any other position, she'd have wanted more, faster, deeper. Instead she wanted only to ride this sensation all the way home. "I beg you not to stop exactly what you're doing."

The only change was a very subtle increase in pressure, offset by a slowing of strokes. "I bet you're standing up like a soldier. I studied that too."

As she visualized her slick, rippling lips, she sucked in deep gulps of air between her teeth, holding each breath in anticipation of her climax. When it didn't come, she exhaled with force, only to find herself even more excited. If this one somehow got away from her, she'd die right here in a tangle of nerves.

And then the magic happened, a burst of vibrations that lasted five or six glorious seconds, the shortest of her life.

"You have killed me." She throbbed around Stacie's fingers, which now were buried deep inside her. "And I died in ecstasy."

"Guess I'll have to roll your dead body off the bed and take care of myself."

"No, no. All you have to do is kiss me to bring me back to life."

Cathryn closed her eyes as their lips met, savoring a tender sensation that went beyond caution about the injured eye. She could no longer pretend this was just another SappHere hookup. The sex was wonderful, but it was obvious too that they cared for one another.

They traded sexual adventures until well after midnight, when Cathryn finally dragged herself from the bed. "I have to go. Everyone's so wound up right now there's no telling what my in-box looks like, and I wouldn't be surprised if they came knocking on my door at five o'clock in the morning."

"If they did, it wouldn't be a SWAT team. They don't knock."

"I really am sorry about that, Stacie. This is going to be hard for us, you know. I'm not kidding when I say I could lose my job for being with you."

Stacie, dressed again in her shirt and panties, followed her to the door. "I know you have a lot more at stake than I do so I'll leave it up to you where we go from here. I hope you can find a way to see me, because I really like you a lot."

"I feel the same about you—even if you're one of those environmental whacko birds—but it's riskier for us now that Depew's guys are checking up on you...and who knows? Probably me too." She realized she'd already made her decision and didn't like it one bit. "Maybe we should cool it."

"That will suck." With a grim smile, Stacie kissed her softly on the cheek. "It doesn't have to be forever."

"It won't be."

As Cathryn drove back to her hotel, she contemplated their parting words. SappHere was a hookup app, and neither of them had walked into this expecting anything else. Yet Stacie was unlike any other woman she'd met, and the fact that their lives were intertwined outside of dating deepened their relationship in a way she hadn't expected.

It probably couldn't come to anything, since they lived in different cities and held wildly divergent views on the one issue that practically defined them both. That didn't mean they couldn't get together for an occasional weekend, a thought that made her more sad than happy because it wasn't fair to have to deal with such restrictions. No boss should have that kind of power over her personal life.

The odor of scotch hit her the moment she opened the door. Depew was asleep on her couch, an open bottle beside him on the floor.

"What the hell are you doing here?"

He sat up and blinked, obviously disoriented. Then he held up a plastic key card. "I'm in charge of security, in case you forgot. When you didn't answer your door, I had to check and make sure you were…secure." He belched.

"I am. Now get out."

"I answered your question. Now you answer mine. Where have you been?"

Lying could get her in a heap of trouble, on the off-chance he was sober enough to remember what she said long enough to check it out. But Stacie had given her the perfect cover. "A friend of mine drove up from St. Paul and we met for a drink downtown. Jane Larsen." There had to be at least a dozen women by that name in the Twin Cities.

His eyes glazed over as he stood, and for a moment she feared he'd throw up. Instead he staggered toward the door. "About your little press tour…you don't need to go crying to Hoss when you want something. I'm a reasonable man. I can always work something out."

It was all she could do not to slam the door behind him. How dare he let himself into her apartment! She knew now to keep everything personal locked in the safe and to double-check the bolt on the door whenever she was inside. Any more visits like this and she'd file a sexual harassment claim.

Except *Don't Make Waves.* Reporting Depew would end her career.

CHAPTER NINE

The dining room at the Weller Regent bustled with business types and Stacie had worn one of her conference outfits to fit in. It made her look more professional and that was important for this meeting. She'd polished off a mixed fruit bowl with toast, and was chatting with Izzy using her laptop's instant messenger app.

"Tankers still coming in all hours of the night. Big staging area in the woods straight across from the cabin. Sneaked out and got the samples you wanted before daylight."

According to the video Ricky had streamed the day before, Nations Oil was getting ready to ramp up its operation when, by their own reports, they should be winding down. Little wonder they were doing it under the cover of darkness. She couldn't wait to get her hands on the new samples and get them tested by a reliable lab.

She hurriedly typed, *"Don't say anything to Jenn about the samples, okay? Don't want to hurt Marty's feelings by using somebody else to do the analysis."*

"Understand. Btw, Ricky said the main board you sent from the hobby store was bent, but he was able to fix it. Should have another drone up and running by this afternoon."

"Sorry about that." She hadn't inspected the cache of supplies Marty had gathered before dropping them off, but probably wouldn't have noticed a damaged board anyway. *"You need anything else?"*

"Bananas. Toilet paper. Deck of cards. Will set the samples out tomorrow morning."

"Great. I'll run your stuff out before sunset. Gotta go."

Colleen Murray entered the restaurant and Stacie waved her over. "I really appreciate this, Colleen. And I think you will too."

The *Star-Tribune* reporter, a woman in her fifties with Nordic coloring typical of Minnesotans, had in fact acted delighted when Stacie called her for a chat over coffee, especially after the promise of new information based on CLEAN's research. She came well-prepared for the interview with a stack of articles on oil spills, copies of all the press materials Nations Oil had released and her reporter's notebook.

"Some of this has to be off the record. I'm sorry, but we have people in the field whose safety could be compromised. I understand you're going on a press tour of the cleanup site tomorrow afternoon. Apparently it was invitation only and our people weren't invited."

"I get so mad when they pick and choose who to talk to. It's like they're reminding us we have to print what they tell us or they'll freeze us out."

"That's exactly what they're doing, and that's why I wanted to talk to you before you went out there. Maybe you could ask a few questions for us."

"Sure, what have you got?"

"More flyover pictures for starters, but they shot down our drone this time." Stacie had printed out several frames of the video Ricky had live-streamed before his drone was destroyed, including a close-up of the staging area. "They're still bringing in equipment. All this came in just three days ago."

Colleen studied the first photo with interest. "That makes no sense. They said yesterday they were ninety percent finished. And why would they be bringing in a bulldozer?"

"To build a dredge pad." She pointed to the second photo, the same view but from a higher altitude. "See how much land they've cleared? They're going to suck up the whole lakebed and pile it in this clearing. Once they find a dump site, they'll haul it off one truckload at a time."

"I don't get it. Why would they need to—" Her eyes went wide. "Are you saying the whole lake is contaminated?"

"That's exactly what I'm saying. They've managed to convince the public, and maybe even the EPA, that this spill has been confined to a small cove inside the containment boom. Ninety thousand gallons. CLEAN thinks it's a whole lot more." She went back to the first photo and pointed to two of the machines that had just arrived. "Take another look at this one. These are grab dredgers, used for scooping up heavy sediment. That's not how you pick up heavy oil. For that, you'd normally use a vacuum and centrifuge."

Colleen sifted through her resource materials and produced a photo of a suction dredger. "One of these."

"Right. You suck the water in, spin it, fill up a tanker with oil and pour the clean water back into the lake. You hardly have any losses, so it doesn't make sense they'd use a grab dredger… unless it's sitting on the bottom—and it's not really heavy oil."

"You think it's bitumen?" She covered her mouth after realizing she'd nearly shouted the words. "That kid from the school paper who got hassled about smoking pot in his car, Ethan Anders…he asked if that's what it was."

"He had reason to think so." Stacie explained how she knew Ethan, and that she'd filled him in on her clandestine kayak mission, though she didn't mention the samples since the negative results undermined her claims. "Nations Oil was fined seven million dollars two years ago by the PHMSA for moving bitumen through an unapproved pipeline in Wyoming. Another incident like that could earn them a fine five times that size."

"Do they actually think they can get away with this? Surely the EPA knows what's in the lake."

She wasn't going to speculate about Nations Oil paying off the EPA, but it wasn't out of the question. "They probably don't have that many inspectors on-site because they're telling everybody this is a relatively small spill. If it's bitumen, it's sitting on the bottom where no one can see it, especially if they aren't looking out past the boom. Obviously Nations Oil figures they'll have to clean it up eventually, but they don't want to get caught doing it because it could screw up their approval on the Caliber Pipeline."

Colleen shook her head. "It still doesn't make sense. How do they think they're going to dredge that lake without anyone knowing about it?"

"By continuing to deny access. Have you been keeping up with all the property transfers out there? A friend of mine says Nations Oil is offering way over the market value for every single cabin on the lake. Why do they keep pushing that if the lake's almost clean?"

"Good question to ask their spokeswoman."

Their spokeswoman. Poor Cathryn would be blindsided again, and would have to bear the brunt of ridicule when her false information was exposed. It was entirely possible she didn't even know about the dredge pad, since they were moving equipment in at night and it was well past the traffic barricade. Nonetheless, Stacie couldn't let her personal feelings enter into this, not when exposing this cover-up could torpedo once and for all Nations Oil's chances of pushing through the Caliber Pipeline. That would be the biggest victory in years for the clean energy movement.

"Oh, and while you're out there tomorrow, look around at the number of tankers. We saw at least four on our flyover, and they're supposed to hold nine thousand gallons each. Why do they need that many if they've cleaned up all but eight thousand gallons?"

Colleen had scribbled page after page of notes, and when they finished, set her reference materials aside and turned her notebook to a fresh page. "Now do I get to hear the story of that shiner?"

After two days, her eye had taken on a purple hue. "On the record or off?"

"You tell me."

Over one last cup of coffee, Stacie shared the story of the raid, being careful not to cast direct aspersions on Nations Oil or the local sheriff's department. She had no ironclad proof the two were in cahoots but a good reporter like Colleen could potentially make hay out of police reports and interviews with the right people. It was even better to have a mainstream journalist telling the story because it wouldn't be written off as slanted to their side.

"One last thing," Stacie said. "You remember we're holding our rally at five o'clock tomorrow in Chester Park, and I think it's going to be really big. I'm not just saying that. People are getting on board with us, and we need to show them there's something they can do. It's a great lineup. Wait till you hear the congresswoman from Arkansas talk about the Exxon spill in her district. It just bubbled up right out of the ground and ran down the street. And one of our speakers is a guy who grew up on the Kalamazoo River in Michigan in a house his great-grandfather built. He used to fish there and go swimming with his dogs. Now he feels like his whole way of life is gone, all because an oil company pushed tar sands through pipelines that were built for conventional oil. They'll be telling those stories here in the not-too-distant future, so I hope you'll be able to make it."

"The press tour's scheduled for three o'clock. That cuts it close but I'll try to get there."

Cathryn had probably done that on purpose so the mainstream press would miss the rally. Smart, but not very nice.

"Don't worry, Stacie. This is more than just a Lake Bunyan story now. Those oil companies have pipelines all over Minnesota, and I intend to write stories that will make people stop and think about what that could mean to their lives. And besides, do you honestly think I'm going to miss anything now that I have all this background?"

"I promise we'll sit on these photos till Thursday morning after your story comes out. It's your exclusive." She stacked the photos and pushed them across the table. "And here's my card in case you have any questions."

When she grabbed the check to pay for breakfast, Colleen forced her to take three dollars. "We pay our own way at the *Star-Tribune*. No gifts, no matter how small."

It was refreshing to know there were still some people who weren't for sale.

* * *

Cathryn lowered her safety mask each time she spoke so her voice wouldn't be muffled. "As you can see, the dredge operator is picking up sediment from the lakebed and transferring it to the truck, where it will be taken to a refinery in Pipe Bend for processing. Feel free to take photos."

One of the TV reporters thrust a handheld broadcast microphone bearing his station's logo into her face, meaning she'd show up on the news in a hardhat with her mask hanging around her neck. Not her best look. "I don't understand, Ms. Mack. Shouldn't the oil be floating on the top?"

Before she could answer, Larry Kratke stepped in to take the question. "The floating oil was our first priority. We removed most of it immediately, but as the hydrocarbons evaporate, what's left grows heavier and sinks to the bottom."

Colleen Murray leaned in close to Larry with a digital voice recorder. "Isn't this the same technique for cleaning up bitumen?"

Larry's eyes showed surprise at the question. "Similar."

"Is there an official estimate on how much oil has been recovered?" The question came from another TV reporter and was directed to Bob Kryzwicki, who headed the EPA's inspection team. Bob had come along on the press tour at

Cathryn's urging, feeling it would put the public at ease to know the agency was performing its regulatory function.

"Our estimate is just over eighty thousand gallons. As Miss Mack here has already explained, the cleanup is actually proceeding ahead of schedule. It gets a little tricky when we get down to the last ten or twelve percent because it's less concentrated."

"How would you describe this spill relative to others?"

"Not minor, not major. On the low end of moderate, I'd say."

Larry added, "It may not look like it with all this equipment around here, but we expect to have this lake back the way it was within another week or so, provided the weather holds out."

"If that's true," Colleen said, "why is Nations Oil buying up all the waterfront properties? I reviewed title transfers at the county courthouse yesterday and saw that three-quarters of these cabins have been sold in the last ten days to a holding company controlled by Nations Oil."

Cathryn hadn't expected such aggressive questioning from Colleen. "I'll take that, Larry. We addressed that in one of our earlier press conferences if you'll recall. One thing that always happens after an accident such as this is homeowners get anxious about their property values and they worry about living in an area that might be environmentally compromised. When we buy their properties, they have money to settle elsewhere immediately, giving them peace of mind. It also protects us from very expensive litigation that can go on for years, litigation that's designed to harass and inhibit our company's legitimate right to expand our business."

"A question for Mr. Kratke," Colleen said, not missing a beat. "Is it normal to pick up heavy oil with a grab dredger? It's my understanding the most efficient process is to use a suction dredger that separates the oil from the water."

"We used a suction dredger to recover most of the oil that was spilled," he answered testily. "As I was saying earlier, the recovery becomes more tedious when all that's left is what's embedded in the sediment. You can't just suck up the lakebed like that. You have to get down there and scoop it up."

Colleen cocked her head as if confused. "I'm curious about the three tankers that were parked in that lot. Why would you have so many—by my estimate they'll hold twenty-seven thousand gallons—when all you have left is about eight thousand gallons, and you're scooping that up with a grab dredger and taking it to Pipe Bend in a dump truck?"

Cathryn's stomach dropped when Larry didn't immediately answer, and she jumped back into the conversation. "I could check the manifest on those if you like. It's likely they're loaded and ready to roll, but can't because the refinery is at capacity."

"Another question for Mr. Kryzwicki," Colleen continued relentlessly. "Has your agency performed tests on the water and sediment outside the containment area?"

"We regularly monitor the margins for leakage, and I can assure you there's no oil outside the containment area."

Another reporter spoke up. "So you've done no tests?"

"Of course we've done tests," he snapped, "but they've shown no evidence of contamination beyond the booms."

With a wave toward their company van, Cathryn said, "If there are no more questions—"

"I have one more," Colleen said, looking up toward the sky. "It's obvious with all the equipment and fumes, this area should be closed to the public out of safety concerns, but how does your company feel about citizens using surveillance drones to monitor the cleanup process?"

Before Cathryn could answer, Depew pushed his way forward. She hadn't even realized he was lurking at the back. With his usual gruffness, he barked, "How did you feel when some dimwit gave you only half the story on the fish kill and made you all look like idiots?"

That was not the impression Cathryn wanted reporters to take away. "I'm not sure what the law says in Minnesota about the use of private surveillance drones, but if they're permitted, there's no reason they can't be used. I think the important caveat is they may very well be misleading, and I'm particularly concerned that amateur film is subject to manipulation."

"So if they're legal, you wouldn't try to prevent their use?"

"Absolutely not. We have nothing to hide."

"Then you deny shooting one down yesterday as it filmed your dredging operation?"

Again Depew spoke up. "We periodically fire shotguns in the air to scare off birds. If we accidentally hit somebody's flying toy, that's just unlucky for them."

Cathryn directed the reporters back to the van and cornered Depew as he climbed into his SUV. "I don't know what you were trying to accomplish, but you can't talk to the press like that. It just makes things worse. Communication is my job, not yours."

"Then you should do it," he shot back. "My job is security, and if you can't keep that bullshit out of the papers, I will." He slammed his door and spun out of the lot, spraying gravel in his wake.

"God, I hate that man."

On the short ride back to the press trailer, Cathryn noticed Colleen, who had taken far more notes and photos than anyone else, still scribbling in her notebook. Not only had she shown more skepticism, she also had displayed a deeper understanding of the technical aspects of oil cleanup. The biggest surprise was her special knowledge of a drone that had flown over the day before, something of which Cathryn wasn't aware. That could only mean she'd talked to Stacie Pilardi.

The rally in Chester Park started in forty-five minutes. With luck, the reporters in the van would rush home to file their stories, and the protest would get no coverage at all from the major media outlets.

Woody and Amy emerged from the lavatory together as soon as she entered the press trailer.

"Whatever you're doing, you guys need to knock it off at work, and I'm not going to warn you again."

At least Amy had the common sense to blush.

"The Clean Energy Action Network is holding a protest rally in Chester Park at five o'clock. We need to be there so we can hear their talking points. I want you both to mingle. Open your ears, clap and cheer, hold signs if they ask you to."

"What are you going to do?" Woody asked.

"They'll probably recognize me from TV, so I'll just stand in the back and look bitter." That shouldn't be too hard.

* * *

Thirty-five hundred people at their protest rally was a couple of thousand short of "doubling every day," but in a small city like Duluth, it was beyond Stacie's wildest dreams. All of the local news stations had hurried over with camera crews after Jenn tweeted pictures of the growing crowd. Nothing pumped up support for the cause like showing people their neighbors cared. No matter what Cathryn said, there was only one responsible side to this issue.

Two-thirds of the crowd were young people, probably college students. Ethan had become a rock star on campus after his false arrest, and his peers were outraged. Dozens of them had signed up for the online training seminars, after which they'd join CLEAN's nationwide network, either to work in their own communities or to come along on a future road trip.

Another common face at their rallies were the aging Baby Boomers, well-educated couples who might have been hippies in their youth. Many of them had the capacity to understand science and logic, and still held onto their dream of a better world.

One of those couples was making its way toward her with Faye, the girl who had dropped out the week before. "Stacie, I want you to meet my parents. Actually I want my parents to meet you."

The Brownings were midforties, Stacie guessed, and dressed in business clothes as though they'd come to the park directly from office jobs.

"Mr. and Mrs. Browning, my pleasure. And thank you for sending in such a generous donation. Believe me, we'll put it to good use."

"Give us a minute," Mr. Browning said, and Faye and her mother stepped away. "I hope you understand about Faye. She's a really passionate young lady and I worried about her getting in over her head. That doesn't mean we don't agree with what you're doing. I'm just being a protective dad."

"I totally get it. We all have to find our comfort level, and that can be lying down in front of a bulldozer or just pulling the lever for the candidate who'll do our cause the most good."

"Faye would definitely be the bulldozer type if we didn't rein her in. For what it's worth, we brought along a few reinforcements tonight. I belong to a sportsman's club and we don't want to see our lakes ruined. Some of my friends are here with their families, and Beverly managed to get a whole group from our church."

"Wow. That's exactly the kind of public reaction we need to win this battle. I hope you'll tell Faye what a huge impact she's made on the environment just by sharing her passion." They shook hands.

Their first speaker, Representative Sheila Rutledge from Arkansas, was slated to kick things off in fifteen minutes. In the meantime, a local band was warming up the crowd.

Stacie worked her way to the volunteer table, where people were signing up for various jobs—door-to-door canvassing, collecting signatures, working the phone bank, holding up placards on street corners—something for everyone.

A couple in their midtwenties had been studying the opportunities and sign-up sheets, and the girl stepped forward and asked, "Is this where we volunteer?" She had a heavy Southern accent, and they were interested in working a three-hour shift on Saturday holding up signs that read *NATIONS spOILed Lake Bunyan* on the sidewalk next to one of the company's busiest gas stations.

As they walked away, Stacie noticed the man's lizard-skin cowboy boots. "Cross them off. They have no intention of showing up, and if they do, it'll only be to cause trouble. They're both employees of Nations Oil."

Walking behind them through the crowd, she saw the young man give a thumbs-up sign to someone in the back. Her eyes followed his to where Cathryn was leaning against a tree sipping bottled water. Outflanking her, Stacie was able to surprise her from behind. Keeping her voice low, she leaned over Cathryn's shoulder and said, "We have a few chairs up front if you'd like to sit."

"Jesus! You scared me half to death."

"Sorry, I wasn't trying to. I sneaked around because I figured you wouldn't want your acolytes to see me talking to you."

"My acolytes?"

"The girl with the Southern accent and the guy in the cowboy boots. They're a little out of place in the Land of Swedish Meatballs."

Cathryn crossed her arms and looked back toward the stage, her chin thrust forward defiantly. "I'm not here to hassle you. It's my job to know what's going on."

"I know. I'm not here to hassle you either. I just hope you'll listen to our program with an open mind."

"And then you'll listen to me? I'll have you know Nations Oil has a long list of green initiatives, like wind and solar, biofuels…and we're constantly working on new technology to improve emissions. All you ever see is a big evil dollar sign."

"No, what I see is a big oily footprint."

"How can you say that?" From her gritted teeth, it was obvious she was trying hard not to make a scene. "We've had spills before and we've cleaned up every one. We've always done our utmost to make sure every single person who's affected gets compensated. The only solution that works for you is for us to disappear completely tomorrow, and that's just not going to happen."

There was a lot of truth to that, but it wasn't about the money. "Fossil fuels are killing the planet. There's no comfort in being just a little bit dead."

"Hyperbole."

"Science." The band's final bow signaled the start of the speaker program and Stacie inched away. "I have to go. You have no idea how much I wish we were on the same team, Cathryn, but it would have to be my team."

* * *

When Cathryn returned to her car, she found a citation on the windshield for improper parking, with a scribbled note that read, *Failure to pull forward*. While it was technically true her wheels were not against the parking stop, they were less than a foot away and not obstructing traffic. She noticed a smattering of tickets throughout the lot, and reluctantly had to conclude it was part of a law enforcement harassment campaign targeting CLEAN's activities.

Stacie sure knew how to put together a powerful and inspiring program, but her public speaking skills left a lot to be desired. Too many nervous fillers, and in a voice that modulated up and down at all the wrong times. It took away the power of her words, which was a good thing as far as Cathryn was concerned.

Unfortunately, the legislator from Arkansas, a feisty African-American woman, more than made up for it. She'd come to urge the citizens of Duluth to use every available channel—protests, letters to the editor, elections and the courts—to demand not only cleanup but criminal accountability for those responsible for the pipeline break. Her vivid description of a small town north of Little Rock where oil ran down neighborhood streets, through the sewer and into a local lake had the crowd ready to gather torches and pitchforks for a march out to Lake Bunyan.

Next was a man from Michigan who grew up along the Kalamazoo River. He told of his dogs wading in the river and stepping out with gobs of tarry oil stuck to their feet. Even more damaging was the news that he'd not caught a single fish in the three years since the spill.

As much as Cathryn wished she could dismiss the rally as a minor, inconsequential event, it had in fact been quite effective. The crowd was much bigger than she expected and far more enthusiastic, and she dreaded her call with Hoss tomorrow in which she'd have to tell him they were organizing for legal proceedings. This was her failure for not controlling the message.

After the speakers, the band returned to the stage and Cathryn took her leave. Traffic slowed considerably on the highway leading out of town toward her hotel. In the distance she saw blue lights, and an ambulance passed her on the right in the narrow emergency lane. As she inched past the scene, she fought the urge to gape but it was no use. A car had left the road and was sitting upside down, its top nearly flattened. There was little doubt someone was seriously injured, if not killed.

Perspective. Some poor soul was having a far worse day than hers.

CHAPTER TEN

"I'm doing my part."

"And I'm doing my part."

"At Nations Oil, we're all doing our part to make this right, and it won't cost taxpayers one dime. In fact, we're working with Duluth Public Schools to start a new Outdoor Education Program to help everyone learn how to take care of this beautiful land we call home."

"Thank you, Nations Oil!"

"Thank you, Nations Oil!"

"And thank you, northern Minnesota, for your trust and patience. We keep our promises."

Cathryn muted the television and kicked off her shoes, ready to relax for the night.

The ad agency had delivered in a hurry, getting their message on the air in a mere twenty-four hours. Hoss had come through with a check for the schools, and another for a regional wildlife sanctuary.

Their advertising blitz was meant to reach everyone in the four-county media market, countering the efforts of Stacie and her supporters. Average people would be less likely to get involved in protests if they believed Nations Oil was behaving responsibly, and they couldn't afford to let CLEAN's campaign grow into a groundswell.

She looked forward to wearing her favorite business suit for the ceremonial presentation of the school check to a classroom of third graders, a nice photo op for the newspapers to go along with their full-page ad. She'd canceled the next day's press conference, and in fact was cutting back to only three a week in an effort to stay out of the news.

There was still no word from Hoss about when she and her staff could return to Houston. The preliminary report from the PHMSA was due early next week, but that was only for the pipeline accident. The EPA's report on the spill and cleanup would take longer, and she desperately hoped he wouldn't make her wait around for that. If they could just get through the next week or so with no more surprises, she was headed back to an office on the East End.

It would be nice if she and Stacie could be together again during whatever time they had left, but they'd have to agree not to talk about work. It wasn't as if they had nothing else in common. There was yoga, movies…incredible sex. Maybe they wouldn't even have to talk at all.

Despite their fundamental disagreement on oil production, she admired Stacie's passion. Anyone who dedicated her life to something she thought would make the world a better place deserved respect, especially since many others with her financial means were jetting off to the Riviera to party on a yacht. Too bad her cause hadn't been world hunger or stamping out some horrible disease.

A sharp knock on the door jarred her from her thoughts, and she realized she'd almost nodded off to sleep on the couch. She didn't have the energy to deal with Woody or Amy tonight, and it couldn't possibly be Depew because it was an ordinary knock, the kind polite people used.

"Who is it?"

"Pizza."

She swung the door open. "I didn't order—"

Stacie, wearing a black cap pulled low over her brow, stood holding a pizza box. "I need to talk to you."

"Get in here before somebody sees you!"

"I'm only going to stay a minute. First of all, this." She tossed her cap aside and pulled Cathryn into a kiss. "This situation sucks. We have to make some time to be together before I go crazy."

"Me too, and I'm working on it already. I used your cover story the other night about meeting up with an old friend from St. Paul. What if I tell them I'm driving down to visit her for the weekend? Can you get away?"

"Yes, absolutely."

"But if somebody catches you here—"

"They won't. I gave the pizza guy a hundred bucks to drive me over in his car. I had to talk to you about Colleen Murray. You need to know this."

"I heard what happened. She's going to be okay, right?"

The horrible accident Cathryn had witnessed on her way home from the rally turned out to be Colleen, whose brakes had failed. According to Amy, she was in traction from head to toe with a badly sprained neck.

"I spoke with her son today. He had somebody check out the car and he says the brake line was deliberately cut. Cathryn, somebody did this." She whispered as though it were a secret she was dying to share.

"Why would anyone want to hurt Colleen?"

"I think you know why—because she was asking too many questions and making the wrong people uncomfortable. The more important question is who, and I think we both know the answer to that one too."

"You think it was Depew."

"Don't you?"

The question shocked her. "Are you serious? You can't just accuse somebody like that. Do you have any proof?"

"What I know is Colleen was working on a big story that would have made Nations Oil look very bad. I gave her some photos that showed your company was building a dredge pad, and those photos disappeared after the accident, along with everything else in her briefcase—all of her notes and resource documents, and her camera too."

"That doesn't prove anything." But she had to admit it made her dreadfully uneasy to recall Colleen's aggressive questions and Depew's rude response. "Why are you telling me this? If you've got evidence Depew's behind it, you should go to the police."

"You want me to go to the people who did this?" She pointed to her injured eye, which had faded to yellow and green. "Look, I know you can't do anything about Depew, but I don't want this to blow back on you. You need to get out of this before it gets even uglier. They could have killed her, Cathryn."

"Quit my job because of Karl Depew?"

"This is bigger than Depew and you know it. It's a whole conspiracy. I should have realized that when the SWAT team showed up. He has enough friends in the sheriff's department to do whatever he wants, and I wouldn't be surprised if he was getting even more help than that."

"Now you're sounding paranoid."

"It wouldn't be the first time the feds stepped in to protect the interests of their friends with money. People like Hoss Bower don't prop up politicians without expecting something in return."

Hoss was definitely cozy with Senator Mike Washburn, but it made perfect sense that both would be interested in economic growth, and the oil industry was a big part of that. "Why do you have to assume everything we do is underhanded?"

"I don't think you've done anything wrong, Cathryn, but somebody is pulling a lot of strings. If there's blowback, your company is going to throw people under the bus. Who better to take the fall than the public face of Nations Oil?"

Cathryn shook her head vehemently. Hoss wouldn't do that to her.

"I don't want to see you hurt, sweetheart. Please get out of this before it's too late."

Sweetheart. "I could say the same to you. If any of what you're saying is true, you're in a lot more danger than I am."

"If people like me run away, the bastards win. I intend to stop them, but I won't be able to protect you if it all crashes down."

"It won't." Passion and courage, with no small dose of recklessness. And yet Cathryn respected her more than ever. "Please be careful."

"I will. Come to the St. Paul Hotel tomorrow night."

Cathryn watched from the window as she got into a station wagon, its lighted sign the perfect cover for a clandestine visit. Stacie had taken a great risk to show up here, all because she believed Cathryn would be the one to suffer from the fallout.

A dredge pad. The containment area was relatively small, manageable with just a few trucks to haul off the sediment. The only reason they'd need a dredge pad was if they were planning to scrape a wider area…like the whole lakebed.

As much as she tried to deny the puzzle Stacie had put together, her own picture was even more complete given Woody's estimate and Depew's cryptic threats. What's more, she knew exactly what was at stake, and it wasn't just a billion dollars in cleanup and fines. The Caliber Pipeline was moving through the Senate committee, and any disruption could kill it once and for all. It represented the future of Nations Oil for decades to come.

For the first time in twenty-two years, she wondered if indeed she was working on the wrong team.

* * *

"Right this way, Miss Pilardi."

Stacie followed Matt Stevenson's receptionist to a conference room, where Jenn and the attorney were already waiting. Several documents were spread out awaiting her signature.

"You're not going to believe what just happened," Matt said. "I called the sheriff's office this morning and told them we were making a property claim for eighteen thousand and change. They said to bring it over, they'd review it and cut a check. When I mentioned physical injuries, they offered an extra six thousand dollars for us to waive any and all future claims against their department related to this incident."

Jenn pumped her fist triumphantly. "Sounds like their lawyers didn't think much of that show of force. They aren't used to having somebody fight back."

"It's more than that," Stacie said. "I think their paid thugs inside the department got cold feet all of a sudden. It was fun while they were roughing up a bunch of tree-huggers, but then Colleen Murray got hurt. My guess is they're crying foul, and this payment is coming directly from Nations Oil as hush money."

Matt nodded thoughtfully. "That all fits. By the way, their offer for the cabin just jumped to half a million. Not bad for eight hundred square feet. How soon can your friends be out?"

"Another week?"

She'd picked up Izzy's samples this morning and divided them into two sets. One she'd deliver this afternoon to the Department of Health in St. Paul, and another—just to hedge her bets in case Nations Oil tried to buy off even more officials—to a private lab that offered environmental mitigation services. Both contacts were provided by one of her well-connected donors. With the results in hand by the end of next week, they could go forward with an all-out media blitz against Nations Oil for acting in bad faith. If they made a big enough splash, the EPA would be forced to come down hard. Best of all, it would help their chances against the Caliber Pipeline.

* * *

Woody clacked away on his keyboard while Amy spoke with a congressional aide on the phone.

Cathryn wasn't accustomed to working with such distractions, especially when her task required concentration. She was writing—spinning, actually—a press release to accompany the PHMSA report, which had landed on her desk early this morning. There was no such thing as a favorable incident report, but this was as close to one as she'd ever seen. The break had occurred beneath the perimeter road, leading investigators to blame it on stress from heavy vehicle traffic crossing above. Nations Oil could reasonably argue the county shared culpability for not enforcing weight restrictions on its roadways.

In response to these findings, her company would launch an immediate inspection across its pipeline network of all segments that might be compromised by traffic. What she didn't say was that ninety-nine percent of these inspections would be conducted from their computer center in Houston, with only a hundred or so inspected manually. They'd look for anomalous pressure readings that couldn't be explained by pumping irregularities, and they might even conduct preventive maintenance in a few places. The reality was accidents like this couldn't be predicted, not when they were caused by variables beyond the control of engineers.

Her phone lit up with a call from Hoss. "Good morning."

"It certainly is!" he boomed. "Too bad you're not here with us in Houston. We're saving a cigar with your name on it."

"I'm afraid I'll have to pass on that, but I hereby bequeath mine to you."

"You twisted my arm. So how do you plan on celebrating?"

"Actually, I have a nice weekend planned. One of my friends from college lives in St. Paul. She invited me to visit this weekend and I think I'll take her up on it. It would be nice to talk to someone who wasn't pelting me with questions."

She'd never outright lied to Hoss before. The only way she could justify the betrayal was to convince herself it was personal and not at all related to her job. Convincing Stacie of that was even more important.

"That's a great idea, Cathryn. Get your mind off work and relax. You earned it."

"Thank you."

"Listen, the main reason I called is Larry tells me he's going to be finished with the cleanup by the middle of next week. I talked with Mike Washburn and he thinks we ought to do a dog and pony show so the press can see what a good job we did. He's thinking about throwing his hat in the ring for a GOP run at the White House, and he needs some outdoor bonafides. But the main reason is so we'll have something to brag about when his committee takes up the Caliber Pipeline."

And maybe after that she could finally get back to Houston and away from creeps like Karl Depew. "We can do that. I assume you'll want it at one of the downtown resorts on Lake Superior."

"Oh, no. Mike needs to have it outside. Find us a nice spot by that lake, something with a pretty view in the background. I want people to see everything back to normal."

She was skeptical, especially given the odor of petroleum and the recent arrival of more heavy-duty equipment, but he wouldn't plan this if he weren't sure. "There's a public park, a boat launch. I'm sure the county will let us use it."

"Outstanding! Oh, and make sure you plan to join the senator and me for dinner on Thursday night. Mike'll like you, but you'd better watch out for him. He's a rascal."

It was hard not to feel she was being whored out, though Hoss was only asking her to be a charming hostess. She had no choice but to comply, knowing it could mean fending off creepy advances from a US Senator while somehow making sure they didn't lose his support.

"Looks like we're going to get out of this with our hide, Cathryn. We dodged a bullet, no small thanks to you. Bryce and some of the others always said we needed a spokesman like Paul Barker who'd go out there and give 'em hell, but I told him we'd catch more flies with honey. Guess we showed them, huh?"

She hated Bryce Tucker and the horse he rode in on. Such an ass, running around bad-mouthing her behind her back. He was no better than Karl Depew. They didn't have an ounce of decency between them.

It was ironic to think she'd described the higher-ups at Nations Oil to Stacie as kind and decent, when their second in command—and likely the next CEO—was anything but, and she'd always known it in her gut. Obviously he had allies within the company, which meant her future might very well be tenuous if he preferred having someone like Paul Barker as spokesman. Hoss was only two years from mandatory retirement, and Bryce was twelve years younger. Her stint on the East End could be short-lived.

She'd managed to ruin a perfectly good day with negative thoughts. Besides, it wasn't as if they were home free. If Stacie was right and the EPA discovered bitumen in their pipes, there would be hell to pay, and there was still the matter of how much oil had actually spilled. As of this morning they'd accounted for all but four thousand gallons, according to Larry. Even if they spun it and squeezed it all out, it was only half a tanker load, yet two more tankers had rolled in this morning. Part of her wanted to ask questions, but the smarter part knew better.

* * *

Colleen's traction apparatus had been replaced by a sturdy neck brace holding her chin firmly in place.

"You certainly look better," Stacie said. "How's the pain?"

"I'm fine as long as I remember not to breathe."

Her son Brian, an insurance claims adjuster from Minneapolis, patted his mother's knee. "She keeps telling me I don't have to yell at her for trying to move. Her neck yells loud enough."

"Any word on when you're busting out of this joint?"

"Doctor says tomorrow. She also said I should take a week off and I told her fat chance for that. I want this story bad."

"That's crazy, Mom. You need to be taking care of yourself, and besides, I still don't think this was an accident."

"All the more reason for me to keep digging. A good reporter doesn't pack it in when someone tries to push her off the story. Especially then." Her eyes turned toward Stacie while she held her head perfectly still. "My editor came up from Minneapolis this morning, something he almost never does. He wanted me to turn over everything to one of his general assignment hotshots but I told him to go to hell. In the first place, I don't have anything to turn over other than what I've already filed. Everything's gone, but I can reconstruct most of it if you have copies of what you gave me the other day."

What worried Stacie most was knowing these guys played for keeps. If they'd targeted Colleen because of her reporting, she might not be safe. "Sure, I can do that, but maybe Brian is right. Nobody's going to think less of you if you take a little break to feel better."

"Screw that. If Brian's right about this not being an accident, there's no way I'm going to hand this story over to someone else now."

If there was one thing Stacie understood, it was tenacity. That was the single most important characteristic of a dedicated activist, someone who was willing to keep charging no matter how many times he or she got knocked down. She asked Brian, "Did you talk to anyone in the sheriff's department about what you found?"

"Nobody's interested. They didn't even dust for prints and by now the car's been touched so many times you couldn't possibly find anything of use. But I'm working another angle."

"My son, the detective."

"Not me. I'm a claims adjuster, so I'm used to dealing with stuff that looks suspicious. That's how I knew the brake line had been cut. You'd be surprised what some people will do to collect on a million-dollar life insurance policy."

Stacie shook her head. "Very little surprises me anymore."

"Anyway, I've asked one my private investigators to look into it. He came by last night and said something interesting."

Colleen groaned as she accidentally moved her neck, and then said, "I told him what happened, that I left before the rally was over so I could go file my story. I didn't really hit any traffic until I got out to the highway, and by the time I needed my brakes, they were shot."

"The investigator said it would have happened a lot sooner if Mom had been sitting in traffic to get out of the parking lot. She wouldn't have been going so fast and it would have been just a fender bender. I think their plan was for people to run up and help so somebody could snatch her briefcase in the confusion."

Stacie liked thinking whoever did this hadn't meant to put Colleen's life in danger. "It would be interesting to know if they got any witness statements at the scene, but I wouldn't hold my breath. It could have been somebody acting like a Good Samaritan until he got his hands on your briefcase and took off."

Brian nodded. "I'll ask him to check it out."

"So how soon can you get me back in business?" Colleen asked.

As much as she wanted to see this story move along again, her first priority was getting the samples to the labs in Minneapolis, and her second was private time with Cathryn. "What say we meet Sunday afternoon at four? I can come by your house if you're out of here by then. I'll bring copies of everything I gave you, maybe even something new that'll put you on Page One come Monday morning."

The florist came in with a towering arrangement in lavender and white. Brian snatched the card and read, "Feel better soon, Cathryn Mack. Who's that?"

Colleen snorted. "The spokeswoman for Nations Oil. She's got a lot of nerve."

"I don't think she's involved," Stacie said quickly. "The people who do these things usually work so far under the radar that only a handful of people in the company know about it. They do it that way on purpose to give everyone deniability. There's no way they're going to involve their public face."

"No wonder she sometimes looks like a deer in the headlights. Makes you wonder who's pulling all the strings, doesn't it?"

Stacie knew exactly who was pulling the strings. "If you feel better before Sunday, do some research on a guy by the name of Karl Depew."

"He was at the press tour."

"Then I can guarantee whatever he told you was a lie."

CHAPTER ELEVEN

The two-and-a-half-hour drive to St. Paul should have been relaxing, but the creepy notion Depew might be keeping up with her whereabouts had Cathryn on edge. She'd made no secret of where she was going, so if he was tracking her car with some sort of electronic device, her story would hold up.

Funny how she'd once thought Stacie was paranoid and now she was the one obsessing over Depew. It made little sense he would care what she did. She'd done nothing to undermine her company, except perhaps to withhold Stacie's conjectures about bitumen and the size of the spill, which she could argue left her in a better position to counter them.

None of her rationalizations would matter if their relationship were discovered. She'd be fired in a New York minute—no ifs, ands or buts. And yet the urge for two more nights together was more than she could resist. It made sense now why people took such extraordinary risks to have affairs outside their marriages, or how young lovers through the ages had forsaken their families to step across feuding lines. The desire for something this special was overpowering, so much that she was willing to ignore the consequences.

She pulled into the valet circle at the St. Paul Hotel, a cultural landmark decorated in the grand style of the early twentieth century with deep red velvet, heavy chandeliers and dark polished wood. Stacie had texted her through SappHere with the room number, allowing her to bypass the registration desk and go straight to the elevators. Her fear of being seen, baseless as it was, caused her to quicken every step until she finally reached the door.

"Thought you'd never get here." Stacie was dressed again in only her plaid shirt and panties. "I wore this just for you."

Cathryn dropped her bag and drew her into a hard kiss, as though the force alone might expel the tension from her body.

"Feels like somebody missed me."

She had no idea what was driving her urgency. They had two whole days ahead of them and yet she felt the clock already counting down their minutes. Still without speaking, she doffed her jacket and kicked off her shoes.

"Whoa, Cathryn. Let me help." Stacie loosened all her buttons and pushed her shirt off her shoulders.

Cathryn slipped out of her bra and snuggled inside the open shirt to press their flesh together, resting her head on Stacie's shoulder. It settled her momentarily, but the longer she held the embrace the clearer it became that the source of her anxiety had as much to do with her feelings for Stacie as her paranoia about Depew. Ordinary physical longings always surged when the chemistry was right, but this was more than sexual lust. She hadn't been drawn to anyone this way in a very long time, and would never have risked so much just for sex.

"I feel like I've been looking over my shoulder all week," she said. "It's crazy to keep doing this but I can't help it. I need to be with you."

"I can't help it either." Stacie lifted the covers and led her into bed. "If my friends had any idea we were here together, they'd all assume it was to squeeze you for information. I promise you, nothing could be further from the truth."

"What is the truth?"

"That when I'm with you, I don't care about anything but us." She pressed her lips to Cathryn's forehead and held them there for several seconds. "And when I'm not with you, I want to be."

Was that physical want, or did she feel the same emotional pull? Cathryn needed to believe she wasn't falling into something one-sided. She could love a woman like Stacie—fighting selflessly for a better world against overpowering odds—but how could Stacie ever feel that way about someone she didn't respect?

Love. They'd known each other not even a month and were as different as night and day. All they had in common was here between the sheets, yet Cathryn could no longer claim her own heart.

As they kissed, her hands wandered, remembering contours and sensitivities, all the little places that caused a ripple or gasp. The smooth curve of Stacie's hip. The warm hollow at the apex of her thigh. And yet after a subtle battle for dominance, Stacie emerged on top.

Cathryn gave herself over. With nearly two full days ahead, there would be plenty of chances to express her feelings. Right now her body wanted to listen.

Warm lips nibbled her neck, and as they drifted lower she pushed her breasts together in a silent plea. When Stacie took them in her mouth, Cathryn dropped her hands between her legs, opening herself to feel the friction of the soft belly as it gently rocked from side to side. If she concentrated on the sensations the way Stacie had described the last time they were together, it might even be enough to climax, especially if she continued to hold her lips apart.

Then a chill crossed her breasts as the wet mouth tracked lower across her navel, and her legs were pushed apart. Stacie must have read her urgency because she didn't tease at all. Her tongue slid the length of her slick folds, alternately soft and flat, and then rigid as it probed her with precision.

With her eyes tightly closed Cathryn envisioned herself climbing, every stroke another step. Focusing only on that, she was able to quiet the emotional noise, but when her climax finally erupted, it was like tumbling from the peak. She feared crashing, coming apart physically and mentally as confusion once again overwhelmed her. Stacie somehow knew her hold was tenuous and eased her down slowly until her body was still.

Their hands found one another as Stacie rested her head upon her thigh, smiling in a way that seemed tender rather than amused. "Are you all right?"

The insight and compassion of that simple question caught her off guard and she nearly blurted out what would have been a ridiculous declaration of love. Instead she retreated to safe territory. "I'm officially wasted. You should be very pleased with yourself."

"You've obviously misunderstood my intentions." Stacie wriggled one of her hands free and gently stroked her stomach, tickling the triangle of hair. "That was supposed to be all about pleasing you, and if you didn't notice that, I'm going to have to do it again."

Ridiculous or not, Cathryn knew what love felt like. This was it.

* * *

"How can anyone say no to bacon?" Cathryn asked, playfully waving a crispy strip under Stacie's nose. "Does this qualify as being obnoxious?"

"Would it make any difference if I said yes?" Stacie loved how easily they moved between passion and mischief, as if they'd known each other for years. "I hate to burst your bubble but you aren't annoying me nearly as much as you think. My aversion to meat is—wait for it—political."

"Why am I not surprised? Everything you do is political."

"Not everything. I drove to West Virginia once for no reason at all."

"You expect me to believe that? I bet you drove there to hook up with some woman you met on SappHere."

"Technically true, but she stood me up. Ergo—no reason."

Cathryn held out a peace offering of sorts, a ripe red strawberry. "Her loss."

"Aw, what a nice thing to say. So unlike you." She bit into thin air as Cathryn snatched the fruit away. "That's the woman I know and love."

The word seemed to startle both of them.

"Figure of speech?"

"Something like that…maybe," Stacie conceded.

On the drive down from Duluth, she had admitted to herself she was falling in love, but that didn't mean she was ready to shout it from the mountaintop, least of all to Cathryn. It was absurd. They'd spent nearly half of their time together hiding who they were. Cathryn would think she was one of those starry-eyed romantics who latched onto everyone she dated—the very sort of person "Marlene" guarded against on SappHere. Trying now to walk it back as a slip of the tongue would be clumsy and rude.

"But don't worry, Cathryn. I've been arrested lots of times but never for stalking."

"Who says I'm worried?"

"Okay, then. I said it. You heard it. We don't have to overanalyze anything." The fact they both were smiling was meaning enough.

Cathryn scooted her breakfast tray into the hallway for pickup. "Let me get this poor dead pig away from you before you organize a protest."

"I'd probably have better luck getting Americans to ride skateboards everywhere than to give up eating meat."

"Speaking of protests, that was a decent program you put together in Chester Park…as much as I hate to admit it. And I was thoroughly impressed that you turned out such a big crowd."

"Thanks. That's high praise coming from a pro like you." Stacie explained their strategy of doubling every day. "I have to get good speakers because I'm not very good at it."

"We all have our strengths. You're a good organizer."

"A lot of people support what we do, but it's hard to get them out of their chairs to be counted. We depend on a few people to make a lot of noise." Then she playfully smacked Cathryn's arm. "Especially when you turn around the next day and flood the airwaves with those ridiculous feel-good ads." In a child-like voice, she squeaked, "Thank you, Nations Oil!"

Cathryn couldn't help but laugh. "What got you started with all this? Or did you come out of the womb yelling at the doctor for having too many lights on?"

"I probably yelled about something but it wasn't that. I wasn't all that conscious of the environment until high school. That's when the *Exxon Valdez* dumped its whole load in Prince William Sound. Such a beautiful place spoiled forever. My dad's shipping business moved a lot of petroleum products, and I realized how easily something like that could happen in the inland waterways. They'd have called it the Pilardi River Spill or the Pilardi Disaster, and I would have felt personally responsible."

"It's hard to imagine you owning part of a company that makes money off shipping oil. I'm surprised you haven't sold out."

"Believe me, my brother Philip would like nothing more than to buy me out, but I like having the power to change how things are done. Dad came around just before he died and helped me push through safer standards that laid a lot more financial culpability on the shippers, which they passed on to the oil companies. My brother still has to honor them if he wants my voting shares." Stacie fluffed the pillows and patted the space beside her.

Cathryn lay on her side, resting her head on Stacie's shoulder. "I admire what you've done with your life. I don't exactly agree with your doomsday scenario for the planet, but

I respect you for standing up for what you believe. And you're right about some of the benefits of oil probably not being worth the costs. It depresses me to see what they're doing to the land in Alberta, and especially to the First Nation people."

Canada's indigenous peoples complained bitterly of fouled air, water and land caused by the tar sands industry. All so oil companies could churn obscene profits.

"Unfortunately," Cathryn went on, "I'm never going to have enough power to stop that kind of abuse."

"People have more power than they realize. Sometimes all it takes is one person speaking up for others to realize they're not alone. You're in a good position to do that because you know better than anyone how the public feels." She was impressed Cathryn would even consider bucking her company's party line. It would take a lot of courage but the first step was realizing change was possible. "You've got a lot to be proud of too. You came out of a tough situation at home and made something of yourself. What drives you to work so hard?"

"Nothing quite so noble as you, I'm afraid. Sorry if that disappoints you, but I'm basically all about me."

"I'm not buying that. I've seen my share of selfish people and you don't fit that bill."

"I didn't say I was selfish. I'm just looking out for myself so I won't ever have to depend on anyone else. My mom put up with a lot of shit because she didn't have anywhere else to turn, and I don't ever want to end up like that. She's been apologizing to me for thirty years, so I guess you could say what drives me is wanting to prove to her that I'm okay."

With her arm wrapped around Cathryn's shoulder, she could feel the muscles tightening in her back. "You're tensing up again. What are we going to do about that?"

"I get this way every time I think about how my father used to treat us. I'd just as soon talk about Depew."

"Then we'd both be in a bad mood. I've got a better idea."

She lit a couple of candles in the bathroom and filled the tub with warm water and lavender scented bubbles from a powder tin in her duffel bag. They eased in on opposite ends and tangled their legs in the center.

"You have the best ideas," Cathryn said. "I need more candles and lavender in my life."

"Everyone needs more candles and lavender. You'd be surprised how soothing it is just to turn everything off for a few minutes a day."

"And we're saving all this water by bathing together. I feel better about myself already."

"That's how it starts. Before long you'll be chaining yourself to a bulldozer."

"Don't bet on it. The closest I want to get to a jail is sleeping with you."

"That's okay. I need somebody on the outside with bail money anyway." She cupped her hands and squirted a stream of water toward Cathryn. "That would be interesting—me getting arrested for protesting Nations Oil and you coming to bail me out. What would your bosses think of that?"

"You mean my ex-bosses. I'd be fired faster than you could say oil slick."

"But then the worst-case scenario would be behind you. We wouldn't have to sneak around and there'd be no more assholes like Depew to worry about."

"And I wouldn't have to worry about my mortgage either because the bank would take my house."

"Nah, you're a survivor. You'd land on your feet."

* * *

Cathryn looked up from her smartphone as Stacie emerged naked from the bathroom and bent over to get something out of her bag. "My, my. I'd sure like to have that in an eight-by-ten glossy."

"You can have the real thing anytime you want it. How soon do we get to do this again?"

"Looks like I'm going to be here at least another week or two."

Stacie looked down at the bed. "Hey, you have two phones."

"D'oh. Of course I do. You think I want the tech guys at work tracking my SappHere dates? The black one's just for work-related stuff. The white one is personal."

She pulled a package out of her backpack and ripped it open, dumping out a pair of prepaid cell phones. "If I'd known that, I'd have only bought one of these. I was going to give you one so we could talk instead of text. What's your number?"

Cathryn recited it and then picked up her personal phone when it rang. "You've reached the Texas Department of Lesbian Services. There is no one available to take your call because there are no services for lesbians in Texas."

"Cheeky."

"How come you need another phone?"

"Same reason, sort of. We have a business plan, so Jenn and the auditors have access to all my calls. Not my SappHere texts though. It's not that I don't trust them, but I like keeping the personal, personal."

"Believe me, I understand." With their business in Duluth nearing its end, they'd have to work around their schedules to squeeze out every minute they could. Cathryn was even willing to take chances. "Are you still staying at the Weller Regent?"

"I can go somewhere else if it's easier."

"No, I like it there. With the parking garage, I don't feel so exposed." It was a half hour until checkout and already she was fantasizing about their next time together. "Can't wait to use my little vibrator tonight, especially since the last person it touched was you."

"And when I want to remember you, I'll just eat a juicy peach." Stacie's main phone rang, the first time all weekend, and her brow wrinkled as she checked the number. "Sorry, I need to take this."

As she disappeared behind the bathroom door, Cathryn closed her laptop and packed the last of her belongings. She couldn't be annoyed at the intrusion since she'd spent practically the entire morning answering work-related emails.

All in all they'd done well to turn off their jobs for the weekend but it was time to get back to reality.

"Is everything all right?"

Stacie smiled. "It's fine. I just need to meet someone this afternoon when I get back to town. And no, it wasn't some hot chick on SappHere."

"Good thing. Fooling around with other women could be hazardous to your health," Cathryn said with a playful sneer. "Should I be on the lookout for any surprises this week?"

"Not that I know of, but the week is young." Her smile faded and when she spoke again, her voice was serious. "I'll do my best not to blindside you again, Cathryn. You should know that one of my friends sneaked out to the lake and took some more samples. I dropped them off for analysis on Friday at the Department of Health. I know what you said about this being heavy oil, but it sure looks like bitumen to me."

"It isn't just what I said. I've seen the preliminary results from the EPA's report. Ninety thousand gallons of heavy crude. That's it, and they're digging out the last little bit right now. Between you and me and the bedpost, I'll admit Nations Oil was careless. They should have done maintenance on that pipeline. I wish I could tell you they learned their lesson, but we both know it could happen again tomorrow. If you ask me, that's an argument for why we need to build the Caliber Pipeline, because there's still a lot of oil in America's future and it ought to be transported safely."

"The reason there's oil in our future is because no one is investing in the alternatives. Our taxes are subsidizing the oil industry, whose profits are already obscene."

"And every government pension fund in America reaps the benefits."

"Come on, Cathryn. You make it sound like it's a public good."

"If you live in Texas, it is. Forty million dollars in wages every year."

"But at what cost to the rest of us?"

"Have you seen what people in Europe pay for gas? How do you think Americans would feel about forking over ten dollars a gallon at the pump?"

"They might as well, instead of hiding the true costs inside our tax structure. What if we taxed all the oil companies at a fair rate and put our subsidies toward clean energy development? High-speed rail, mass transit, green space, retro-fitting public buildings with eco-friendly technology."

Cathryn had heard it all before, and knew exactly where to push back. "That might work for people in New York, but what about the farmers and plumbers in Kansas? Or the teachers and nurses? They all have to get to work, and you can't move a rural population with mass transit."

"But there's no good reason their cars and trucks can't be electric with zero emissions. Our tax dollars should be going toward that technology." Obviously, Stacie had heard it all before as well.

"And where do you think all that electricity comes from? You can't store wind and solar power."

The amazing aspect of their point-counterpoint, Cathryn realized, was that both were passionate, maybe even a little agitated, but so far neither had risen to anger. They just disagreed. That didn't mean it was a pleasant conversation, and she wished they'd stuck to their pact not to talk about work.

"They can't store it right now. Let's see if research dollars can change that," Stacie said. "We have to pull our investments out of the past and look to the future. You don't start a diet by saying you're going to eat all the junk food in the world first. You guys have already picked the low-hanging fruit. With every year that goes by, a gallon of gas costs you more money, more energy and more resources to produce. And it's taking a bigger toll on the planet. I understand the profit motives. They're selfish as hell, but at least they're rational. What I don't get is how seemingly intelligent people can deny the science and justify destroying the planet their grandchildren are going to inherit. The only thing I can figure is they must be counting on passing their money down so their family can blast off in a spaceship to an unspoiled world."

"You're one to talk about money, Stacie. You've never not had it." With that retort, Cathryn knew she'd stepped over the line, and felt bad immediately.

Stacie was clearly stung and reacted by retreating across the room, where she folded her arms and assumed a defiant posture. "That's true for Hoss Bower too. His family practically started the Texas oil boom, and he's never wanted for anything in his life. The difference between Hoss and me is what we do with our money. He spends his to make more. I spend mine to make better."

"I'm sorry I said that. It was out of line." She rubbed her face in her hands and sighed. "I should never have brought up work. I don't want us to end our weekend like this. The rest of it was so sweet. We both have our jobs to do, and I know you're not deliberately trying to hurt me. I'm not deliberately lying to you either."

"I know," Stacie said, nodding solemnly. "This is all so ironic, you being the voice of an oil company. Why couldn't you have been just an ax murderer instead?"

"You'd really prefer that?"

"Wouldn't matter. I've already let my feelings slip out. As crazy as it is, I've managed to fall in love with you."

A warm shudder caused her to smile. "That's got to be the most unromantic declaration of love I've ever heard."

"It was pretty awful, wasn't it? Let me put it a different way." She kissed each of Cathryn's hands and guided them around her neck. "I'm crazy about you, and I'd go even crazier if you felt that way about me too."

"That was marginally better. Now kiss me while I pretend to act like I'm still thinking about it while in fact my little heart is doing cartwheels around the room."

"Cartwheels, huh?" Stacie kissed her gently at first but then with enough passion to nearly drive them back into bed. "This…what we feel…it's precious. We have to find a way to make it last."

They could do that, but only as long as they kept their relationship hidden from their friends and co-workers. Cathryn appreciated her privacy, but she didn't care much for high-stakes secrets. The stress of worrying she'd be found out would wear on her over time. The question was whether or not Stacie was worth it. Right now the answer was yes.

* * *

Stacie juggled the steering wheel with her elbows while adjusting the earbuds she had plugged into Marlene. "Okay, I've got it now. What were you saying?"

Jenn was still chuckling with her news. "Izzy was crawling around in the woods and got into a bed of poison ivy. He called begging us to bring him some itch cream. Marty's in the pharmacy right now picking it up."

So far Stacie had handled all the secret drops. "Did he tell you where the culvert was? I usually pull off just past the first bridge on State Road 194. That way I can walk along the edge of the woods over to Lake Bunyan Road."

"Yeah, he told us to come just before dark. That's about three hours from now. He's going to sneak out around midnight to pick it up, if he can last that long."

"That's dangerous. They'll be out on patrol."

"He sounds pretty desperate. What about you? Did you have a good time? You should be well past the U-Haul stage by now, or is this a different woman?"

For obvious reasons, Stacie had shared very few details about who she was seeing, a fact made easier by staying at the hotel downtown. One of these days she'd come clean with Jenn, but not until this episode was well behind them. "I had a great time but that U-Haul thing is a little tricky since neither of us lives in Duluth. But if I need any help moving, you'll be the first person I ask."

The call she'd taken earlier in the bathroom was from Brian Murray, who had some urgent news to share. She bypassed her hotel and followed Marlene's directions to Colleen's house.

Brian met her at the door, his eyes burning with anger. "We got the son of a bitch."

"Are you serious?" She followed him into the living room where Colleen, still in her neck brace, was sitting on the couch. Stacie joined her and carefully patted her knee. "Feeling better?"

"Anything's better than being in the hospital."

A stack of photos sailed across the coffee table as Brian pulled up another chair. "See for yourself. There were some pictures from the rally in the newspaper, and my investigator noticed you could see the parking lot in the background in one of them. He went down to the paper and asked the photographer if he could look through all his shots, and there was this one." He laid out a photo and pointed to a blurry figure squatted beside a car. "That's Mom's car, and you can tell this guy's messing with it."

The figure had a full head of dark hair and appeared to be wearing jeans and a red T-shirt, but his face was unrecognizable from this distance. "Is this the clearest picture he had?"

"From that angle, yes. So then he looked through the pictures of the crowd to see if he could find anyone dressed like that, and here he is on his way over to the car." In the second photo, the man was walking from the rally toward the parking lot, but this time he was facing away from the camera.

"Could have been anybody."

"Could have…but then here's the money shot."

The third photo caused her stomach to drop. The man—same jeans and T-shirt with dark, bushy hair—stood behind the volunteer table. It was Marty Wingate.

"Oh, shit. I know him."

That explained what happened to her first set of samples, and also how the SWAT team had found them at the farmhouse. Marty was selling them out to Depew. He'd been seeing Jenn for three months, and while CLEAN had tangled with Karl Depew on several occasions, she never once considered he might try to infiltrate their group. That kind of subterfuge required cunning and patience, and Depew favored the sledgehammer approach.

There was another possibility, one she could barely bring herself to acknowledge—the feds. Big Oil had lots of important friends. They bought a lot of influence with their campaign contributions and what they expected in return was for the government to do their bidding. Organizations like CLEAN got in their way.

It was no accident the SWAT team had treated them like terrorists. That's how they justified what they did, as if disrupting the fossil fuel industry's profits were a threat to national security.

No, it couldn't be the feds, she realized. They could be unscrupulous but there was no way they'd allow an undercover agent to have a sexual relationship with a target. Marty "belonged" to someone else, or perhaps he was an independent contractor like all the former cops and military tough guys that made up Depew's security brigade. They weren't bound by laws, nor apparently ethics.

Based on the investigator's speculation that the accident should have happened in the parking lot, Marty probably hadn't meant to hurt Colleen, though he was still responsible for her injuries. "Brian, you realize we can't prove he did this from a blurry photo, even if we've got him kneeling next to your mom's car. He could say he dropped his keys or something, and all the other physical evidence has been compromised."

"I'm not interested in proving anything. I just want to beat the shit out of him."

As tempted as she was to let that happen, Stacie had other problems, including the fact that Marty was about to discover the location of their drop zone at the lake. She needed to warn Izzy.

"Can I keep these photos?"

"Sure. He gave me digital copies."

In exchange for Brian's promise not to track down Marty and beat him to a pulp, she gave up his name and the fact that he might have a Colorado driver's license, since that's where he and Jenn had met. His investigator could dig into Marty's background and find out who his contacts were.

The moment she got back in her car, she dialed Izzy. "You guys need to bug out fast. This new boyfriend of Jenn's, he's somebody's snitch and now he knows where you are. If you go anywhere near the culvert, you'll be walking into a trap."

With Izzy looking at an online map of the perimeter road, they planned an alternate rendezvous location and a pickup time an hour before Jenn and Marty were to drop off the lotion. Once her friends were safe, she'd figure out how to break the news to Jenn. Even more important was seeing that Marty got what was coming to him.

CHAPTER TWELVE

"This doesn't make any sense," Woody said. His hair was standing on end from where he'd rubbed his head in frustration. "I must be reading it wrong."

Cathryn walked around his desk to peer at the spreadsheet on his screen. The tables charted the flow of oil from one pump station to the next, beginning at the Provincial Oil Fields and ending at the port in Hartford, Illinois. "What's the problem?"

"These are the numbers from twenty-four hours on each side of when we first heard about the spill. We had over half a million gallons go through the pump station at Canosia. That's the last one before the rupture. The next one's down at Cloquet and here's what passed through there."

"A hundred thousand and change."

He tapped the numbers into a calculator. "So that's about four hundred thousand gallons we have to account for."

"Ninety thousand of which was spilled."

"Right. Larry said the contractors got down here and sealed the leak within six hours, so the rest of it had to be stuck in the pipe. It couldn't go down to Cloquet because they'd shut down the pump."

"And they recovered it and trucked it down to Hartford. That's what all those tankers were doing here when we first arrived."

"That's what I thought." He clicked a tab to switch to a new spreadsheet. "Except if you look at the transport logs, they couldn't have moved that much."

At nine thousand gallons each, there weren't enough tankers to move it all. "You're still missing at least two hundred thousand gallons." That was a lot of loose change, but she was convinced they were overlooking something obvious.

"The first tanker convoy was subbed out from Childers Oil in South Dakota, and we paid mileage for them to go back to Sioux Falls. Since when do we ship oil there? It should have gone down to Hartford."

"Woody, there's no way two hundred thousand gallons of heavy crude just disappears."

He threw up his hands and shook his head. "That's why I'm pulling my hair out, because here's where it gets really screwy. Thirteen hours after they shut off the pump, another two hundred thousand gallons went through Canosia. Why would you send oil through a pipeline you know is broken?"

Woody was right. The numbers made no sense, but Cathryn was even more convinced the flow management software had somehow failed. "The time stamp has to be off or something. That would explain it. These numbers must be for the wrong date."

"It isn't just the time stamp, Cathryn. The pressure went down too and so did the temperature. It's like they flushed the pipes or something."

"Weird." They needed high pressure and heat to move heavy oil.

"I'm going to print this off and go ask Larry about it," he said. "The answer's probably staring us in the face, but if it isn't, then something's wrong with the software."

Cathryn had studied reports like these for years and never had trouble making sense of the numbers. If there were a glitch in the software, it would show up across all their pumping stations, not just the two on either side of the spill. There was another explanation…and she didn't like it. Using the thumb drive on her keychain, she downloaded Woody's files to study later.

Amy entered the trailer, her eyes wide with excitement. Cathryn had sent her to the other side of the lake to scout the public park for next week's press conference with Senator Washburn. "You won't believe what I just saw. There's a bunch of storm troopers over there on the other side of the lake. They've got guns and helmets and who knows what else, and they're going from one cabin to another. No idea what they're looking for but they scared me half to death."

Cathryn knew exactly what they were looking for—Stacie's friends, the ones who were flying drones overhead and taking pictures of the cleanup. The show of force was exactly like the one at the farmhouse where Stacie had been hurt. As much as she hated to admit it, there was little doubt Nations Oil was behind this one as well.

When Amy stepped into the restroom, Cathryn sent a message through SappHere. "*SWAT team at cabin now.*"

Moments later her pocket dinged. "*Got it covered. Thx.*"

* * *

Two cars were parked at the farmhouse, but that wasn't unusual because the volunteers often rode into town with Jenn. Stacie hoped that was the case today because what she needed to do required total secrecy. After checking the house to make sure she was alone, she set to work in the room Jenn and Marty shared.

It bothered her to violate their sacred rule against getting into other people's belongings, but she had to know for sure if Marty Wingate was a spy. All night she'd tossed and turned, halfway convincing herself it was only circumstantial, that maybe Marty really had just dropped his keys near Colleen's car and she was getting paranoid over nothing. The text this morning from Cathryn, however, made that unlikely. It couldn't be coincidence Depew's SWAT team stormed the cabin only hours after Marty learned where it was.

Any real evidence of his ties to Depew was probably in the grungy gray backpack he carried everywhere he went. She found his clothes in the bottom dresser drawer, and her careful pat-down of his cargo shorts yielded a surprising find—three neatly rolled marijuana cigarettes. "That son of a bitch." Even if by some miracle he turned out to be clean, he was jeopardizing their legitimacy by bringing drugs into the house.

His laptop and phone were missing, probably in his backpack, and unless he was stupid, password-protected. The closet held their duffel bags—both of them empty—and three sleeping bags, one of which was hers. She hadn't used it since the night of the SWAT raid, and Marty and Jenn hadn't needed theirs because they'd lucked into a bed with sheets and a blanket.

If he'd hidden anything in the house, it had to be in another—

Why was his sleeping bag on top if he hadn't used it at all?

She stripped its casing and unfurled it on the bed, noticing at once a bundle in the bottom. A leather shaving kit for a man who didn't bother to shave. She unzipped the bag and dumped the contents—several more cigarettes, rolling papers and a plastic bag containing about two ounces of marijuana, probably the same stash the SWAT team had "found" in their kitchen that went missing immediately after the raid. And an Ohio driver's license with the name Martin Winthrop.

There also was a small cloth bag with a drawstring top. She loosened it and shook out at least a dozen tiny electronic gadgets, each no bigger than a button. Transmitters. So that's how Depew's people had known which tires to slash, which windows to break and which cars to pull over.

With a shudder, she realized Marty also knew each time she went to meet Cathryn, though he couldn't put that together unless he was tracking her too, and there was no reason he'd do that. She'd been to Cathryn's hotel only twice, once in a rental car and again with the pizza delivery guy.

It was too late to worry about Cathryn now. She needed to neutralize Marty. Kicking him out of the house wasn't enough. She wanted to kick him in the teeth.

Izzy would know what to do, but the idea rapidly taking shape in her head was well outside the lines. CLEAN activists had a long, deliberate history of playing by the rules, and she couldn't ask anyone to do something that might result in serious trouble with the law.

She dropped the cigarettes, including the ones in the drawer, inside the plastic bag and set it aside. Then she rolled everything else back inside the sleeping bag and returned it to the closet.

For good measure, she emptied her backpack to make sure she wasn't carrying around a transmitter, and then tucked the drugs into the outside flap where she could get to them easily. It took her only ten minutes to find the transmitter in her Prius, taped to the bottom of the driver's seat. Though tempted to pull it out and crush it beneath her heel, she imagined a couple of scenarios where it might come in handy, especially if she could make Depew think she was somewhere else.

With the rally behind them and Nations Oil touting the end of their successful cleanup, Jenn had shifted the volunteer focus toward collecting signatures door-to-door for their petition against the Caliber Pipeline. Beyond that, there was little left to do but continue the sidewalk protests at Nations Oil's gas stations and write letters to the editor. They'd enjoyed some fine moments during this campaign, like exposing the video of the fish kill and drawing thousands to their rally. Forceful protests, like blocking the highway into the cleanup site, would serve no useful purpose, and might even garner sympathy for the oil company.

Stacie wasn't surprised to find only a handful of volunteers in the usually busy office. Nor was she surprised that Marty was hanging out in the break room eating chips and playing with his smartphone. His backpack lay on the floor at his feet.

"Hey, Marty. You busy?"

"Not really. You need something?"

"I just realized I have to be in two places at once. I was supposed to meet with one of the county commissioners at one thirty but I got a call from Jeff Johannesson about fifteen minutes ago. He's a chemistry teacher over at Bainbridge High School. I talked to him at the rally, and he offered to have a look at that other duck I plucked out of the lake the day I went out in the kayak." She'd found only one duck, the one he supposedly took to his father's friend at Bemidji State, but he had no way of knowing that. "I must have really screwed up those samples I gave you because Jeff ran some tests for me and he's pretty sure it's bitumen."

"No shit." Now that she knew who he was, his dopey manner got on her last nerve.

"Yeah, and he wrote up a report for us and saved a few of the feathers that still had oil on them. That's the last of it though. If we lose those, we'll never be able to prove what we've got. Anyway, he has a break from class at one forty-five, but I can't be there on account of my meeting."

Marty shook the last of the chips from a bag into his mouth and mumbled, "I could go if you want me to. Where is it?"

"That would be great. I can drop you off. My meeting shouldn't last more than twenty minutes and I'll swing back by and pick you up." She pushed past him toward the restroom. "I need to pee real quick. Can you let Jenn know where we're going?"

Stacie listened at the door for him to leave and hastily slipped the bag of marijuana into his backpack, shoving it all the way to the bottom. Then she went back inside and flushed the toilet, exiting the restroom just as he returned.

"She said good luck with your meeting. What's it about?"

She groaned and rolled her eyes. "We got some complaints about approaching people outside the Target store. I just need to smooth things out so we don't leave a bad impression."

To Stacie's relief, he didn't seem the least bit suspicious as they drove toward the school. He probably was scheming already about how to compromise this new piece of evidence.

"How do I find this Jeff Johannesson?" he asked.

"Apparently they won't let just anybody walk into the school, so he told me to meet him outside by the box office at the football field." When they stopped at a traffic light, she took out her phone. "I'll text him that you'll be there instead of me."

At the school he pulled his lanky frame out of her car and slung his backpack over his shoulder. "You want me to wait here?"

She looked at her watch. "Yeah, give me half an hour."

When she turned the corner out of sight, she pulled into a parking space and looked up the nonemergency number for the Duluth Police Department, an entirely separate entity from the county sheriff's office that was apparently working with Depew. Using her second prepaid phone, the one she'd intended to give Cathryn, she placed a call.

"Look, I don't want to get involved or anything, but I need to tell somebody about this. There's a guy hanging out at Bainbridge High School by the football field. I think he might be dealing drugs. I saw him out there a couple of days ago meeting up with some kids and now he's back. That's all."

She immediately turned off the phone, wiped it down and stomped it with the heel of her boot until the plastic casing shattered. Piece by piece, she ground the electronic parts into a mangled mess and wrapped them inside a brown paper bag. Then she got out of the car and walked half a block up a hillside street that afforded her a view of where she'd left Marty. Within minutes a patrol car with two officers arrived and confronted him. One of them searched his backpack and produced the bag she'd put there. Once she saw him handcuffed, she started back to her car, dropping the paper bag in a trash can along the way.

* * *

It was after eight o'clock when Stacie walked into the farmhouse. Alex and the Mauneys were watching TV in the living room, but the kitchen was dark and all the dishes stacked neatly in the drainer. The lamp was on in the back bedroom where Jenn was sitting amidst a stack of papers and pounding away on her laptop. A pencil protruded from her curly hair.

"Hey, where have you guys been?" Jenn craned her neck to look out toward the kitchen. "Where's Marty?"

"It's been a really tough day, sweetie. We need to talk." Stacie closed the door and leaned against it as she sank to the floor. "I don't know the best way to say this, so I'm just going to put it out there. Marty Wingate isn't who he says he is. In fact, that isn't even his name. It's Martin Winthrop, and he's been working for Karl Depew for the last four years." She related how Brian Murray's investigator discovered the photos from the rally, and that she'd searched his things and found the transmitters in his sleeping bag. "That's how those guys always knew where we were. They were tracking our cars."

Jenn absorbed it, denied it, cried about it and ripped her tissue in a thousand pieces. "Is there any chance at all you've made a mistake? I've been sleeping with this guy for three months."

"I saw his driver's license, Jenn. He's from Canton, Ohio. And I met with Brian again this afternoon and had his investigator run a trace on him. He served seven years in the army, and that's probably how he hooked up with Depew. We've always known these guys would try to infiltrate us eventually."

"So he's the one who tipped them off about where our cars were parked and when we were out driving around."

"That's not all he did." Stacie went on to explain how he'd probably tossed their first set of samples. "But I got some more from Izzy and they're being analyzed at the Department of Health in St. Paul."

"Izzy!"

"Don't worry. I picked them up last night about an hour before you made the drop. And I got word this morning Depew sent another SWAT team to sweep the cabins on that side of the lake." Left unsaid was who had shared that tidbit.

"That creep. Why did they pick me?"

"Because you were single, straight…and you had access to everything related to our organization." Including their confidential donor lists. Depew could smear the organization by selling their list and making donors think CLEAN had violated their privacy. Even worse, he could send everyone notices saying their credit card information had been compromised.

"Don't worry, I never shared my passwords with him, but now I know why he was always messing around with my laptop. I thought he was trying to see if I'd been emailing other guys. He acted that way sometimes…jealous. I wouldn't have hidden things from him if I felt like he trusted me, but I didn't think I should have to prove anything." Her face was swollen and red from crying, but if the twitch in her jaw was any indication, hurt feelings were about to give way to fury. "Part of me wants to kill the son of a bitch in his sleep, but the other part wants him to see it coming so he has time to shit his pants."

"I don't think we have to worry about him coming back. He's in the city jail on suspicion of selling drugs."

"Oh, my God. What did you do?"

"I can't tell you, Jenn. It's for your own good…and mine too, I guess."

"If you set him up, he's going to tell the police."

"I know, but Brian says he was kicked out of the army for drugs, and he's been arrested twice for possession. With a record like that, he's going to have a hard time getting anybody to listen. Besides, they were his drugs. I found them here in the house, probably the same bag they found the night of the raid."

Stacie had been careful to cover her tracks even beyond making sure they couldn't trace the phone call back to her. She also had temporarily removed the tracking device from her car and left it under a rock in a parking space behind their office building. After seeing Marty arrested, she circled back and picked it up again. To anyone who was watching its signal, she'd never left the building.

"We need to tell the others we found out he was working with Depew, and all of them should search their backpacks and purses for transmitters. Not necessarily to throw them away—just to be aware of them. Depew might still be tracking us, and it might not be a bad idea for him to think this was only about the drugs, and not because we've figured out who Marty is." It gave her special satisfaction to think Depew would burn him over his marijuana habit. "I'd rather we didn't share any more details than that. There'll probably be an investigation, and the less people know, the better."

Jenn sniffed and reached for another tissue. Marty had done a lot of horrible things, but as far as Stacie was concerned, the worst was taking advantage of her best friend. It bothered her a lot that she couldn't make him pay for that, but she wasn't going to lose a minute's sleep about sending him to jail for something he didn't technically do. Even if he hadn't gone to the school to sell drugs, they were his. At least now she had both him and his stash out of the farmhouse.

CHAPTER THIRTEEN

The truth was inescapable, Cathryn admitted as she shuffled papers around on her dining table. Nations Oil had indeed spilled a lot more than reported, and it appeared the ninety thousand they'd admitted to actually was an intentional discharge into the lake. The answer was in the tanker logs. The tankers rushing in from Sioux Falls had weighed in full at the state line checkpoint on Interstate 90, but empty on the return. Nations Oil owned reservoirs on that route, meaning the trucks had carried full loads of heavy crude to Canosia, where they pumped it into the pipeline. Nations Oil officials were waiting at Lake Bunyan to watch ninety thousand gallons pour into the lake before capping it. Additional tankers from Thunder Bay then collected what was left in the pipeline and trucked it down to Hartford. That's how they'd convinced the federal agencies they were pumping heavy oil.

Underneath what they'd spilled on purpose were at least 200,000 gallons of what was probably bitumen, which presumably originated on the far western edge of the Provincial

Oil Field. It was possible the designation was wrong, but now that she'd seen firsthand the lengths to which her company would go to deceive the regulators, she wouldn't be surprised to learn it was actually piped into Provincial from the Cold Lake Oil Sands.

Cathryn was no longer sure whose side she was on. The woman she loved had dedicated her life to taking down the oil industry, while she'd defended it every step of the way. Now it was clear Stacie and CLEAN were right about practically everything. Did she really want to be vice president of a company as dishonest and deliberately destructive as Nations Oil?

There was no way Bob Kryzwicki didn't know about the bitumen spill, which meant Hoss had bought off the EPA. For all she knew, the PHMSA report was fraudulent too.

The worst of it was Depew. Under orders from Hoss and Bryce, he'd treated Stacie and her friends like criminals when all they were doing was exercising their constitutional rights to free speech.

Now Hoss was ready to bring her home and make her a vice president, and the price was higher than simply averting her eyes from their wrongdoing. She'd be a part of their corruption, just as guilty as any of them.

She gathered the documents and thumb drive and placed them in an envelope in her safe. There had to be a way to turn this around, to root out the corruption inside her company and restore the public trust. The question was whether or not she was brave enough to take that on.

Her head pounded with a stress headache. What she wouldn't give to have Stacie kneading the muscles of her neck and telling her everything would be okay.

After changing clothes, she spread out her mat and lit the lavender candle Stacie had given her last weekend. Her movements were fluid, as though warm, clean oil coursed through her veins to lubricate her joints. For nearly an hour she stretched and posed until her muscles trembled with fatigue. She pulled herself into the lotus position to meditate, and instead of closing her eyes, focused on the tiny flame. It danced from side to side, much as she imagined how she flickered between her choices. A chance for prestige and money on one side, a free conscience on the other.

As she stared at the yellow glow, she momentarily lost all awareness of her body. In this sublime ethereal state, she felt centered, fully at peace. She had to choose her conscience.

And love.

* * *

One knock. Then three. That was their signal.

Stacie opened the door and waved Cathryn inside. "Where's your suitcase?"

"I can't stay. Our CEO is flying in tonight and we have a seven o'clock breakfast meeting at the North Shore Resort. If I'm gone all night, people will notice."

She didn't like the anguish in Cathryn's voice and had a feeling it was more than just worry about getting back to her hotel before her co-workers discovered she was gone. "Is something wrong?"

"Everything is wrong, Stacie. I don't know who I can trust anymore."

Only then did she notice Cathryn was carrying a large manila envelope, which she tucked beside her in the armchair. Something told her to play it cool, to let Cathryn come to her with whatever had her so upset. "You can always trust me. I mean that, no matter what."

"Even if I have evidence that practically everything you accused my company of doing is true?"

That certainly explained her anguish.

"Not only that, it's even worse than you thought."

Stacie listened with stunned amazement as Cathryn walked her through what she'd found in the company's flow records and tanker logs. "I always knew those guys were crooked but I never dreamed they'd go so far as to dump that much oil on purpose to cover their tracks. That's just diabolical."

"After what happened in Wyoming, they—or rather we, as in Nations Oil—can't afford to get caught pumping bitumen again, especially right now. I don't even think it's about the fines. It's about getting the permit for the Caliber Pipeline through the Senate. The hearings start next week, and all they have to do is keep up the charade a little longer. Hoss says the votes are there, and once it passes, there's very little chance of it being rescinded, even if all this malfeasance comes out later."

Malfeasance was too nice a word for what Nations Oil had done, especially considering Colleen could have been killed. "Cathryn, why are you giving me this?"

"I don't even know. Maybe because I'm an honest person and I don't want them to get away with it."

"If I go waving it around, people will want to know where I got it."

"You can't show it to anyone, Stacie. I'd lose my job. I just thought if you knew for sure it was there, you could figure out a way to make it public."

"Yeah, well…thanks to Big Oil's smear campaign, we don't have a whole lot of credibility with the public. Most of them think we're whacko terrorists, remember?" She was convinced Cathryn no longer felt that way. "Colleen's out of the hospital now and ready to get back to work. I could pass this on to her and explain that she has to be careful not to reveal you as a source. I bet she could back trace that information in the tanker logs and the weigh stations, and make it look like she found it on her own."

"She knows her stuff. That day she had the accident, she was on the press tour asking a lot of uncomfortable questions."

With Cathryn already so distressed about her company's actions, Stacie contemplated not saying anything about Marty, but knowing just how far Nations Oil had gone to cover up the truth might strengthen her resolve.

"What happened to Colleen wasn't an accident." She shared the details of Brian's investigation and her discovery of Jenn's new boyfriend as a spy. "So not only did he almost kill somebody and spy on us for Depew, he had sex with my best friend under false pretenses. That's practically rape in my book."

Cathryn visibly shuddered. "I can't stand Depew. I wouldn't be surprised at all if he was behind Colleen's accident because he showed up at the press tour and practically yelled at her when she asked about one of your surveillance drones."

"Marty's out of the picture now, locked up on drug charges. It's possible he'll turn on Depew if he feels enough heat. Nothing would make me happier than seeing that asshole in jail too."

"All the numbers are in here, and my notes too so you can make sense of them." Cathryn lobbed the envelope onto the bed and stood. "I have to go. I'm really sorry."

"I understand." She hooked Cathryn's arm as she walked by. "I'll forgive you for not staying the night but you aren't getting out of here without kissing me."

It wasn't their usual kiss, the kind that escalated in passion until they tore off their clothes and tumbled into bed. This one was deliberate, overflowing with emotion.

I love you.

I care about your feelings.

You're safe with me.

"Cathryn, no matter what happens, all of this needs to end with you and me together. I don't know how we're going to do it, but I've waited a long time to feel this way about someone and I'm not letting you walk out of my life."

The arms around her waist tightened as warm lips pressed against her neck. "I want the same thing you do."

Yet they both knew there was only one way to overcome their differences.

* * *

The small ballroom was set up with five tables seating ten each, appointed with fine china and crystal. One table was reserved for Hoss and whomever he invited to join him.

Cathryn was among the first to arrive and chose the table farthest from Hoss, assuming the usual pecking order. She lost all interest in breakfast when Karl Depew entered and pulled his chair up beside hers. The rancid odor of last night's scotch mingled with his overpowering cologne, and it was all she could do not to wretch.

"I ain't seen you all week, Cathryn. Where you been?"

Where your grammar? She'd overheard him speaking authoritatively to his men and knew this folksy approach was phony. "My job keeps me very busy, and when I'm not working, I appreciate my private time."

"We all have to eat. What do you say we—"

Larry Kratke joined them, groaning and holding his head. "I'm never drinking again."

Depew got up and slapped him on the back. "You did good, Larry, my boy. At least you weren't puking your guts out like Bob. I thought we were going to have to call the EMTs."

That confirmed for her that Bob Kryzwicki was chummy with the people he was supposed to be overseeing, probably in violation of the EPA's ethics code. Even the investigators needed investigators. She could hardly wait to see their conspiracy unravel.

A scandal this large likely could lead to congressional hearings and even criminal investigations. It was hard to imagine Hoss or Bryce allowing themselves to be implicated in anything more serious than "improper oversight," for which the board of directors would dock a few hundred thousand from their obscene bonuses. The windfall from getting the Caliber Pipeline approved would make up for it a thousand times.

The best outcome would be seeing Karl Depew hauled off to prison. He was paid well to get his hands dirty, but that meant taking on all the risk. Maybe Bob Kryzwicki could have the cell next door.

Woody and Amy approached their table, but after a scolding look from Depew, sat off to the side with a handful of Larry's assistants. Of course it was a corporate caste system, but she resented Depew thinking so highly of himself.

Gregg O'Connor's legal team arrived en masse and claimed a table for themselves. They'd been staying at this luxury resort all along, meeting clients in plush conference rooms, eating with linen napkins and probably hitting the strip joints every night. Those guys lived like kings, but the showy part was because they'd needed to make a good impression on the property owners who came to negotiate their sale.

Cathryn didn't have to impress anyone. Other than the brief flurry of attention they'd gotten from the flyover drone, interest in the pipeline rupture had fallen off just as Depew had predicted. Colleen's upcoming story could change that, but it wouldn't make any difference if the Senate vote on the Caliber Pipeline came first.

A familiar voice shouted from the hallway, "Let's get this show on the road!" Hoss entered the room all smiles, flanked by Bryce Tucker and Norma Garrison, vice president for human resources.

Norma, whose platinum hair was teased and sprayed bigger than a Texas breadbasket, seemed out of place at an event like this…unless it was only a stopover on their way to negotiate a new acquisition. Other than that, she rarely traveled.

"Morning, y'all!" Hoss took his place at the reserved table and pulled out the chairs on either side. "Larry, Cathryn. Y'all come on over here to the grownup table. You too, Gregg."

Cathryn and Larry traded hesitant looks and meekly went over to take seats beside their boss.

"Larry tells me we're wrapping up. They're dredging up the marsh and hauling it up to International Falls to see if we can squeeze any more oil out of it. Wouldn't want to waste a single precious drop," he added, drawing a chuckle from the room. "Come Wednesday morning, we'll all be looking at a shiny new lake, courtesy of Larry's hardworking crew. Let's give him a hand."

Larry nodded sheepishly at the applause. He certainly deserved recognition for his work, but it was inconceivable he didn't know what still sat on the bottom of the lake.

"Also want to give a shout-out to Gregg and his team. They've completed acquisitions for all but two of the lakefront properties, and he tells me they'll be finalizing those today. Let's hear it for legal."

One of those holdouts had to be the cabin where Stacie's friends had been staying.

Gregg stood to acknowledge the applause and added, "One other thing I'd like to update…it just came through last night. There's a public park across the cove from the spill site. We've negotiated with the county to keep that closed to the public for a period of one year so our environmental team can nurture the lake back to its natural state."

"And speaking of that public park," Hoss said, "Cathryn's putting on a big shindig out there on Thursday to celebrate getting this cleanup behind us. I'm sure you all know my good friend, Senator Mike Washburn. He's going to be there. It's mostly a press event, but Cathryn tells me any permit for a county park has to be open to the public. That means the crazies will probably be out in force." He pointed toward the back of the room. "I'm looking at you, Karl."

Depew laughed along with everyone else. "Are you calling me a crazy?"

"I just call 'em as I see 'em. We've had our share of troubles with those tree-hugging idiots, but you have to hand it to Cathryn here. She slapped them down like a pro. Everything they flung at us, she turned it around and flung it right back. Slickest thing I ever saw."

She managed a small wave to acknowledge their round of applause. These guys were so confident, dead certain they could outmaneuver anyone. And why shouldn't they think that? If the regulators were in their pockets, there was no stopping them.

"And that's why, ladies and gentlemen, I flew up here for this special meeting. I have the pleasure of announcing a couple of promotions. As of today, Larry Kratke is our new Senior Vice President for Operations."

Larry's jaw dropped and he leapt from his chair to shake Hoss's hand. Senior VP. He'd just vaulted over half the people on the East End.

"And while I'm at it, let me also introduce our new Vice President for Communications, Cathryn Mack."

It was all she could do to stand on her wobbly legs as she accepted her boss's hug, turning her face away from the audience so they couldn't see her look of shock. Somewhere the Fates were laughing their asses off.

After the celebratory breakfast, she followed Norma to a meeting room to sign some papers. It was indeed a six-figure raise, but her salary paled next to her stock options, which would be worth millions if the Caliber Pipeline went through.

As she signed on the dotted line, she pictured Stacie's face peering over her shoulder. There had to be a way to reconcile this. Stacie couldn't expect her to give up her dream, especially if it meant working within the hierarchy to change how things were done. She had a voice now.

Hoss came in, still smiling like a Santa Claus who had just delivered presents to a children's hospital ward. "I knew this day would come, sweetie. Oh, scratch that. I'm not supposed to call women things like that. You won't write me up, will you, Norma?"

She looked at him sternly over her reading glasses. "Not this time, but don't push it."

"Seriously, Cathryn. I'm really glad to have you on board. Did you get a chance to look at the handbook?"

Cathryn had no idea what he was talking about, but then Norma pushed over a stack of bound documents.

He put his hand on her shoulder. "You'll have to study those, but let me tell about the biggie. Officers are different from employees. The Securities and Exchange Commission lays out the rules for officers, called fiduciary duties. Basically that means you always act in the company's interest, and you never do anything that might hurt the stock value. Those boys at Enron didn't get that memo, and they went to jail."

She easily read between the lines. His little chat had nothing to do with stock value. Now that she and Larry knew where the bodies were buried—in this case, where the bitumen was buried—these new positions bought their silence.

As she walked through the lobby of the resort, she took note of the majestic view of Lake Superior through the three-story glass wall. The perks associated with her position wouldn't kick in until she returned to Houston, which meant another week at the residential hotel, and the miserable trailer at the cleanup site. The next time she went out on the company dime, however, it would be in style.

Amy sat in a leather armchair staring forlornly through the glass.

"What's up?" Cathryn asked.

"Oh, nothing. Just waiting for Woody. We rode together."

"Where is he?"

"You didn't hear? He got kicked upstairs to assistant vice president, Larry's old job. I couldn't believe it. The guy's only twenty-five years old."

Suddenly the pieces fell into place. Woody's discovery of the tanker logs had set all this in motion. As an assistant VP, he technically was an officer too, which meant they all were bound to the same loyalty oath. "Good for him. He's a bright young man, and I wouldn't be surprised to see him running the place one of these days."

Amy smiled weakly. "I was kind of hoping there'd be something in it for me, but Bryce said you were going to retain your duties as spokesperson."

"Don't let that get you down. You're only twenty-eight, and I was a lot older than that when I took the reins. I'll see to it you get some good opportunities and when the time's right, you'll be ready."

On the drive to her office, she acknowledged that she'd made her decision. Convincing Stacie she could change the corporate culture from the inside wouldn't matter much. Someone in her position couldn't possibly have a relationship with the head of an activist group whose main goal was to wipe them out of existence.

If they played it cool, they could see each other occasionally and maybe take secret vacations to Europe or the islands. Already they'd proven they could manage their differences.

Who was she trying to kid? That kind of masquerade was a betrayal to both sides.

CHAPTER FOURTEEN

Freshly shaven and wearing a tie and sport coat, Izzy looked downright handsome.

"You clean up really well," Stacie said. "How come you don't have a girlfriend?" In her fantasy world, Izzy and Jenn would fall in love and have a dozen eco-friendly children. Too bad there wasn't even a spark of chemistry between them.

"Who says I don't?"

They were sharing the backseat of the Prius with John and Rita in front, on their way to the Department of Health in St. Paul where they had an appointment with a state inspector who had found their test samples interesting.

The Mauneys would drop them on a street corner and continue on to a shopping mall, a ploy to confuse whoever was tracking their movements. They'd all agreed it was better to leave the trackers in place today and use them to their advantage. The only time Stacie would leave hers behind was when she met Cathryn.

Speaking of Cathryn, that particular conversation with Jenn and Izzy was now off the table. Her status as a pseudo-whistleblower inside Nations Oil afforded her anonymity, even from Stacie's closest confidantes.

She'd gotten two SappHere texts over the weekend asking to get together, but had been caught up with Jenn and Izzy planning CLEAN's next event, a protest at the hoopla Nations Oil had scheduled for next Thursday at the lake. Running out on the preparations would have raised questions she wasn't ready to answer.

According to Jenn, Cathryn had given a press briefing the day before to announce that Senator Washburn would have the honor of reintroducing several species of fish and a pair of wood ducks. It was shameful they were willing to sacrifice even more of those poor creatures in the name of public relations, and she hoped it wasn't Cathryn's idea.

"This is it," Izzy said, and they hopped out at the stoplight. "You ready for this?"

"Just the way we practiced." Their meeting was riding on the hope that Nations Oil hadn't already spread its tentacles inside the state regulatory office. It was imperative they convince someone outside the EPA to get involved, depending on the results of the tests.

The Department of Health was situated amidst a maze of public buildings, with the Environmental Health Division housed on the third floor. After a twenty-minute wait on hard plastic chairs, they were ushered into the office of Jack Douhat, whose nameplate read Supervisor, Environmental Impact Analysis Unit. He had thinning hair and a bushy brown mustache, and in his short-sleeved shirt and tie, it was hard to imagine him as anything but a career civil servant.

"You're here about the samples?"

"Yes, sir. Do you have the results?"

"I do," he said, opening a file to peek inside. "Would you mind telling me where these came from?"

"I'm happy to, but first I'd like to know what you found." She'd paid in advance for the analysis as a private citizen, listing the location only as a public lake.

He gave her a copy of his report, a table of numbers and chemical names she couldn't pronounce. "Here's the particle breakdown. If I were to put it in layman's terminology, I'd call it tar sands."

"I knew it!"

"And you say you found this in a public lake?"

Izzy took over, dropping his business card and a brochure on the supervisor's desk. "I collected those samples personally from Lake Bunyan at the site of the Nations Oil spill. The company claims they've spilled heavy crude, and they also claim they've contained it to a small area of the lake. This sample was taken from well outside that area."

Stacie couldn't come right out and accuse the EPA of collusion, but she had to raise the possibility their investigation was compromised. "Mr. Douhat, I'm afraid the EPA inspector that's working on this has been misled by the company."

"We're sending more samples to the chemistry department at the University of Minnesota, and also to the EPA in Washington," Izzy added. That wasn't true, but there was always a chance Nations Oil would persuade Douhat to lose those results, so it was important to make him think there were more.

They walked out with exactly what they came for—a promise to open an investigation immediately. The problem was "immediately" didn't actually mean right now. There was paperwork that had to be submitted first—vehicle requisitions, mileage, per diem. The Caliber Pipeline could be approved by then.

* * *

The text read, "*Dinner?*"

Cathryn had never been so relieved. She was desperate to hear from Stacie again, to convince her not to share the story with Colleen or anyone else in the press.

She texted the address of a Chinese restaurant on the north side of town. From what she'd gathered over the past few weeks, Depew and his men rarely ventured beyond the nearby steak and Tex-Mex restaurants.

As she neared her car, Depew appeared on the walkway, staggering slightly. It was nearly eight o'clock, which meant he was two hours drunker than usual. "Where you going?"

"I promised an interview with *Minnesota Monthly*. We're meeting for dinner."

"So that's what it takes. How about I interview you tomorrow night over a steak?"

"I'm here to do my job, Mr. Depew. I suggest you focus on doing yours." Without waiting for his retort, she got in her car and drove out. Less than a mile down the highway, she turned off on a county road that would take her into town on a roundabout route just in case he'd had her followed.

Stacie's Prius was in the lot of the strip mall, and she waved from a table for two. "Sorry I couldn't get away earlier. After we canceled our weekend at the hotel, I made plans with Jenn and Izzy and couldn't run out on them."

As Cathryn took her seat the waitress delivered two plates. Hers appeared to be chicken with broccoli.

"I hope you don't mind that I ordered for you. She told me the kitchen got slammed with a bunch of takeout orders."

"It's fine." Cathryn's hands were shaking so badly she couldn't manage her chopsticks. It didn't matter since her appetite had vanished.

"You okay?"

"Stacie, I'm scared. Did you give those papers to Colleen?"

"Not yet. She's working with copies of the stuff I gave her before the accident. This is a huge story, Cathryn, and it's complex. I'm sure it'll take her a while to put it together."

"I've changed my mind. If that story hits the news, I know they're going to trace it back to me."

"Don't worry, I'll make sure Colleen protects you." Stacie nonchalantly continued eating, her expression giving away no sign she was concerned.

"It won't work. There are only three people who saw those numbers, and the other two will know it was me."

Stacie put down her chopsticks and gave her a skeptical look. "You told me this was about being honest."

"It's complicated."

"Matters of conscience usually are. If they weren't, everyone would always choose to do the right thing."

"You don't understand. Hoss just promoted me to vice president. Now I have a legal obligation to protect the stockholders. If I do anything to damage the company, they could sue me. Or worse, I could go to jail."

"But in the meantime, your company gets to screw over the whole country. They used to call that a criminal enterprise. These days it's just business as usual."

"You don't even care what I just said? I could go to jail for talking to you." Cathryn pushed her dinner aside and leaned across the table, pressing her hands together as if she were getting ready to pray. "Look, I'm in a position now to change things from the inside. I have a seat at the table, and I can use my clout to push back against what they're doing."

"Seriously? How are you going to push back against this, Cathryn? Are you just going to let them get away with lying about what's on the bottom of that lake?"

She resented Stacie's holier-than-thou attitude. "I guess it's easy for you to sit there in judgment when you get to go home to your privileged life. You've never known what it's like to struggle, to wonder if you're going to be able to hang on just one more day. I know what that's like, and I'm never going to live like that again. You can sneer all you want about what other people do for money because you've never not had it."

"How much is enough? Does Hoss Bower need more millions? What about Karl Depew? You don't think he tries to have people killed for minimum wage, do you?" She waved her chopsticks in the air for emphasis. "Guys like that are never going to have enough money, and they don't care who they hurt to get it. I know you're not like that. You just want to be safe and secure, and I don't blame you. Walk away while you still can. If this blows up in your face, you'll be damaged goods. Hell, your bosses might even be marched off in handcuffs. You think anyone will hire you with that on your résumé?"

It was clear Stacie still cared about her, and it was the only leverage Cathryn had. "Please, Stacie. I made a mistake giving you those papers. I'm begging you not to give them to anyone. You'll destroy me."

Stacie sighed and threw up her hands. "I can't believe you're asking me to save a bunch of greedy bastards who don't care about anything but their bank accounts."

"I promise you the lake will be cleaned up. We've bought up all the property. Cleanup crews will be moving into those cabins by next week, and they plan on being there at least a year. Every square inch of that lakebed will be dredged, and then all those properties will go back up for sale and people will get their lake back. That's going to happen whether you break this story or not."

"And why shouldn't Nations Oil be held accountable for lying in the first place about what was in the pipeline and how much was spilled?"

"Because it will hurt me." She searched Stacie's face for any hint of compassion. "I'm not negotiating with CLEAN on behalf of Nations Oil. I'm asking you on behalf of me. Just pretend you never got those papers."

"Fine. The game's over anyway. I took the samples down to the Department of Health and they came back proving it's bitumen. They'll be starting their investigation soon and all that money Hoss Bower paid the EPA inspectors won't matter a bit. But you'll be free and clear."

Cathryn hardly cared about the bitumen being discovered, as long as it wasn't traced back to her. "Thank you."

The uncomfortable silence lasted a couple of minutes while a boisterous foursome was seated nearby. Stacie leaned forward and, keeping her voice low, asked, "Do you still love me?"

She wasn't prepared for that, and instinctively answered, "Yes, of course I do, but..." Their feelings for one another wouldn't be enough to overcome this rift. "After our event at the lake on Thursday, my work is finished. It looks like I'll be going home to Houston on Friday. If we continued to see each other, we'd have to keep it hidden from everyone. My company could never find out. I'm just...I'm not sure I can handle living like that."

Tears flooded Stacie's eyes but she tipped her chin upward, defiantly refusing to let them fall. "That's okay. I can always return to my privilege in Pittsburgh. Have a nice life, Cathryn." She slapped a twenty-dollar bill on the table and lurched from her seat, knocking over a water glass as she stormed off.

* * *

"I heard you had an opening for a roommate," Stacie said as she dropped her duffel bag on the floor.

Jenn was sitting up in bed typing away on her laptop. "This is a surprise."

"I figured it was time to circle the wagons. Is everything still on track for Thursday?"

"So far we've got fifty-six commitments, and they're all promising to bring three or four people each. That'll give us a couple of hundred, but I think we can pick up a few dozen more by tomorrow. They're going to muster at a couple of motels down near Carlton and caravan to the lake on Thursday morning."

Only a handful of trusted locals knew of their plan, which gave them a good chance of keeping it under the radar until the last minute. If Marty had still been embedded as Jenn's boyfriend, he'd have already alerted Depew and the sheriff's department to what they were doing.

Even though Stacie had held off on handing over Cathryn's explosive documents, the truth was coming out. By Thursday afternoon, everyone would know about Nations Oil's extraordinary efforts to deceive the public. The outcry would serve its purpose, killing the Caliber Pipeline as it was heating up for a Senate vote. Cathryn, like all the others involved in the cleanup at Lake Bunyan, would probably be collateral damage.

Stacie sank to the floor with her back against the wall and stretched out her legs. "I've got something to tell you, Jenn."

"The last time you said that, my whole life turned upside down."

"It's my life this time. You remember Cate, the woman I hooked up with the first night we got here?"

"The one who's been keeping you busy on weekends?"

"Yeah, I didn't know it at the time—and you're just going to have to take my word for that—Cate was Cathryn Mack, the spokeswoman for Nations Oil."

Jenn slammed her laptop and tossed it aside before jumping up to pace the room. "I can't believe these assholes! They got to you too."

"Not exactly. I met her through a dating website where most people are anonymous. I found out who she was when I saw her on the news that night we sprung the video. When I confronted her, she was just as shocked about who I was. She's naïve…not stupid, though. She just didn't want to believe her company was behind the raid or all the vandalism. After she saw my black eye, she started coming around, and when I told her what happened to Colleen, she gave me a file that proves Nations Oil dumped heavy oil on top of their bitumen to fool the regulators. But now she's gone back over to the dark side."

"They're all snakes, every last one of them. They can shed their skin, but they'll never be anything but cold-blooded reptiles."

Stacie kicked off her shoes and pointed her toes upward to stretch her calves. A candlelight yoga session would feel great right now. "I'm really sorry about Marty. I should have been a lot more sensitive about your feelings when I told you the news. You loved the guy, and now I realize it must have felt like a kick in the gut."

"It wasn't your fault. Once I found out he was a bastard, I didn't waste much time worrying about my broken heart."

"I see what you mean. I wish I could say that about Cathryn, but I think deep down she's a decent person, and I still love her."

Jenn squatted down and patted her knee. "That's because you're a lesbian and you can't help yourself. If you guys could just stop falling in love so fast, you wouldn't have these problems."

There was no denying Jenn was right this time. Stacie had led with her heart instead of her head, blissfully pretending Cathryn would be the one to give up everything. There was no scenario in which they both got to be happy.

"Speaking of Marty, I talked to Matt today," Jenn said. "He sat in jail for a couple of days and then somebody bailed him."

"I'm not surprised. He was in some pretty deep shit and they couldn't afford to let him start singing."

"Apparently he's been turned over to his parents in Ohio, but he has to come back for trial in October. You don't think he'll make trouble for anyone in particular, do you?"

By anyone, Jenn obviously meant her. Stacie had thought quite a bit about that very question. It must be clear to Marty by now that she'd set him up, but by implicating her, he might call unwanted attention to his criminal activities with Depew. "Be careful what you say to Matt. I trust him totally, but he's an officer of the court and we don't want to put him in a bad spot. As for Marty, let's just drop it and let those chips fall where they will."

In hindsight, it might have been better to let Brian Murray handle him. She hated to think her rash action might somehow result in him making a deal that got him out of taking responsibility for Colleen's wreck. That was way more important than bringing drugs into their house.

"We're on the cusp of a big victory, Stacie. I think tomorrow, just to be safe, we should spread out...see if we can get some of the locals to take us in for the night. I don't want any more SWAT team surprises."

"Good idea." They both knew it wouldn't make any difference at this stage because their plan was already in motion and didn't depend on any one person leading the way. Still, they both wanted to be there to see it go down. "We'll have a lot more friends next week because people will see how effective we can be in fighting against Big Oil. When this is over, I want to take CLEAN up a few notches. We need offices and full-time staff. Health insurance, pension, the whole nine yards. We're here to stay. And I want you to take over as executive director."

Jenn slumped back on the bed shaking her head. "Not me. You're much better at schmoozing than I am."

"But you're better at organizing and talking to the media. That's what a good ED has to do. I still plan on schmoozing, but I want to do it on a different level. We need a national board of directors that's so big and powerful that Congress has to listen to them. Those snakes in the oil industry aren't going to just slither off in the grass after this. They'll keep working under the table until they get more legislators on their side, and that's where the next battles will be fought. I want to be ready."

"I don't know, Stacie. I wish I could say yes but...I just can't see myself working in an office. This is going to sound weird, but I actually like the road."

That sure threw a wrench into her plans. "I knew Izzy would say that but I was hoping you were ready for a change."

"Maybe in a few years. I'll take the health insurance and pension though."

CHAPTER FIFTEEN

"Don't bunch them all together," Cathryn yelled, stomping through the wet grass at the park. "Three on each side. Didn't you look at the diagram?"

Her event started in forty minutes and the contractors still weren't finished setting up the stage. There were six chairs in all, left to right for her, Bryce Tucker, Hoss Bower, Senator Washburn, Bob Kryzwicki and the county administrator. The backdrop was the public boat launch and beyond it, Lake Bunyan, sparkling in the morning sun.

Why on earth had they chosen to hold this event in the morning? If they didn't drown in the dew, they'd be carried off by mosquitoes.

Amy rushed over from the event truck. "He wants to know if you want a podium or just a standing microphone?"

"The podium with our logo on it, of course," she snapped. How could someone who professed to be a public relations professional not realize you took every opportunity to promote your brand?

Cathryn had ordered one hundred folding chairs for the press and visiting dignitaries, which so far included every elected official in the county, and representatives from all the relevant state and federal agencies. Technically, the event was open to the public, but she didn't expect much of a turnout among ordinary citizens. The people who actually cared came to rallies, not self-congratulating corporate ceremonies.

Citing security concerns over Senator Washburn's presence, Depew had successfully lobbied officials for the establishment of a free speech zone, a designated area for protest activities. It was located at the far end of the parking lot, where the activists would be visible only as people arrived or left the event. Anyone who wanted to carry a sign or shout slogans had to remain inside the yellow tape, and violators would be arrested.

"I ordered two amplifiers, one on each side of the platform." She couldn't risk having the senator's remarks drowned out by distant shouts of "Nations spoiled!"

Hoss and Senator Washburn were currently touring the spill site with the other officials. For the time being, the dredging equipment had been moved to the tanker lot well out of sight, and crews had collected the booms. To the casual observer, the lake was clean, though the cove in the distance that had borne the brunt of the spill was now stripped of its vegetation.

Already she was dead on her feet. She'd barely slept since her wrenching talk with Stacie, and got up each day half expecting to read a horror story on the front page of the paper. No news was good news, and it gave her hope Stacie would keep her word. Even if the story somehow broke, she was confident they would do everything they could to mask her identity as the one who leaked it.

Amy stepped away to answer a call on her cell phone, and then returned. "Some of our guests have started to arrive. Would you like me to stay here and supervise the crew, or should I go up to the parking lot and escort them back down here to their seats?" From her meek tone, it was clear she feared setting Cathryn off on another tirade.

"You should go meet them, Amy. You always make a great impression on people." There was no excuse for Cathryn taking out her frustrations on others, especially Amy, who was already smarting over watching everyone else move up the corporate ladder.

Cathryn needed to get control of her faculties. Since her promotion five days ago, she'd been unable to meditate, and the muscles in her neck were so tight her head throbbed all the time. The worst part was the creeping feeling that getting this Lake Bunyan episode behind her wouldn't be enough to settle her spirit. She'd still have to deal with the inner turmoil of her role in her company's deception, and now the grief over losing someone she loved.

"The flowers?" A worker appeared before her with two arrangements.

"One on each side of the podium." Nothing like waiting till the last minute.

Several TV crews were jockeying for the best position from which to cover the event. It wasn't every day a high profile senator came to a community like Lake Bunyan, and the rumors were already percolating that Washburn would toss his hat into the next presidential ring.

Senator Mike Washburn, their key to the Caliber Pipeline. Just this morning, at Hoss's "suggestion," she'd written a personal check to his campaign fund, the maximum amount allowed under federal elections law. That nice raise would come in handy, considering she'd now be expected to spread it around.

With the stage finally assembled—and not a moment to spare—the event crew retreated with their truck to the parking lot and the gates opened to allow the general public to enter the park. The sheriff's department provided two dozen deputies for security, and the state had sent ten uniformed troopers. Scattered among them, and apparently giving the orders, were Depew's men, all of whom seemed dressed for Halloween in camouflage pants, black T-shirts and caps, and mirrored sunglasses. They'd swept the area several times, and were taking up positions by the stage and around the perimeter of the audience area.

The parking lot was designated for media and invited guests only. All others would have to park along Lake Bunyan Road and walk at least half a mile to the park, another of Depew's obstacles to limit general attendance. This wasn't really meant to be a public celebration. It was pure theater for the media and local officials.

Cathryn swatted a mosquito on her ankle and noticed with chagrin her cream-colored pumps were stained with dew, permanently ruined. She couldn't wait to leave this misery behind. Houston had its problems with humidity and bugs, but at least her office wasn't outdoors.

Amy approached her with three women and two men, and introduced them as county commissioners. Cathryn made small talk about how much she'd enjoyed her stay in their beautiful area, and after a few minutes, directed them to reserved seating in the first two rows. It was then she noticed the seats behind them had begun to fill in, at least forty citizens with dozens more streaming in. The commissioners fanned out to shake hands as if their election were the next day.

She tugged Amy to her side. "What are they doing?"

"That's how people are in the Midwest. They're probably trading recipes for casseroles and Jell-O salad."

The growing crowd shouldn't have surprised her, not after Stacie and her group had turned out thousands at Chester Park. They were concerned citizens, the foundation of democracy. The bedrock of America. The Heartland. These were the words she'd use in her introductory comments when she thanked them all for coming.

"We should have ordered more chairs," Amy said. Her cell phone chirped with news of another arrival, and she hurried back to the parking lot to escort more dignitaries to their seats.

"Excuse me, Miss Mack?" A young man wearing powder makeup and eyeliner approached with a cameraman following close behind. "I'm Kip Goddard, KLS-TV in Duluth. I wonder if we could ask you a couple of questions before the program gets started."

"Of course." She'd rather have postponed everything until the end, but Nations Oil was at the mercy of a friendly press. As they readied their equipment, she took out her compact and touched up her face.

"First, describe for our viewers the purpose of this event."

"As you know, we've had a very unfortunate incident here at Lake Bunyan, an oil spill caused by stress on our pipeline resulting from unexpectedly heavy traffic on Lake Bunyan Road. While we couldn't have predicted something like that, we're holding ourselves accountable, and showing the citizens of this county and the entire nation that we're trustworthy stewards of the environment. We've kept our promise to clean up the spill, and we're here today to celebrate that."

"We've been told by county officials that Lake Bunyan will remain closed to the public for at least one more year. Why is that, if as you say, the lake is clean?"

"We very much regret the need to keep the lake off-limits, but this area has an extremely fragile ecosystem. Over the next few weeks, we'll gradually be reintroducing various species of hatchlings, fingerlings and waterfowl. I've been told several lakes in Minnesota have a few extra ducks."

If only the rest of her day ended on such a light note.

When she turned away from the camera, she was stunned to see the seats were all taken and a hundred people or more were standing in the back and on the sides. Approaching the press section to mild applause was Colleen Murray, walking gingerly on the arm of a young man and a woman whose cap was pulled low over her eyes—Stacie Pilardi.

* * *

Jenn's suggestion that they scatter about in private homes on Wednesday night had proven prescient. Before clearing out, they removed the tracking devices from their cars, leaving them in the driveway inside reusable water bottles with the CLEAN logo. Matt reported that deputies conducted a pre-dawn raid on the empty farmhouse, ostensibly in search of more illegal drugs, a fact that made Stacie uneasy.

Today's civil disobedience was sure to make national news, but she had no intention of being arrested. Her job was to talk with the media afterward and make sure they knew it was bitumen at the bottom of the lake.

John and Rita were leading the protest contingent that had been corralled inside the "free speech" zone. It was absurd the Supreme Court permitted such arbitrary restrictions under the guise of protecting the safety of attendees and protestors at public events. They'd ruled, however, that such constraints could not be implemented based solely on the content of the message. CLEAN put the lie to that by having a couple of their activists carry hand-painted placards that read *Mark Washburn for President!* Those individuals were permitted entry inside the park, and Jenn made certain other members of the media made note of the disparity. Their photos would be grounds for a lawsuit against the county alleging suppression of their rights, which they planned to file this afternoon. It was all part of the constant battle.

They sat through introductory remarks from the county administrator, followed by rosy assessments from the company's CEO and operations officer. In between, Cathryn had taken the podium and artfully delivered a summary of previous statements along with an overview of what the next speaker would say. She was very good at her job, smooth and articulate, and she looked fabulous in a low-cut tan suit.

Stacie could hardly bear to think about Cathryn returning to Houston tomorrow and ending their relationship. Such a waste of love—for both of them. She'd lain awake half the night trying to imagine how they might get past their differences and salvage what they felt for one another. The prospects were grim.

"Next, I'd like to introduce Bob Kryzwicki of the Environmental Protection Agency, who will talk about the standards his agency measures to ensure compliance. Bob?"

Up until now, CLEAN's record for protest-related arrests was forty-one. That's how many activists showed up two years ago to blockade the road into a drilling site in Colorado after an oil company won a permit from the state legislature as a last-minute addendum to a hard-fought budget bill. Big Oil and their legislative stooges were like cockroaches in the dark, but CLEAN was about to turn on the lights. Izzy had conceived their plan when Nations Oil announced they were holding the event in the public park not far from where he'd taken the samples they'd turned over to the state inspectors. He was an adrenaline junkie who thrived on taking risks, and she wasn't surprised when he too turned down the leadership opportunity she offered.

"Thank you, Bob. We appreciate the clarification of the EPA standards and look forward to your final report. And now, ladies and gentlemen, I have the pleasure of introducing our next speaker, who will share his thoughts about the oil industry and its role in national security. Please join me in giving a warm welcome to Senator Mark Washburn."

As the audience came to its feet in thunderous applause, all of the CLEAN activists—one hundred sixty-three, not counting Stacie—began shedding their clothes to reveal bathing suits underneath. En masse they darted toward the shore before security could get into position to block them. Some swam toward the center of the lake while others frolicked in waist-deep water, splashing and laughing, and even dipping underneath the surface.

Senator Washburn's aides shuffled him offstage immediately and back to the parking lot, with Hoss Bower and Bryce Tucker on his heels. Cathryn had the catbird seat, high on the stage from where she could watch the mayhem unfold.

The uniformed deputies stopped at the water's edge, seemingly reluctant to get wet, but Depew's men weren't the least bit daunted. They waded into the lake in pursuit of the swimmers, bringing them one by one back to shore where they were bound with plastic handcuffs and seated in rows.

All the while, TV cameras captured every glorious moment.

"What's that black stuff all over them?"

Reporters and their camera operators defied the security guards and rushed toward the activists. "Zoom in here and get a picture of this for our viewers," one reporter said, bending low to point to a girl who had been dragged from the lake. Her whole body was streaked with tarry oil.

The commotion lasted for thirty minutes, during which everyone who had anything to do with Nations Oil disappeared, including Cathryn.

Every single swimmer was arrested, and Stacie couldn't have been prouder of their feat. As Izzy marched by, he spun around to flash her an awkward two thumbs-up with his wrists bound together. Matt would have his hands full arranging bail for this many people, but it was worth every nickel. Never before had CLEAN made such a splash—literally and figuratively—and this day would live in activist lore for years to come.

"Pardon me, are you Stacie Pilardi, director of the Clean Energy Action Network?" It was Ethan, whose question caused three reporters and a cameraman to rush toward her.

She provided background on the organization and confirmation of the substance they'd seen on the swimmers. "We collected samples from the lake prior to evacuation that suggested bitumen had settled on the lakebed. As you may know, tar sands are diluted for transport, and when the pipeline ruptured, this dilbit as it's called spread across the surface of the lake. The diluents evaporated rather quickly, causing the oil to sink to the bottom. We knew it was there, and we gave Nations Oil ample time to acknowledge that fact, but they did not."

If only she could go further into her explanation, but now that officials knew of the deception, they'd surely discover the deliberate spill of heavy oil on top of the bitumen that was accidentally leaked.

"How were you able to organize today's demonstration?"

"People all over the country care passionately about this issue. We're tired of seeing the oil companies get away with destroying our lakes and rivers, killing our wildlife and ruining our pastimes, and we're tired of politicians who cozy up to their interests in return for campaign contributions. I don't mean to criticize any of you standing here—I know you're stretched thin and you're expected to cover a lot of news with just a handful of reporters on a tight budget—but it takes a lot these days to get the media's attention. Nations Oil tried to pull a fast one on all of us. Go after them and make them answer the hard questions. Then go talk to people and find out how they feel about having their favorite fishing hole ruined forever so a bunch of millionaires who live somewhere else can make even more money. I bet they'll tell you they don't want the Caliber Pipeline coming through their backyard, or anyone else's backyard. We're all ready for clean energy."

As the reporters hustled off to file their stories, the event crew came in with their truck to dismantle the stage and pack up the chairs. From where Stacie was standing, it appeared the authorities had called in school buses to transport the arrested protestors. They'd probably be taken directly to the courthouse for processing, since the jail couldn't accommodate so many. She was looking forward to Izzy's triumphant tale once he was released from custody.

Besides Stacie and the event crew, there was only one other person still in the park. Cathryn sat beneath a pavilion at a picnic table, her face a puzzle of what looked like misery and amusement.

"Sorry about your day," Stacie said sincerely, looking about to make sure they weren't being watched. "I honestly hated what this was doing to you."

Cathryn shrugged. "I never said we didn't deserve to be caught. I just didn't want to be the reason. Are you going to share those papers I gave you now?"

"There's no need. The cat's out of the bag. The investigators should be able to piece it together on their own...the new investigators, that is. I imagine Bob Whatzisname from the EPA is already looking for a lawyer."

"The lawyers are going to do a good business for the next couple of years. I'll probably need one too."

"Maybe, but I don't think any of this will land in your lap. You haven't done anything wrong."

Cathryn chuckled. "You should be proud of yourself, Stacie. After this debacle, there's no way the Senate is going to approve the Caliber Pipeline."

"Not this year, anyway. Nations Oil still has lots of friends though. If history's any judge, we'll see a fine that looks enormous to the average Joe but barely scratches your company's annual profits. Bower might get pushed out of the plane, but you can bet your ass he'll have a golden parachute. This type of corporate behavior isn't going to change until guys like him are the ones marched off in handcuffs."

"Don't hold your breath on that one. Hoss Bower's too big to jail. I'm sure he's hedged his bets in all the right places." Cathryn looked away, clearly ashamed to be a part of their scheme. "That's something I admire about your people. You take a stand even when you know there will be consequences. Guys like Hoss…they have enough money to guarantee they'll never have to face the music."

Though her dismal observations were nothing new to Stacie, she was heartened to know Cathryn had finally come around to seeing things the way they really were. She still hoped some intrepid prosecutor would pursue criminal charges all the way to the top as long as Cathryn didn't get caught in the web.

The event truck's engine roared as its tires spun in the mud. Finally it got traction and pulled out, leaving only trampled grass and gobs of tarry mud. A victorious battlefield for Stacie, but for Cathryn and Nations Oil, it was Waterloo.

Stacie joined her on the bench. Side by side, both of them stared out toward the lake. "What happens now?"

Cathryn checked her watch. "I was supposed to fly home tomorrow on the corporate jet, but I have a feeling it's roaring down the runway without me right this very second. I thought maybe I'd call my friend down in St. Paul and see if she wanted to get together one last time tonight at the Weller Regent before I head out."

"That sounds like a really good idea. I'm sure you'll have a wonderful time." One more night. The only reason at all to say no was to avoid the agony of knowing it would probably be their last time. In the heat of the moment, Stacie might blurt out that she hoped Cathryn got fired so they could be together forever. "I guess I'd better get over to the courthouse with my checkbook. Let's hope nobody fingers me as the mastermind."

"I'll slip you a shiv in a cake."

CHAPTER SIXTEEN

The protestors, many of them still wet and with oil streaking their skin, were packed shoulder to shoulder eight rows deep in the county courthouse for their arraignment. Matt Stevenson hadn't yet entered a plea, hoping a sympathetic judge might dismiss the charges altogether.

Stacie didn't mind fair charges, and in fact, preferred to have CLEAN activists plead guilty to misdemeanors, as it cemented their resolve. These days, however, there was an ominous trend of prosecutorial overreach—menacing charges with stiff sentences designed to intimidate those who might consider protesting in the future. This was that.

The Honorable Susan Lindquist wrinkled her nose and stared down from the bench at the gallery. "I don't want any of you to take this personally, but you're having quite the malodorous effect on my courtroom."

That she had a sense of humor was a good sign. Judges who were all business were less inclined to consider the motivations behind acts of conscience.

The assistant district attorney, who looked to be in his late twenties, was likely salivating at the prospect of padding his conviction numbers with a roomful of defendants. "Your Honor, in addition to unlawful assembly, the defendants are also charged with trespass, interfering with the duties of law enforcement officers and resisting arrest."

That was pretty much everything possible, since there was no resulting injury or property damage. By piling on redundant charges, he clearly hoped for jail time.

Matt calmly interjected, "My clients did not resist arrest, Your Honor. On the contrary, they allowed themselves to be handcuffed, and they followed every order given."

"I breathlessly await an explanation for why the defendants engaged in this forbidden frolic."

Stacie looked down and covered her mouth to stifle a chuckle.

"Yes, certainly. In the wake of its devastating oil spill at Lake Bunyan, Nations Oil held an event today—which was open to the public, I might add—and announced they had completed cleanup. My clients had reason to believe that assertion was untrue, and as you can see by the oil that still clings to their faces, they were correct. This was an act of civil disobedience to expose wrongdoing by a corporation, and perhaps by the very agencies charged with regulating their conduct."

Swiveling from side to side as though casually entertaining herself, Judge Lindquist asked the prosecutor, "Is the county really prepared to prove a hundred and sixty-three people interfered with law enforcement and resisted arrest?"

"Those are the charges listed in the police report, Your Honor. In accordance with the laws of Minnesota, it is my job to prosecute those charges."

"So it is. Were there any damages or injuries?"

"No, Your Honor."

She turned to Matt. "Civil disobedience has a longstanding tradition in this country. However, it is not without consequences, and I trust your clients understood that when they took this action."

"They did, Your Honor, and they are fully prepared to accept society's punishment, but not for crimes they did not commit."

"Very well, then. In exchange for their guilty pleas for unlawful assembly and trespass, I'd suggest the State collect fines of, say…five dollars apiece, and time served. I hope that works for everyone, because I'm not inclined to grant other charges."

Sweet victory! The prosecutor got his convictions and her group got off with a token fine and no obligation to return to court at a future date. Too bad the corporate puppet masters would throw thousands of dollars behind Judge Lindquist's rival during the next election cycle.

Stacie caught up with Jenn in the hallway, where she'd been thanking everyone for coming on such short notice and executing their plan perfectly.

"Look how happy they are, Stacie. You remember how exhilarating our first time was?"

"I'll never forget it." The Battle of Seattle in 1999, where forty thousand gathered to protest policies of the World Trade Organization.

"You think it's safe to go back to the farmhouse tonight?"

"I don't see why not. There's not much point in harassing us now." It was time to think about packing up and heading home. They'd trained enough locals to ensure the real cleanup would be monitored, and Jenn would rally the troops back to town if there was trouble. "Uh…I won't be coming home tonight."

Jenn gave her a sidelong look. "You have another date with the enemy."

"I do," she said, scuffing her foot as though confessing to childhood mischief. "But I don't think she's the enemy. She was out of the loop on this."

"Are you sure you can trust her?"

"It doesn't really matter because I can't help myself." She recalled her first date with Cathryn and laughed. "But if anything happens to me, you can tell them it was Cate with a C."

She was already checked in at the Weller Regent, since they'd left the farmhouse in anticipation of another raid. It was silly she hadn't given Cathryn her room number, but now she had an excuse to call. On her prepaid cell phone, she tapped the button for recent calls, expecting to see Cathryn's number. It wasn't there.

"Oh, shit." Either her cheap cell phone didn't remember numbers…or she'd used the wrong one to call the police on Marty.

* * *

"*RM 317.*" The text message came from SappHere instead of Stacie's prepaid phone. It occurred to Cathryn the ensuing investigation into Nations Oil's misconduct could very well result in all of her phone records being subpoenaed, and maybe even her texts from SappHere. Perhaps they'd accept her explanation of meeting a woman named Marlene and let it go at that. If not, there was nothing she could do about it now.

Hoss hadn't left town after all. He was holed up at the North Shore Resort with Bryce and the lawyers plotting how they were going to get out of this mess. The corporate jet had whisked Washburn back to DC and was returning for all of them in the morning. The Nations Oil brass, which now included her, were flying home just the way they'd arrived a few short weeks ago.

Stacie's face fell once again when she realized Cathryn hadn't brought her overnight bag.

"I'm sorry, change of plans." She explained the situation with Hoss. "But I have two or three hours. How about we forget all about the oil business and enjoy our time together?" She took Stacie in her arms and they kissed, gradually tumbling to the bed.

"I have just one condition," Stacie said. "This can't be goodbye. I don't know how we're going to do this, but I'm not letting you walk out of my life."

Cathryn knew her willingness to risk coming here was proof her feelings for Stacie were strong enough to withstand the stress of hiding their relationship from everyone who mattered. Weekends, vacations. They could even spend time at her home in Houston and no one would ever know. She'd lived in her townhouse for four years and not once had anyone from Nations Oil stopped by.

"It's not goodbye, I promise."

They spent their first hour fully clothed, trading kisses and deep, soulful gazes. Cathryn ran her hands through Stacie's short brown hair and committed to memory every fragrance, wrinkle and feature, whatever she might conjure to soothe her longing when they were apart.

Stacie gently pushed her onto her back and began loosening the buttons on her shirt. "Every time we've done this before, I couldn't wait to touch you. It made me feel power and privilege to know someone as beautiful as you was giving herself to me. All I wanted was to make you feel so wonderful that you'd remember me forever. That isn't enough anymore."

Cathryn arched in anticipation of feeling Stacie's hands on her breasts. From their very first night together, it had been about comfort and physical pleasure, a welcome respite from the demands of work.

"Now I want more than to touch you. I want to make love with you so you'll know all these feelings inside me. I'm so lucky I found you, and nothing would make me happier than to know you felt just a little of that for me."

"Of course I do. You're making a real difference in my life, and that's the biggest compliment I could ever pay you." As she'd gotten to know Stacie and the reasons she worked as an environmentalist, it was impossible to dismiss her as one of the crazies she used to deride so easily. There wasn't a selfish bone in her body, and she showed remarkable restraint given how she was persecuted by the likes of Depew. Cathryn respected her, and though her work was very different, she strived to conduct herself with integrity like Stacie's.

They stripped off their clothes and fell together again, with every kiss, touch and gesture conveying a message of solemn devotion. The clock moved like a pinwheel, spinning their time away too fast.

"I have to go," Cathryn said.

"I know."

"You're on top of me."

"I know that too. It's part of my strategy to keep you here." Stacie eventually rolled off and slipped on her panties and shirt as Cathryn too got dressed. "I'd like to go somewhere with you, a vacation or something. Not that I don't love worshipping your glorious body, but I believe there's a lot more to both of us than what we've been able to show each other in a hotel room. I want us to laugh and be ourselves."

"I want that too." In the meantime, though, Cathryn saw no choice but to hide, especially with her job on the line. The board of directors could can the whole slate of officers, and who would blame them if they did? It would solve a lot of her personal problems, but she hadn't climbed to the pinnacle of her career to have the rug pulled out from under her feet. If she could hold onto her job, she would.

Stacie walked her to the door and snaked her arms around her neck. "I'm going to start back to Pittsburgh tomorrow. Whatever you do, don't walk out this door and change your mind about me."

"I love you, Stacie." She savored one final kiss and walked out, not daring to look back lest Stacie see the tears pooling in her eyes.

What if she couldn't do this?

* * *

The driveway was blocked by a car from the Bunyan County Sheriff's department, leaving Stacie no choice but to park on the grass. She expected to find the farmhouse in disarray again after the SWAT raid. The storm troopers knew they wouldn't find anything, but screwing with activists was such irresistible joy. Still, it was hard to believe they'd wreck the place again after having to pay damages the first time. She hoped Jenn was inside giving a full accounting of what they'd broken this time.

"We didn't hear you pull up," Jenn said as she sprang from the couch, her eyes darting furtively over Stacie's shoulder.

Deputy Gustafson, wearing a tight brown uniform shirt with dark green pants, emerged from the dining room. The house appeared to be in order, suggesting Jenn and the volunteers had straightened it already, or perhaps the thugs hadn't tossed it after all. So why was a deputy paying them a visit?

"That's the Prius for you. The engine cuts off whenever I slow down so I can sneak up on practically anyone."

"Deputy Gustafson has a few questions for you about Marty." Though her voice was calm, Jenn's eyes were wide and anxious.

"I hope he didn't put me down for a character reference. I've got nothing good to say about someone who'd sell drugs to kids."

"Can we step outside, Ms. Pilardi?"

Not good. As his former girlfriend, Jenn should be the one answering questions. And no one should be answering to the sheriff's department in Bunyan County, unless Marty had somehow gotten his case transferred back over to a friendly jurisdiction. That wouldn't be surprising.

The screen door closed behind them, and the deputy led her to a corner of the wide porch. "When Mr. Winthrop was arrested, he was in possession of two ounces of marijuana. That's a felony in Minnesota."

"Yeah, I always worry about the first-timers who come along on our campaigns. There's no way to know what they're really like until you spend some time with them. We don't tolerate drugs, Deputy. It's in our training materials, and everyone has to sign a pledge. I can show you Marty's if you want to see it."

"Yes, I'd like a copy of that if you don't mind."

"We're not just drug-free. We have strict rules about weapons and alcohol too, anything that might get us in trouble. You have to understand, Deputy, we get hassled a lot because we ruffle the wrong feathers. We've had two raids on this house on account of someone spreading false information about us. We aren't terrorists, and we don't deal drugs. The people who were staying here came here from all over the country because they care about the environment. If we don't stand up and make these oil companies take responsibility, no one else will."

Gustafson looked up from a small tablet where she'd been taking notes. "Do you think it's possible somebody set him up with those drugs?"

The danger in offering up too many details was getting caught in a small lie that would unravel her entire story. "I thought about that at first, but then I heard he'd been kicked out of the army for marijuana."

"The thing is, Mr. Winthrop says you sent him to the high school to see a man by the name of Jeff Johannesson, who I haven't been able to find. And while he was there, the Duluth Police Department got an anonymous call that he was out there selling drugs. Do you know anything about that?"

"Unbelievable!" Stacie sighed deeply and shook her head, still determined not to lie. "That's how it is with guys like Marty. Whenever they get caught doing something, it's always someone else's fault. I bet you hear that all the time."

"I sure do," the officer said cynically. "The sheriff just asked me to check everything out. Can you give me a rundown of where you were last Tuesday?"

"Sure thing." She opened the calendar function on her phone and stepped closer so the deputy could see. "I had a couple of conference calls that morning, and then I went to the office for a while." Too bad she couldn't produce the GPS coordinates of the tracking device to back up her story.

"He said you told him you had a meeting with a county commissioner, but I checked that out and your name didn't show up on anyone's calendar."

The thoroughness of this investigation was disturbing. "That's because it's not true. I didn't have a meeting. I don't know why he said that, unless he was just trying to concoct something elaborate to make it more believable. I'm telling you, I had no idea he had anything to do with drugs, or he wouldn't have been part of our group."

Gustafson nodded blankly, as if tepidly accepting her explanation. She started for her car but turned back. "Do me a favor, would you? Leave me a number where I can catch up with you in case I have any more questions."

Ugh. Stacie had hoped that would be the end of it, but this case wasn't going away as long as Marty Winthrop was pointing fingers and Depew was pressuring the sheriff's department to follow up.

Jenn joined her on the porch as the deputy drove away. "What's going to happen?"

"Nothing, I hope. I told her guys like Marty always blame everyone else for their problems."

From the sound of it, Gustafson was working only with Marty's version of events and not any of the actual evidence, which meant his case probably hadn't been transferred after all. This was all a special favor to Depew. Now she had to hope no one looked into the phone she'd used to make the call.

CHAPTER SEVENTEEN

The fiasco at Lake Bunyan had made national news with humiliating video that caused even the wooden-faced, baritone anchor of the most-watched news network to chuckle. Even worse for Cathryn, it kicked off with her rosy introduction of Washburn, who was now getting unwanted attention from the Senate Ethics Committee.

The flight back to Houston would undoubtedly be the most miserable three hours of her life, and after yesterday's disgraceful incident, that was saying something. She was the first to board the plane and took her usual seat in the back.

She was startled moments later when Woody stepped aboard, for the first time wearing a bolo instead of his usual necktie. No doubt he'd pick up a big hat too as soon as he returned to Texas. Amy was right to feel cheated at how he'd been promoted so many levels above his old job, and there would be lots of other petroleum engineers on Bryce's team who would feel the same way.

He set his briefcase on the center seat. "This is a far cry from being crammed into a regional jet. It could take some getting used to, but I'm willing to give it a try."

"You might want to start by not taking Hoss's chair."

"Oops!" He moved to the seat across the aisle from hers. "I really appreciate having the chance to work under you, Cathryn. There's no way I'd have this job if you hadn't been such a good mentor."

There's no way he'd have this job if he hadn't stumbled across the tanker logs. "I enjoyed having you on my team, and I hope my next technical assistant is as smart and hardworking as you." It never hurt to be gracious, especially since he could very well be her boss someday.

Her personal phone chimed with a message from SappHere. *"Miss you already. Safe travels."*

She answered back to say the same and dropped her phone in her briefcase. It wasn't fair she'd finally met someone she could love with all her heart, and they were doomed from the start by circumstances. If she had one wish, it would be—

"Where the hell is Depew?" Hoss demanded angrily as he stormed aboard the plane. Judging by his red face, his blood pressure was in the danger zone. He was followed by Bryce and Gregg. Poor Larry would be left behind in Duluth to oversee the cleanup.

"I saw him this morning at breakfast," Woody said.

"Call him and tell him to get his ass here."

"He's coming now, Mr. Bower," Juan said, scurrying down the steps to take Depew's bag.

"Sorry I'm late, fellas…and ma'am," he added, tipping his hat. "It takes all day to get it through those thick skulls that locked down means nobody gets in."

Bryce, whose face was nearly as red as Hoss's, poked a finger in Depew's chest. "For what we paid you, we weren't expecting a bunch of imbeciles. Everybody did their job but you."

Though it always made her uneasy when Bryce went off on someone, Cathryn didn't mind seeing Depew on the receiving end. If he weren't such a bastard, she might have volunteered the observation that the activists could have discovered the bitumen on the lakebed before he ever arrived on the scene, which happened to be true. It was much more satisfying to watch him squirm.

Hoss loosened his collar, which Cathryn hoped would calm him down. "How did we get blindsided like this? I thought you had somebody on the inside."

"I did, but he got himself arrested on a drug charge. He says that woman set him up, Stacie Pilardi, the head of that crazy ecoterrorist outfit." Depew swiveled toward Gregg. "By the way, he needs a lawyer who can plead that down. It wouldn't do to have him start singing."

"Goddammit, Karl!" Bryce yelled. "What the hell do you think we hired you for? You put all of our asses on the line and now you expect us to take care of your man? We paid you for security services. If he's got anything to sing about, that's your problem, not ours."

"Excuse me," Gregg said, craning his neck to make eye contact with Cathryn and Woody in particular. "I need to remind everyone that, as general counsel, my presence makes this a privileged conversation. If you're called upon to give a deposition, you're not required to divulge anything you hear on this plane. In fact, your responsibility as officers of the corporation requires that you safeguard all information from private company meetings, including this one."

Especially this one, she thought. She gripped her armrests as the jet roared down the runway and burst into the air, quickly gaining both altitude and speed.

The men, locked in a pissing match, hardly seemed to notice.

Now it was Depew who was red in the face. "Don't think for a minute you're going to hang me out to dry, Tucker. Remember our little powwow at Jackson Hole last year? I recorded every second of it because I knew you sons of bitches would get all high and mighty if things ever went south. You're up to your necks in this, all of you, and I can prove it if I have to. Bribes, vandalism, roughing up the protestors. You signed off on every bit of it, and you told me to stop that reporter who was fixing to tell the whole world about you dredging the lake. My guy sitting in jail—the one you don't want to help—he was following your orders, and that's what he'll sing about if you don't get him out."

Hoss whirled to face Tucker. "You told him to take out a reporter?"

"I had to, Hoss. Larry called and said she was asking about the dredgers like she knew something. She had pictures of our dredge pad in her briefcase. Somebody was feeding her information."

"Do we have any idea who it was?"

Depew spoke up. "It probably came from that drone we shot down. Our inside guy said there was somebody holed up in one of those cabins, but we swept the whole lake twice and didn't find them."

"Maybe they were playing your guy the whole time," Cathryn said, relishing the chance to twist the knife. "I don't know what the range is on those drones, but it seems like they could have been flown in from outside the perimeter."

Depew scoffed. "You give them a lot more credit than I do."

"We gave you too much credit, Karl," Hoss spat, and spun back toward Tucker. "What are we getting from Larry on the EPA?"

"He met last night with Kryzwicki, and he's on board."

"He damn well better be. His head's on the chopping block too."

As the lead inspector for the EPA, Bob Kryzwicki was more vulnerable than anyone. He'd signed off on a preliminary report saying the spill was heavy oil and they'd accounted for all of it. Walking that back at this point would require an elaborate fabrication.

Bryce went on, "The story is we found out about the dilbit when everyone else did. Turned out we had a slow leak, one that's been building up out there for several months. We never looked for it because we didn't know anything had gone missing. Woody here, he's already fixed the flow reports to back that up."

All eyes turned toward the back of the plane where Woody suddenly sat up straight like a schoolboy called on to recite his lesson. "That's right. I made a little software adjustment that shows a slight drop in volume going all the way back to January. It looks like a calibration issue. It's too small to trigger an alarm, and it looks like it could have been evaporation."

"And the tanker logs?"

"Gone."

Hoss shot him a thumbs-up sign along with a wink, and turned back to Bryce. "So how are we going to explain the fact that it's dilbit and not heavy oil?"

"Jesus, Hoss," Gregg said, his impatience clear. "If we have to pay another fine for running dilbit, let's just do it and make this mess go away. The regulators want a scalp of some sort, and that's the easiest one to give them. What matters most is convincing them we didn't know any of it was there. If we get greedy over the dilbit, they might decide to take everything to a grand jury, and somebody could end up going to jail."

The question was who. Taken together, all the pieces of their story were a house of cards. One person deviating from the company line could bring it crashing down around them, and she worried they were setting Woody up to take the fall. History had shown the cover-up could be punished even more than the crime.

"Who'll be taking depositions, Gregg?" she asked.

"The EPA, for starters. We'll all have to get on the same page for that, including Bob. My guess is they'll want to talk to Hoss and Bryce, and then Larry and a few of his supervisors. If we can sell them on a slow leak, it might stop there. If not, the SEC could take a much harder line. They'll want to talk with you, since you were putting out the daily updates. If any of your public statements are contradicted by the facts at hand, they'll take that to mean we misled investors."

In other words, she could be held responsible for repeating the lies they fed her.

"Don't you worry, Cathryn," Hoss said, reaching back to slap her knee. The paternalistic gesture, which he probably meant to reassure her, filled her with dread. "Gregg will fix you up with a good lawyer and you won't have to admit to anything."

So his plan was to have her stonewall the regulators. Even if she survived that, she'd never again be effective with the press as Nations Oil's spokesperson. Nor could she go before the shareholders and stock analysts. With her credibility in the toilet, she was completely useless as head of communications, and not just with Nations Oil. She'd be damaged goods forever—just as Stacie had said.

Hoss leaned back in his chair and looked around the executive cabin. "So how many people know about this, and more important, have we taken care of all of them?"

"Well," Bryce said, "it's everybody here on the plane plus Bob and Larry. He told a couple of his fellas they'd have to stick around another week or so until the EPA signed off, but they don't know about the other leak. We're all set to bring in private contractors from Calgary as soon as everybody else bugs out."

"All-righty, then we're all good. Anything else?"

The conversation shifted to damage control for the Caliber Pipeline. Hoss planned a trip to DC hoping to convince the Senate committee to delay their hearing until the ruckus died down. If they took it up now, their answer would be an unequivocal no.

Cathryn stewed over how casually they'd swept her situation aside. For the next few months, she'd be up to her neck in legal troubles while they were wheeling and dealing for their next fast buck. If the EPA bought this bogus story, their problems were practically over while hers had just begun.

Stacie was also right about all of these guys. They were greedy bastards, corrupt to the core and without an ounce of decency.

By the time they landed in Houston, she wanted nothing more than to get away from all of them, and she bounced down the stairs and paced as Juan unloaded their luggage. It was only when she reached the executive terminal that she realized she'd left her briefcase at her seat, and she stalked back to the plane. At the top of the stairs, she stopped in her tracks to hear Hoss's voice.

"…that Stacie Pilardi. It's time to take her out—permanently. I don't care how you do it, Depew, but she's fucked with us for the last time."

"That's right," Bryce said. "Cut off the head of the beast, the body dies."

"And don't go sending those imbeciles of yours out to do this. When I pay the top dog, I want the top dog. You've got till Saturday."

"Don't worry, Hoss," Depew said. "I'll enjoy this one. She's good as dead."

* * *

Stacie's niece hugged her at the door of her family's elegant colonial home in Bradford Woods, arguably Pittsburgh's premier neighborhood. "Good thing you made it back before I left, or I would have made you come see me in Buenos Aires." She was leaving in a couple of days to study abroad for her senior year.

"Who knows? I might just do that anyway." Turning to her brother and his wife, she added, "Great to see you again. Thanks for dinner."

"Take care, Stace," Philip said. "See you next Wednesday at the board meeting."

CLEAN's explosive exposé at Lake Bunyan was still hot news, even in Pittsburgh. Most of the board would applaud her triumph, while those heavily invested in oil stocks would treat her with scorn. She'd take pleasure in sitting among her detractors to gloat.

At Philip's suggestion, she'd requested bids from several consulting companies to assist in CLEAN's reorganization. She'd leave it to the pros to decide where their new offices should be located, but the default was right here in Pittsburgh. The only factor that might change that was if Cathryn somehow decided to leave Nations Oil and take a job somewhere else. Stacie was willing to move, but not to a place where she'd have to hide.

As she left her brother's driveway, she noticed in her rearview mirror the headlights of a car as it pulled from the curb. It was downright creepy to know she was being followed everywhere she went.

Marlene's ring startled her and she pulled over to take the call, noticing the car behind her do the same. "This is Stacie Pilardi."

"Thunderbolt Security calling. May I please have your security code?"

Her secret phrase was *Shut up, Marlene.*

"I'm calling to report a brief interruption of service on your phone line, but it appears to have been restored. We suspect it was only a power surge, but if you'd like, we'll send someone to check it out."

"The alarm reset itself, right?" That was a special feature designed to keep it from triggering during thunderstorms.

"Yes, ma'am."

"I'm sure it's fine. I'm on my way home now, and if I see anything suspicious, I'll give you a call."

The road to her house was narrow and dark, similar to the one that circled Lake Bunyan. As she swung wide to collect her mail opposite her driveway, her headlights picked up a vehicle on the shoulder about a hundred yards past her house, though the car that had been following her had faded from view. A handoff?

She disabled the house alarm via remote and pulled into the center of her two-car garage. The transparent tape she'd stuck on the door into the house was still in place, but that did nothing to calm the shaking in her hands as she worked the key into the lock. A quick check confirmed everything was just as she left it, the surface light still on over the stove. As she dropped her mail on the counter, she realized something was different—the boning knife was missing from her kitchen block.

She inhaled deeply, catching a repulsive scent. Pungent cologne.

This was a bad idea. She should have let Thunderbolt send their security guards, and they could have escorted her through the house.

Her heart was pounding so hard she could hardly catch her breath. One misstep and it could all be over before anyone could stop it. With her courage waning, she tiptoed back toward the door, visualizing her safe retreat. In only seconds, she'd be safe in her car.

"Not so fast, little lady." Depew stepped out of the alcove, twirling her missing knife.

Though she'd known he was there, his voice sent a chill up her spine. "How did you get in here?"

"The same way I do everything—without a goddamn soul finding out." He took a menacing step toward her, holding up a canvas bag. "Got your jewelry and that nice new laptop you bought after we smashed up your other one. A robbery gone bad."

"If you think killing me is going to stop our movement, you can forget it. Someone else will stand up and take my place."

"You mean your little friend from Colorado? I'll take that up with Hoss and Bryce. She just might have an accident too. Hell, I bet Marty Winthrop would like to do that himself."

"There's something you ought to know before you come any closer." She tapped the side of her head. "You have a little red dot right around your ear and another one in your armpit."

His sneer faded and he turned his head ever so slightly to find himself on the end of a targeting laser.

"What the—"

"FBI. Move and you're dead."

She hoped like hell he didn't lunge for her, because they'd kill him and rob her of the chance to see him shackled.

CHAPTER EIGHTEEN

Stacie never dreamed she'd find herself back in the St. Paul Hotel. The feds could have brought this case anywhere, but they wanted a jury of Minnesotans to hear how Nations Oil had nearly pulled a fast one and left them holding the bag. Until the indictments came down, the investigation was secret.

The US Attorney had arranged her trip to testify to the grand jury tomorrow about Karl Depew, not only his attempt on her life, but also the intimidation and harassment campaign he'd waged to thwart their efforts against the oil company. Matt warned he might also delve into Marty's accusations that she'd set him up, since that was loosely related to this case. While he never came right out and told her to lie, he reminded her she could invoke her Fifth Amendment rights against self-incrimination and refuse to answer. As far as she knew, there was no one who could corroborate Marty's story, but there was still a question about whether or not they could trace the cell phone she'd used. Or maybe she actually had used the right phone and the other one just hadn't saved a record of her recent calls. A girl could dream.

Voices from the room next door carried into the hall, and she pressed her eye to the peephole in time to see a gray-haired woman walking away. After a couple of minutes, she opened her SappHere app and found Cathryn standing by. *"Guess who's back in St. Paul."*

"How soon can we meet?"

"How fast can you open the door to the next room?"

Moments later the lock rattled and the door opened between them. Cathryn bowled her over with a bear hug. "You scared me to death with that stunt you pulled in Pittsburgh. That son of a bitch could have killed you."

"It scared me too, and that was even knowing I had two FBI agents hiding in my house. It was creeping me out. They'd been there for three solid days, and there were two others following me around to make sure the bastard didn't try to blow up my car or something."

"I hope he goes to prison for a hundred years."

"He very well could. It looks like a slam dunk. There was a video camera on top of my refrigerator and we got every word of it on tape. The dumbass even mentioned Hoss and Bryce."

"Those guys…I still can't believe they did this."

This had to be hard on Cathryn, seeing people she'd once respected behave so ruthlessly. "Where does Nations Oil think you are?"

"Visiting my poor sick mother in New Mexico."

"Hope she feels better soon. How did your testimony go today? I know you're not supposed to talk about it. I just want to know how you're holding up."

"Fine, I guess. The US Attorney wants me back in the morning for a few more questions, but I can't imagine why. We've covered pretty much everything today."

"I don't suppose my name came up." Even if it had, Cathryn wasn't allowed to tell her, because all of the grand jury proceedings were secret.

"Why would it? I haven't told anyone but my lawyer that we know each other."

That was a relief. If they could just get through one more day…

"Enough about lawyers and grand juries. I missed you." Cathryn kissed her hard, forcing her tongue inside and sliding a hand up her shirt.

"I missed you too." Stacie wasted no time undressing, and lay back against the pillows with her legs open. Under Cathryn's heated gaze, she swirled two fingers through her folds until they were wet enough to paint her nipples with the slickness.

"That's so hot." Cathryn dropped the last of her clothes and sat facing her at the foot of the bed. "Do it some more. I want to watch."

"You mean this?" Again she delved into the wet heat, this time with long, languid strokes.

Cathryn stared as if in a trance, moving only to lick her lips.

"Touch your breasts," Stacie said. "Make love to them the way I do."

Memories of their first night together on the couch flooded back as Cathryn lifted her breasts and pressed them together. Her fingers teased the nipples until they stood erect, and it was all Stacie could do to remember she too had a show to put on.

"I want to feel those right here," she said, spreading her lips wide.

Cathryn crawled forward and guided a breast between her legs, pinching a nipple to keep it stiff so she could rub it up and down.

"Oh, that's perfect." It wasn't enough friction to make her come, but it sent her hand into a frenzy. When Cathryn's tongue suddenly darted between her fingers, she pulled them away and used both hands to massage her own breasts. In only moments, a climax rumbled through her and she pulled a pillow to her face to muffle a scream.

Cathryn knew her body so well, and not only the touches that brought her to climax. She had the perfect caress, the gentlest nuzzle and hands filled with emotion.

They needed more moments like this, time alone to explore their feelings for each other. Everything they'd shared so far had been secret, fleeting, forbidden. They deserved better.

"I want you to come away with me, Cathryn. We need a long vacation together. I don't care where. I just want to talk about us…and what we want."

"I want this." She smiled sweetly from where her head still rested on Stacie's thigh, her fingers tickling the soft curls where her mouth had been.

"Be serious."

"I am. I want this, and I don't want it with anyone but you. That's probably the most serious thing I've said to anyone in five years."

Not with anyone but her. That meant something, but they couldn't just say it. They had to make it happen.

"Cathryn, I want more than what we can steal in a hotel room. Who are you when we aren't sneaking around? How do you like to spend a rainy day? What kind of books do you read? Who are the people you care about? I can't know these things if all we ever get is a few hours here and there."

"So come to Houston."

That was the craziest thing she'd ever heard in her life.

"Seriously, Stacie. What better place to champion clean energy than the oil capital of America? Come to Houston and live with me."

"I have a better idea. You come to Pittsburgh."

"My job is in Houston. Yours is wherever you are."

Yes, Cathryn's job was in Houston for now, but only because it would look bad to fire the person who blew the whistle on a vast criminal conspiracy. What Stacie couldn't understand was why she'd want to stay in a job where they were sure to treat her like a pariah. "Do you honestly think you'll have the confidence of your board after you testify against your bosses? Your actions could end up costing them a billion dollars."

"I'm not the one who broke the law. When this mess is over, the people who did will be gone. The board will have to reorganize the company under leadership they can trust to do the right thing." She scooted up to the pillows and tucked Stacie's head against her chest. "Look, I know how you feel about the oil business, but you can't judge our whole company on the actions of a few greedy people."

Naïve or hopeful? The obvious rejoinder was to remind her she'd once described the man who just ordered her murder as kind and decent, but Stacie wasn't trying to score points. This was a pivotal discussion about their future.

"So let's say I pick up and move to Houston. Then what?"

"I don't have a crystal ball, but if you're asking me what I want, it would be for us to be together every day. One day, I hope we'll feel strong enough about our feelings to make a commitment to each other."

That's the future Stacie had in mind too, and they couldn't even start down that path unless one of them said yes to moving. "I love you and I want to be with you, but here's what I need to know. What will our life be like in Houston? How are you going to juggle working for an oil company and having a girlfriend whose mission in life is to put all of you out of business?"

"I never said it would be perfect." She stuck out her tongue. "But I don't tell the people I work with about my personal life. It's not any of their business, so they don't have to know who you are."

"That's your solution? To keep our relationship in the closet? We've been doing that for these last few weeks and it's driven both of us crazy. You'll be looking over your shoulder every time we go out, and I'll have to pick up all my things and hide in my room if the doorbell rings. How can either one of us live like that?"

"Can we please just drop this for now? We hardly have any time together as it is, and I don't want to spend it fighting about something we can't fix."

No matter how many times they broke this down, it always circled back to the same place. Cathryn valued her career above everything, and it would devastate her if she were forced to give it up.

Stacie could only hope she didn't have to. If they got through this awful mess without her bringing down Cathryn too, she would move to Houston after all. Hell, she might just get an office with a view of the refineries.

* * *

Cathryn awakened in the night to an empty bed. By the light that crept in around the curtains, she made out Stacie's silhouette in the chair. "Is the thought of moving to Houston really that depressing?"

"I'll do whatever it takes for us to be together. That includes coming down to Texas and trying it on for size."

That was all she needed to hear. Love had a way of smoothing out most differences as long as they put each other first. She'd do the same for Stacie. "I'll compromise too. Once I get my reputation back, there will be other offers. Headhunters call me all the time, but I've never wanted to jump ship before. Now I have a reason to consider it."

"I'm glad to know that…really glad."

Cathryn patted the sheet beside her. "Come back to bed, sweetheart. We have a long day tomorrow."

"I know." Stacie sighed. "That's actually why I can't sleep. I've been worrying about my testimony."

"You said it was a slam dunk."

"The Depew part is…but there's something else I'm afraid they'll ask me about."

"What is it?"

"Remember I told you about the guy who sneaked into our group, the one who was working for Depew and caused Colleen to have a wreck?"

Cathryn listened in disbelief to Stacie's confession of how she'd set him up to be arrested. It wasn't like her to break the rules.

"They were his drugs though. I found them hidden in his sleeping bag, so he was guilty of possession."

"Why would you do something like that?"

"Because the guy was scum. I'm not proud of myself, Cathryn. It's probably one of the stupidest things I've ever done."

She couldn't disagree. These matters were best handled by the police, not by vigilantes. Still, it was hard to feel anything but contempt for him after all the people he hurt. "What's done is done, Stacie. He deserves what's coming to him."

"He probably deserves more than that. If I could have trusted the sheriff's department, I would have turned in the photos from the rally and let him face the music for Colleen. I would have handed over the drugs too. But I knew some of those deputies were getting money under the table from Depew. Now he's telling anybody who'll listen I set him up, and I have a gut feeling they're going to ask me about it in the grand jury."

"They can't make you testify against yourself. Just refuse to answer."

"That's the other problem." She put her head in her hands and groaned. "I may have made the stupidest screw-up of my whole life. Remember that time we were here in the hotel room and I called you on my prepaid cell phone? It's possible I used the same phone to call the sheriff."

It took Cathryn a moment to unravel what she was trying to explain. "Are you saying I could be..."

"If they track down those phone records, they won't know who made the call. But they will know whoever did it called you too. I've been driving myself crazy about this. They might ask me if I know you. Hell, they might even ask you tomorrow if you know me."

"Shit." Admitting that would be tantamount to resigning from Nations Oil.

"And if all that isn't bad enough, the fact that I've just told you everything means you'd have to testify against me if you were asked to."

Cathryn threw back the covers and wrapped herself in a hotel robe. "Is there another chair?"

CHAPTER NINETEEN

Margaret McCullough was a named partner in one of Minnesota's oldest law firms, and Cathryn was lucky to have hired her before anyone else at Nations Oil could. At seventy-one, Meg knew the system cold and everyone in it. Even taller than Cathryn at five-eleven, she still wore high heels, and the shoulder pads in her pinstriped suit gave her a ferocious appearance.

Their limousine stopped at the courthouse steps and Meg touched up her blood-red lipstick. "The prosecutor should wrap up with you in a couple of hours. Remember, if they ask you about anything we haven't gone over, stop talking immediately and ask to see me."

Though Cathryn had been given immunity in return for her testimony against Nations Oil executives and Karl Depew, this was a wide-ranging investigation that also had implications for the Securities and Exchange Commission. She couldn't afford to inadvertently incriminate herself in the manipulation of stock information, and now she had to worry about informing on Stacie too. All of it was complicated by the fact that she couldn't have Meg in the room with her during questioning.

It had pained her to testify against Woody, but there was no way to avoid it, not with the US Attorney holding the copy she'd made of the original flow records and tanker logs. If he was smart, he'd accept a plea deal in return for testimony against Hoss and Bryce. Even then, the poor guy's career in the oil business was already over at only age twenty-five.

Woody wasn't the only one who needed to save his skin. According to Meg, most of Depew's men were already in the wind, but one had come forward to describe their bullying tactics and payments to local officials, and a ranger from the Department of Natural Resources admitted to accepting a bribe to file the false report on the fish and bird kill. Bob Kryzwicki would soon be begging for a plea deal, but the evidence against him was so strong he had nothing of value to trade. The US Attorney seemed only slightly interested in Gregg, but had Hoss, Bryce and Larry squarely in his sights.

Then there was Depew, who Meg said was still being held in a Pittsburgh jail. Whether he talked or not didn't matter, since his attack on Stacie had been videotaped. He'd get what was coming to him.

"Stay close to me and don't speak to anyone," Meg said. By anyone, she meant the reporters who hung around the courthouse all day in case something juicy dropped.

The palatial corridor of the courthouse was lined with wooden benches, and Cathryn scanned them one by one until she spotted Stacie sitting with Matt Stevenson, her attorney from Duluth. She'd slipped out of the hotel a half hour before Meg's limo arrived. Both attorneys knew about their relationship but agreed they should avoid being seen together in public, as it might invite questions about a conspiracy of their own.

"Don't even look over there," Meg said sharply, leading her into a stark waiting room where there were no windows or art, only stiff metal chairs. She unrolled a cushion from her briefcase and allowed it to self-inflate. "You don't practice law for forty-five years without learning a few tricks."

"Do you have any tricks for..." Cathryn stumbled over whether or not to bring up Stacie's dilemma. "What if they ask me about something I don't want to talk about?"

"For instance?"

With an eye on the door in case someone came in, she reluctantly related the story of Marty and the drugs, finishing with Stacie's fear that her phone number had been compromised. "What do I say if they ask me if we know each other?"

"You answer them truthfully."

"And then what? I might as well serve her up on a silver platter."

"Cathryn, you have no choice. Your immunity deal depends on your cooperation, which means answering anything they might ask. Besides, you wouldn't be serving her up. Admitting you know her is only circumstantial. They'd still have to prove she was the one who made those calls, and it's doubtful they can do that."

A uniformed bailiff entered through the side door. "They're ready for you, Miss Mack."

Meg held up a finger. "Tell the court I'm still meeting with my client. I'll knock on the door when we're finished."

Cathryn waited until he left, and whispered, "What happens if I just say I don't really know her very well?"

"That's called perjury, and they send you to prison for it. On top of that, it would cancel your immunity deal and you could be tried as a co-conspirator alongside your boss. Cathryn, my job is to look out for you without regard to how anyone else is affected. I'm advising you not to do anything to jeopardize your deal."

In other words, there were no good choices except to pray Stacie's name never came up.

Meg rapped sharply on the door. "Let's get this over with."

The grand jury room bore very little resemblance to a courtroom. Eighteen jurors sat behind long tables arranged in a U, with microphones interspersed so they too could ask questions. Cathryn's chair was at the front corner opposite a raised bench where the judge, an African-American woman of about sixty, sat with the prosecutor and court reporter.

The prosecutor, US Attorney Vincent Halperin, was a trim, handsome man in his early forties whose boyish blond hair and taste for designer eyeglasses made it a good bet he'd be drafted someday for higher public office. He began with a rundown of the formalities, reminding her she was still under oath, *blah-blah*, was granted immunity from prosecution in exchange for her truthful testimony, *blah-blah*, and had the right to request a conference with her attorney at any time.

"Miss Mack, I want to pick up where we left off yesterday with regard to the senior officers at Nations Oil in this apparent plot to subvert lawful regulation by the Environmental Protection Agency. I'm particularly interested in any discussions you may have witnessed or participated in involving Nations Oil's general counsel, Gregg O'Connor."

It became apparent as he guided her through detailed testimony about the conversations on the plane and in the hotel that he wanted very much to also capture Gregg in the conspiracy web. Though she had no recollection of Gregg's specific role, she attested to his concerns about covering up the paper trail Woody created with his initial report on the discrepancy between the pump stations, and his agreement to bring in Karl Depew for security.

"We're almost finished, Miss Mack. I just have one more topic I'd like to ask you about. Do you know Stacie Pilardi?"

After all her rumination and talks with Stacie and Meg, she still hadn't settled on a plan. And now her time was up. "She's the head of the Clean Energy Action Network."

"Yes, of course. We all know that. What I'm interested in is whether or not you know her personally."

"Personally? What do you mean?"

He studied her for a moment, clearly taken aback by her hesitation. "Have you ever met her? Had a friendly conversation with her? Talked with her on the phone?"

"Yes."

"Yes to which?"

"Each of those."

Until now, Halperin had conducted virtually all of his questioning in a casual manner from his chair behind the bench. Now, because he'd obviously picked up the scent of blood in the water, he squeezed behind the court reporter and paced menacingly near her chair. "Did you happen to have a telephone conversation with her on the morning of July twentieth?"

If she concentrated, she could probably match up Stacie's test call on her prepaid cell phone to that specific date, but not if she simply refused to think that hard. Technically speaking, the majority of their phone communications had been SappHere texts, which Halperin probably didn't know about. "We communicated by phone on more than one occasion, but I can't be sure of all the actual dates."

Apparently the jurors also had picked up on her reluctance to elaborate. Several were leaning forward in their chairs and virtually all of them were frowning.

"What did you and Miss Pilardi talk about?"

"She tried to convince me of my company's wrongdoing, and I tried to convince her we were operating within regulations, which I believed at the time to be true."

"So your relationship was adversarial?"

"No, I wouldn't say that at all." So far she was holding her own. "I respected her even though we disagreed, and I believe she also respected me."

"How often did you and Miss Pilardi speak by phone?"

"Not very often."

By his scowl, Halperin was clearly agitated that he wasn't getting what he wanted. "Not often, and yet you have no idea of the dates?"

"You asked about a specific date, and I told you I didn't remember."

"So you did." He returned to the bench to retrieve his notes and studied them pensively. "In any of your conversations with Miss Pilardi, did she ever mention a man by the name of Martin Winthrop?"

There it was, the kill shot. By asking about "any" of their conversations instead of only those they'd had by phone, he left her no room to dance around it, no way to avoid implicating Stacie. If she said yes, he'd surely hammer away until he got the whole story.

"I'd like to speak to my attorney."

Unfazed by her request, he glared at her fiercely. "Let me remind you, Miss Mack, your immunity agreement compels you to testify truthfully."

The judge's gavel broke the tension in the room, and she calmly said, "That's enough, Mr. Halperin. She asked for her attorney, and my stomach tells me this is a good time to break for lunch. You can resume your questioning at two o'clock."

Meg was on the phone in the waiting room and seemed surprised at her early return. "Did everything go all right?"

"They asked about Stacie. I don't want to tell them."

"We went through this. You have to."

Cathryn shook her head adamantly. "No, she could go to prison. I can't do that to someone I love."

* * *

Stacie gripped Cathryn's hand as they followed Matt and Meg off the elevator at the seventh floor of the Hennepin County Courthouse in Minneapolis. "You guys go ahead. We need just a minute."

Meg stopped short and made a dramatic display of checking her watch. "A minute is exactly what you have. If Cathryn isn't back in front of that grand jury at two o'clock, she'll be held in contempt."

"One minute, I promise," Stacie said. She flitted her fingers to send the attorneys down the hallway, and took both of Cathryn's hands. "Are you absolutely sure you want to go through with this?"

"I can't let you go to jail. Halperin's questions…he put me in a box. No matter what I say, he's going to use it against you. Meg says this is the only way."

"Meg is brilliant, by the way. But this is for real. We're going to walk out of here—"

"Minute's up!" Meg shouted from the end of the hall.

"I love you," Cathryn whispered. "I'm sure about that. And I'm sure you'd do the same thing if I were in your shoes."

No question. "I would, and I love you too."

"Then let's do this."

Margaret McCullough was indeed a genius, and it didn't hurt that she also knew all the right people in local government. Otherwise they'd never have been able to pull this off so quickly.

A receptionist led them into the chambers of Judge Charles Willis, a grandfatherly figure who was eating lunch at his desk. "Meg!"

"Charlie!" She met him at his chair and they shared a hug, a clear sign they were old friends. "Thank you so much for doing this on short notice."

"Anything for you." He held out both hands toward Cathryn and Matt. "Is this the happy couple?"

"You're half right." She nudged Matt aside and pushed Stacie and Cathryn together. "This is. They just got their license downstairs, and we all have to be back in federal court in St. Paul in…forty-two minutes."

He looked at her skeptically. "Is any of this for real?"

"We love each other," Stacie said emphatically.

Meg tapped her watch. "Forty-one."

"Yes, of course." He picked up a laminated placard from his desk. "This solemn agreement between—"

"Cathryn and Stacie."

"This solemn agreement between Cathryn and Stacie has permanent legal standing, and we are serving as witnesses to it. Cathryn, will you have this woman to be your wife, to live with her in the covenant of marriage? Will you love her, comfort her, honor and keep her in sickness and health, and forsaking all others, be faithful to her as long as you both shall live?"

"I will." Cathryn said it without a moment's hesitation and squeezed her hand.

Permanent legal standing. Permanent as in forever.

"...for as long as you both shall live?"

"I will," Stacie said.

The judge craned his neck toward them. "I don't suppose either of you brought rings."

"They plan to go ring shopping later," Meg said impatiently. "We really need to run, Charlie."

"Very well. By the power vested in me by Hennepin County, Minnesota, I pronounce you married. You can kiss in the elevator."

* * *

Cathryn settled again in her seat at the front of the grand jury room as Halperin paced the area between her and the jurors. By the wrinkle of his brow, his mood hadn't improved since she'd raced out of the room earlier.

It was hard not to notice that several of the jurors looked as though they were ready for a nap. Warm room, full bellies. Always a risky combination.

"Miss Mack, before I continue my questioning, I'd like to recap briefly for the jurors where we left off. You told us you and Stacie Pilardi had communicated several times by phone, but you couldn't be sure of the dates. Is that correct?"

"Yes, it is."

He held up a calendar of July with the twentieth circled in red and turned to show it to the jurors. "Records indicate that Miss Pilardi checked out of the St. Paul Hotel on July twentieth shortly after a call was placed to your phone. That was a Sunday morning about eleven thirty. I know dates can be confusing, but I wonder if perhaps you remember getting a call on a Sunday morning, perhaps one in which she mentioned being in St. Paul. Does that ring a bell?"

There went her deniability. He had pinpointed the moment Stacie tested her phone, and it was all but certain he'd matched it to the phone used to report Marty selling drugs.

"Miss Mack?"

"On the advice of my attorney, I'm invoking spousal privilege."

There was a sudden shuffle in the room as the jurors leaned forward in their chairs as though their movements were choreographed.

"Excuse me, you're invoking what?"

"Spousal privilege. I'm declining to answer any more questions about my wife, Stacie Pilardi."

The red in Halperin's face clashed violently with his pink shirt. "You and Stacie Pilardi are married?"

"That is correct."

"As of when?"

Cathryn glanced over her shoulder at the clock mounted behind her as she produced a copy of her license. "About forty minutes ago."

He stormed across the floor to snatch the paper from her hand. "This is an outrageous miscarriage of justice. Your Honor, I'm asking you to compel this witness to testify."

"Let me have a look at that." The judge adjusted her glasses to inspect the document. "Hmmm…it appears everything is in order, Mr. Halperin. If Ms. Mack wants to invoke her privilege not to give testimony regarding her spouse, that is her right, even for events that occurred prior to her marriage."

"But this was clearly orchestrated to circumvent justice."

"The law makes no such distinction. Do you have any further questions for this witness?"

Halperin raised a finger and started to speak, but then pretended to look at his notes, which appeared to be upside down. "When…how did…were you ever…?" He was too flustered to put together a complete thought. "No, nothing more, Your Honor."

"Very well, the witness is excused. And Ms. Mack?"

Cathryn braced for a scolding.

"Congratulations."

* * *

"My breasts have never been so clean."

Cathryn chuckled but had no intention of stopping her soapy massage. She and Stacie fit together very well in the claw-foot bathtub, especially facing the same direction with Stacie leaned back against her chest. Candles and champagne added to the romantic atmosphere. It was after all their wedding night. "My arms aren't long enough to reach any of the other fun spots. I suppose I could scrub your neck." She planted a kiss behind Stacie's ear and gently nibbled her lobe.

"I'm your wife now. You can do anything you want."

"That's right…my wife. I promised to comfort you until death do we die, or something like that. It all happened so fast. I can't remember everything I said I'd do. Was bathing on the list?"

"Yes, I think so. The biggie was something about forsaking all others. Just think, most people visit Minnesota and go home with little Viking hats or painted wooden loons. You and I go home with a wife."

"Exit through the gift shop," Cathryn added with a chuckle.

"I feel that way. This is a gift."

They'd had only nine hours to process being married, but the changes began immediately for Cathryn, and there wasn't even a moment of second-guessing what she'd done. "I feel settled. I know that's weird. Weddings are supposed to be such a big deal…all the excitement, planning every detail…but we packed all that stress inside a thirty-minute ride across the river and then it was over."

Stacie let some of the water out so she could warm their bath. "I feel settled too. You're probably not going to believe this, but after that weekend we sneaked off and spent here at this hotel, I told myself you were somebody I could spend my life with. My friend Jenn laughs at lesbians because we tend to fall in love so fast, but I've never really been one of those. In fact, I've always had the opposite problem. As soon as I realize I have feelings for someone, I start throwing up a bunch of obstacles for why it'll never work. Once I convince myself it has nowhere to go, my feelings start to fade away."

"A self-fulfilling prophecy."

"Exactly. And then I met you. I didn't even have to conjure up any obstacles. There were a million reasons not to fall in love with you, but I couldn't help myself."

"I love you," Cathryn murmured, clasping her hands tightly around Stacie's soapy belly. "I was with Janice for nine years. We spent the first five growing closer and the last four growing apart. Relationships are a lot of work. You have to sacrifice and compromise, and you can't keep score. All those promises we made today, Stacie…we'll have to work hard to keep them."

Stacie squirmed around so they were facing and wrapped her legs around Cathryn's waist. "Being married already makes us stronger because we can't just throw up our hands and walk away. I intend to work hard at this, and like I told you last night, I'll start by moving to Houston to be with you."

Cathryn loved Stacie's smiling brown eyes and look of joy at presenting what she was sure was the ultimate wedding gift. "I love you even more for being willing to do that, but I'm not sure Houston is the right place for us after all. I've been thinking a lot about what you said and you're right. We'd basically have to be in the closet and I'd always be paranoid about someone from work finding out. That's not any way for married people to live."

"What about your job?"

"I think you were right about that too. Nations Oil can't fire me for being a whistleblower, but they can make my life miserable at the office. I'll never be on the inside again."

"There could be worse things than being cut off from people like that."

"That's the real problem, all the people like that. I walked out of that grand jury room today thinking about all the indictments that are coming down. It was bad enough when it was just polluting and bribery, and then doctoring the paper trail to cover everything up. To think Hoss Bower and Bryce Tucker ordered Depew to kill you…and it was only a stroke of luck I happened to hear about it. I never dreamed they'd go that far, but you weren't surprised at all. Whoever takes over Nations Oil will probably do the same things, but he'll try harder not to get caught. I need to get out of there right now and let everyone know I'm not like that."

"I didn't want to be right." She rested her forehead against Cathryn's chin for a moment and sighed. "You know what I think we ought to do? You just gave up your whole life for me—your job, your home, everything you had back in Houston. That's the most profound expression of love I could ever imagine. I think I should do the same. I've been looking at making some big changes at CLEAN. Maybe I'll just put the organization in someone else's hands and walk away. We'll start a whole new life together."

Such irony. If Stacie had walked away sooner, Hoss and Bryce would never have ordered her murder. Cathryn could have eased out of the oil business slowly on her own terms and no one would have been the wiser.

That realization should have been irritating but Cathryn was surprisingly unmoved by its logic. The truth was she felt relieved to be free of the culture of corruption now that she knew how pervasive it was. "I left Nations Oil because they had no scruples. Why would you leave CLEAN when you still believe in everything it stands for?"

"Because I don't want you to look at it every day and remember what it cost you. You don't have to decide anything now, but it's on the table. Just think about it."

While it might make life easier to have a clean break from such a tumultuous beginning, she couldn't imagine Stacie doing anything else. "I don't need to think about it. The answer is no."

"Cathryn, you don't—"

"No," she said more forcefully, hugging Stacie to her chest. "One of the reasons I fell in love with you was because of how passionate, how determined you were. And always so unselfish. Even if I disagree with you sometimes, you fight for all of us. I'd never want to change that about you."

"Wow…if you weren't already married, I'd snatch you up so fast."

"I love you too." They shared a soft kiss. "Let's just get this grand jury behind us. Hoss thinks I'm in New Mexico visiting my mother for a few days. I can't do anything until the indictments come down, but I'm going to resign as soon as that happens."

"I'll come to Houston for the time being if you want me to. We can wait it out together. What do you think you'll do next?"

"Who knows? Contact the headhunters, I guess. I have some money in savings and I can put my townhouse on the market."

Stacie grinned. "Did you just forget you were married? Your wife isn't going to let you worry about money while you look for a job that makes you happy."

Her wife. To love, comfort, honor and keep. Until death do they die.

CHAPTER TWENTY

"My client wants immunity from prosecution," Matt said, nodding toward Stacie across the conference table. "Without her testimony against Martin Winthrop, you'll be letting a very dangerous man walk."

Halperin shook his head dismissively. "Counselor, I'm not going to lose any sleep over a guy holding a couple of ounces of marijuana. My number one concern is the credibility of your client's testimony against Karl Depew. She's at the center of the government's case, and right now stands accused of fabricating evidence and filing a false report. If in fact she's done those things, it will damage us, and you can guarantee the defense will use it to discredit her testimony."

Though the US Attorney seemed to be working hard to maintain his professional demeanor, Stacie could feel his hostility. Obviously he was still pissed about their impromptu wedding.

"The jury won't care once they know why she did it," Matt said.

"That's a very tough sell, Mr. Stevenson. Your client already has a substantial number of arrests and convictions. I should think someone as dedicated to her cause as Miss Pilardi would consider her integrity paramount and come forward with the truth."

"She does and she will, but these circumstances are different. All of her previous convictions fell under civil disobedience. Those were courageous acts that inspired others also to stand up against corporate power and money that bullies its way past the will of the people. And by the way, she does that because the government—including the Justice Department—does a pretty poor job of looking out for the interests of the people. Her arrests so far are admirable to those who share her cause. A criminal conviction, however, might alter her standing in the eyes of potential backers of her organization, and she's not willing to jeopardize their support, not even to give you the full picture of Martin Winthrop's malicious involvement in this conspiracy."

With Cathryn's testimony blocked because of spousal privilege and Stacie refusing to testify with regard to Marty, the US Attorney knew he was missing major pieces of the puzzle. Stacie was prepared to lay it all out there, but had to press her advantage while she still had leverage.

Halperin's jaw twitched with irritation. According to Cathryn, he was convinced they were hiding something bigger than setting up a stool pigeon, and in fact he was right. Stacie wanted nothing more than to tell him about Marty's involvement in Colleen's accident, but she couldn't get to that without incriminating herself.

"I can't give you immunity unless I know what you're going to say, and it's up to me to decide if your testimony is worth thumbing our noses at a justice system that's been in place for two hundred and forty years. If the jury finds Winthrop guilty of drug charges, I don't want to get sued later should that prove to be a wrongful conviction."

"Fair enough," Stacie said, relaxing in her chair for the first time since the negotiations began. "In the first place, the drugs that were in his possession were his. I found them stuffed in the bottom of his sleeping bag. And yes, I sent him to the school on a bogus errand and called the sheriff's department. I considered him too dangerous to confront and didn't want him coming back to our house."

"Why was he dangerous?"

She started at the end of the story with the discovery of how Marty had tampered with Colleen's car. "You should interview Brian Murray and his private investigator, and get the photos from the newspaper so you can see for yourself."

"Something else, Mr. Halperin," Matt interjected. "There's definitely someone inside the sheriff's department working with Depew. Whoever took Ms. Murray's briefcase expected that accident to happen near Chester Park and was probably providing security for the protest rally. But Ms. Murray left the event early. Since she avoided the stop-and-go traffic, the accident was more serious and happened several miles away. I think if you check the duty roster, you might find one of those responding officers came directly from the park."

Halperin grimaced and shook his finger at her. "I wish you'd brought this evidence to the police in the first place. Ms. Murray's case is potentially as serious as what Depew did to you, and this drug arrest needlessly complicates our case."

"I didn't trust the police," she said adamantly. "If Depew had gotten wind of it, Marty would have vanished. Then you'd have no one to hold responsible for an accident that nearly killed somebody. It's not like I went out and bought drugs to plant in his backpack. He may not have intended to sell them to kids outside a school, but they were still his drugs. Do a saliva test on the rolling papers if you don't believe me."

Matt gave her a slight nod as Halperin buried his head in his hands. He'd been fairly confident all along her information was worth immunity. "Look, my client is eager and willing to give truthful testimony against Martin Winthrop on a number of charges, including drug possession, vandalism, stalking and attempted murder. You said it yourself—if not for her, you might not have a case at all against Depew. But I can't let her risk criminal prosecution."

"Very well." Halperin tossed his pen on the table in resignation. "Is there anyone who can corroborate your story? Your new wife, perhaps?"

"She only knows what I told her."

"I did not appreciate that stunt, by the way. The people of Minnesota didn't grant lesbians and gays the right to marry so they could abuse the justice system."

"The people of Minnesota can rest easy then, Mr. Halperin. We married because we love each other, and because Cathryn didn't want to be forced to say something that might hurt me. I'm sorry if that offends you. No matter how this case ends, at least she and I get to come out of it happy."

* * *

"It's like wearing a turtleneck with a cardboard scarf. Who does that in August?" Colleen tugged at her neck brace and fanned herself with her lunch menu, which she'd insisted on keeping for just that purpose. "It's worth it though. This is going to be the biggest story of my career. My editor's given me a whole team—two reporters, a researcher and a graphic artist. Just to think only a year ago they were considering downsizing me with all the other satellite reporters."

"Good thing they didn't," Stacie said. "This story deserves a lot of attention. I only wish you could be in Houston for the frog march. That should be happening any minute now."

Colleen knew all about the grand jury because she and her son had been called to testify. "We sent a stringer with a photographer. They're already camped out in front of Nations Oil's headquarters. Just wait till you see tomorrow's front page."

"Save me a copy. I'm flying out this afternoon."

The indictments hadn't been formally announced yet, but Stacie had a pretty good idea who was on the list—five of the company's officers, Bob Kryzwicki, and Depew. Then there was Martin Winthrop, who faced multiple charges, including attempted murder and felony drug possession. For Stacie, the biggest surprise was Deputy Sharon Gustafson, who faced a litany of charges, among them accessory to attempted murder, since she was the one who had left Chester Park in pursuit of Colleen's car.

"I'll save you all the papers for your trophy case," Colleen said. "Halperin says he expects more charges, including all those goons who worked for Depew. No telling how many on the EPA staff will be implicated. Kryzwicki couldn't have pulled this off by himself. They'll probably pick up a few of Kratke's underlings too. I can't believe they aren't going after Cathryn Mack. She was the biggest liar of all."

Stacie's heart jumped at hearing her name and leaned across the table to keep her voice low. "About that...off the record, okay? This can't be common knowledge yet."

Before Colleen could answer, the waitress returned with their salads.

"Cathryn was the only one telling the truth, or at least the truth as she knew it. They were feeding her bogus information every day."

"How do you know that?"

"She's the whistleblower. None of this would have come to light if she hadn't stepped forward."

"Oh, my God. You have to go on the record, Stacie. That's the backbone of the story."

"I know, and you can have it first. But she's still an officer at Nations Oil, and you have to sit on it until she's out. There's no limit to what these people will do. One of those attempted murders was me. They put out a hit, and if Cathryn hadn't contacted the FBI, Depew would have killed me in my house."

"Unbelievable. The biggest story of my life just got even bigger."

Stacie chuckled and dug into her salad. With her mouth half-full, she said, "I can relate to that. When all those people walked into the lake...man, that was our biggest protest ever, and by far the most successful. Not only did we expose the fact they were hiding the rest of the spill, we killed the Caliber Pipeline, at least until the next company steps up and tries to ram it through."

"That's a lot to celebrate," Colleen said, raising her water glass in a toast.

"You don't know the half of it," she said, thinking about her secret wedding. Back on the record, she talked about what their victory meant for the future of CLEAN. "This shows we can be effective. We have the government's attention now, and that will help us bring in more donors and volunteers. Everyone likes a winner."

Throughout lunch, Colleen peppered her with questions about Depew's campaign to scare off and discredit the protestors. "Is he just some cowboy out of control?"

"I wish that's all he was. Guys like Depew are all over the place—oil, fracking, timber, livestock—wherever big business meets pushback from the public. Most of the guys are ex-military, like private cops without any rules or accountability. They consult with Homeland Security and make us all out to be terrorists, and they get local law enforcement on board by throwing money at them for equipment and overtime, and making them feel like the last line of defense. They tap our phones and email without warrants, put tracers on our cars, destroy our property and have us arrested for no reason—all with impunity. It isn't just Depew who's out of control. It's the whole system."

"How soon do you think I'll be able to talk to Cathryn Mack?"

"I'm not sure, but I'll ask her tonight."

"You two stay in touch?"

"Yes, if everything goes according to schedule, I'll be picking her up at the airport in Pittsburgh." Try as she did, Stacie couldn't suppress her grin. "She's my wife now."

* * *

Each of the padded leather chairs in the executive boardroom of Nations Oil cost more than all the furniture in Cathryn's old office. The boat-shaped granite table sat beneath three crystal chandeliers and held polished brass name placards to mark the officers' pecking order. This was Cathryn's first executive meeting, and also her last.

The room fell silent as Hoss took his regal armchair at the head of the table. "Before we get started, I want to welcome two new faces to the East End." He introduced Cathryn and Woody to tepid applause.

She smiled faintly and offered a wave of acknowledgment. It didn't escape her notice that several of her new colleagues didn't even bother to look up. There was no way of knowing how many were aware of the circumstances under which she and Woody were promoted, but the cool reception told her they weren't impressed. It wouldn't matter after today.

"As you all know, we've had quite a bit of trouble since our last meeting." He hit the highlights of the debacle at the lake, and added that they were already working to manage the fallout. "From a public relations standpoint, this was an unmitigated disaster. It's possible we may get fined again for running bitumen through that pipeline, but our engineers are looking into whether or not we can argue this was extra-heavy oil that's been sitting out there so long the diluents evaporated. I've been assured by the EPA that we'll be cleared of wrongdoing related to the size of the spill we reported. The preliminary report on that should be coming out"—he checked his watch—"right about now."

That would be another nail in their collective conspiracy coffin, Cathryn thought. There was no end to their hubris. The only fly in their ointment was Depew, who had disappeared after the FBI had used his phone to send a short text to Bryce Tucker saying he'd taken care of business. Apparently they thought he was in hiding, but Hoss had stopped in her office twice to ask if she'd heard from him. They were definitely spooked.

"Clifford, what are you hearing from the analysts?"

As VP of Investor Relations, Clifford Blake had been taking a beating from the analysts on Wall Street ever since the incident at the lake. "It's a volatile situation, Hoss. They're estimating this cleanup could cost us half a billion dollars."

Hoss nodded grimly, conceding the point.

"But the bigger issue is Caliber. There's growing skepticism about our ability to secure approval, and that's affecting our long-term outlook. We might be looking at a downgrade next quarter."

"I'll talk with Mike Washburn again and see where we stand," Hoss said. "It might not be a bad idea to let Caliber percolate for a while. We can bring it up again next time somebody starts yelling about a new jobs bill."

Stacie would consider that a victory, especially since there was zero chance Nations Oil would win approval once the honchos at the head of the table were arrested. According to the SappHere text she'd just sent from Minneapolis, that should happen any minute. Cathryn had been scared to death Hoss or Bryce would get word of the grand jury, but so far they seemed oblivious. Facing them in court eventually was unavoidable, but she didn't want to be confronted at work without protection.

Cathryn jumped as the conference room door burst open amidst objections from Hoss's administrative assistant. In walked a team of six men and two women, all dressed in dark suits. Federal agents riding in like Cathryn's personal cavalry.

Hoss planted both hands on the arms of his chair and pushed himself up. "Excuse me. This is a private meeting."

The first man through the door walked straight to the head of the table. "I'm Special Agent David Peavey of the Federal Bureau of Investigation. Harold Bower, I'm placing you under arrest for conspiracy to defraud federal regulators, bribery of government officials, illegal dumping of hazardous material, obstruction of justice and attempted murder for hire."

"What the—"

The agents scattered around the table, surrounding the conspirators as the other corporate officers watched agape.

"Bryce Tucker, I'm placing you—"

"Now hold on here," Hoss demanded as the arrests continued. "I'm sure there must be some mistake. Why don't you take this up with our attorney and we'll all sit down and settle this like civilized people?"

"This attorney?" Another agent smugly nudged Gregg from his chair and pulled his hands behind his back. "Gregg O'Connor, I'm placing you under arrest for conspiracy to defraud federal regulators. You have the right to remain silent—"

"—obstruction of justice and attempted murder for hire—"

"Elwood McPherson, I'm placing you under arrest for obstruction of justice."

"Me? I didn't even do anything!" Woody shouted back, looking at Cathryn with pleading eyes.

So many voices talking at once, forceful and monotone, shrill and indignant, all mingling with the metallic sound of handcuffs ratcheting into place.

"Cathryn Mack?" A female agent appeared at her side. "I've been instructed to escort you from the building for your safety. Do you have everything you need?"

"Yes." She slung her purse over her shoulder and began walking the gauntlet of shocked faces.

Hoss and Bryce were glowing red with fury, and she was glad for their handcuffs and the federal agent on her shoulder.

"What have you done, Cathryn?" Hoss demanded.

Her hand shaking, she took a letter from her purse and laid it in front of their human resources head, Norma Garrison. "I've resigned, but not before telling the US Attorney all about this company's crimes, including how you and Bryce sent Karl Depew to—how did you put that—cut off the head of the beast."

"At least he did," Bryce spat.

"Shut up, you ignorant ass!" Gregg was the only one who seemed to grasp how much trouble they were in.

"Actually, he didn't," Cathryn said, resisting the urge to slap his face. "Stacie Pilardi is alive and well, and Karl Depew is sitting in jail thinking about all the ways he can screw both of you to shave a year or two off his sentence."

The agent led her as far as the attached parking garage. "I would advise you not to go home right now. The press will be swarming your house soon, and everyone in this building will be calling and stopping by to find out what you know. Mr. Halperin would appreciate if you didn't talk to any of them."

"I have no intention of going home." Her living room was stacked to the ceiling with boxes, each marked for shipping or Goodwill. The sooner she got out of Houston, the better. "I'm going straight to the airport and flying out to Pittsburgh to be with my wife."

Cathryn exited the parking lot and pulled into a loading zone where she had an unobstructed view of the building's entrance. Four black SUVs were parked in the circle, surrounded by a media circus waiting to capture the fall of the mighty. The frog march, where accused criminals were paraded like trophies. For the sake of everyone on the planet, she hoped they fell far enough to put the other oil companies on notice.

It was true what Stacie had said about one person being able to make a difference. Cathryn would get the credit for this, but her courage came from someone else.

CHAPTER TWENTY-ONE

Stacie loved the way her car fell silent as its hybrid engine died, leaving only the sound of tiny rocks crackling beneath her tires as she coasted into the garage. "Welcome home… perhaps."

Cathryn was like a zombie, wide-eyed and barely able to move on her own. In the last week, her whole world had been turned upside down, and while she admitted it was all for the best, her body and spirit appeared to be shutting down against the drastic changes.

"I'll bring your suitcases in later. Let me show you around."

Their first stop was the kitchen, and Stacie decided against describing the scene where Depew had confronted her. Cathryn had been through enough shock today. From there, they walked into the great room with its vaulted ceiling, wood-burning stove and towering windows.

"If it weren't dark, we'd be looking out on the Monongahela River. It's gorgeous all the time, but especially at sunrise."

Cathryn hadn't said a word since they turned into the driveway, but was looking around with interest. Her eyes were drawn to the balcony above, from where the FBI agents had drawn Depew in their deadly sights. "Are the bedrooms upstairs?"

"One of them. The master is back here." She led her through the foyer and into her cozy bedroom suite, which also featured floor-to-ceiling windows with the same view of the river.

"It's bigger than I expected. I thought you'd be more conscious of your carbon footprint."

Stacie knew a tongue-in-cheek response when she heard one and was glad Cathryn was able to show a little humor, even if it seemed only to mask her nervousness. "Damned zoning restrictions. It was the smallest one they'd let me build, and the neighbors had a fit when I covered the roof with solar panels. That said, I bet they appreciate that I don't annoy them with lawn mowers and leaf blowers. The whole yard is nothing but native vegetation, all except for the stone path I laid down to the dock."

"You have a boat?"

"A kayak. We could get another one if you wanted to go together." She wrapped Cathryn in her arms from behind and rested her chin on her shoulder. "That could be fun, huh?"

"I don't know…I've never done that sort of thing before."

"Look, sweetheart, I know it's all scary."

"I'm not scared…just a little overwhelmed," Cathryn said wistfully, making eye contact in the window's reflection.

"No wonder. Look at all that's changed for you in just the last week. I don't want you to be anxious about being here. It's just a house. My home is with you now, and if you don't like it here, we'll find something else—anywhere you want to be."

"I feel like I need to hit the Pause button, you know? I've just made a whole bunch of long-term decisions and I need some time to try everything on. Does that sound okay?"

"It sounds like I married a really smart lady. There's no hurry, and I don't want you to feel rushed into anything." She spun Cathryn in her arms and pulled her down for a kiss.

There was no lack of enthusiasm in Cathryn's lips, but her trepidation was evident when she broke their kiss and looked at her with concern. "Will you say that a week from now if I'm still refusing to come out from under the covers?"

"Ha! If there are covers involved, I'll be under there with you." That produced the first genuine smile she'd seen since the airport. "Come on, let me show you the rest of the house. I think you're going to like it a lot."

The bedroom above the master doubled as an office, with a futon and a desk that faced the river. From there they crossed the balcony to Stacie's favorite room, which was directly above the kitchen. Instead of turning on the light she snapped on her butane lighter and set it to several candles.

"You have a whole room for yoga?"

"This room keeps me sane." With windows at the corners, it too had a grand view of the river. "I sit up here at night imagining boats going up and down the river, and all they can see is the glow of my candles."

"It's peaceful."

"We could use a little peace tonight, don't you think? When's the last time you treated yourself to a yoga session?"

Cathryn shook her head. "Almost two weeks ago."

"I bet you're in knots." She handed Cathryn a pair of leggings and a tank top. "I picked these up for you. What do you say we unwind a little?"

Moments later they were bouncing their legs against the floor to loosen up. Stacie led with stretches and curls, and watched as the wrinkles on Cathryn's forehead slowly dissipated. Lunges, salutations, planks and bridges, all working up a light sweat and causing their muscles to quiver. Their last pose was the eagle, balancing on one foot with the other wrapped over the knee and behind the calf. Arms forward, twisted, palms together. Facing one another with the candle between them, Stacie dipped as low as she could without losing her balance, only to see Cathryn go deeper. And deeper…all the way to the floor until she released into a half-lotus. It was the most amazing display of body control she'd ever seen.

Cathryn's physical strength shouldn't have surprised her. Every time she'd faced adversity in her life, she overcame it through hard work and perseverance. Stacie was sure she could do that again—especially if they did it together.

* * *

From her side of the queen-sized bed nearest the window, Cathryn watched the orange line of the horizon grow brighter behind a wooded hill across the river. The Monongahela. Lazy and green, from what she could see. And gorgeous at sunrise, just as Stacie had promised.

It was hard not to feel they were on display—naked in bed in front of a wall of windows—but Stacie assured her the glass was reflective. They could see out but no one could see in, at least not during daylight. Like everything else, that would take some getting used to.

There was much yet to wrap her head around, but the biggest piece came easily—lying here in bed with her wife and knowing she always wanted to wake up with her.

"I bet you're wondering how to call room service," Stacie murmured, spooning her warm body to Cathryn's.

"It probably involves pressing a few buttons. I can experiment to see which one works."

"Mmm…pressing buttons might get you more than breakfast. How did you sleep?"

"Pretty well, since you wore me out." After yoga, they'd shared a bath and spent the hours until midnight making love. "Not that I'm complaining. Speaking of wearing me out, do I get to meet your little friend in the light of day?"

"You mean this?" Stacie stretched over to the nightstand for her vibrating wand. "She was very pleased to meet you."

"The feeling was mutual." From the beginning, she'd been comfortable with all of their sexual explorations, but now that they were committed to one another, there was a new level of trust she'd never felt with anyone before. It gave her confidence the other aspects of their life together would fall into place, and sooner rather than later. Security…knowing Stacie too was dedicated to their relationship, and together they'd find the best fit.

Cathryn shuffled through her suitcase for a pair of shorts, and when she drew out a dark blue T-shirt with a Native American design, Stacie snatched it from her hand and put it on. "I guess I'll wear something else."

"Get used to that. It's my way of always having you close to me."

"I'll try to remember to buy things you like." As she wriggled into a tank top, it occurred to her that no one ever had asked to keep her close.

While the coffee brewed, they cut up fruit and made toast, setting it all on a wicker tray, which Stacie carried down the flagstones to the dock. On one end was a covered picnic table.

"This doesn't suck at all," Cathryn said, sitting on the table with her feet on the bench for a better vantage point to watch the river. A breeze swirled around them and raised goose bumps on her bare arms and legs, but it wasn't at all unpleasant.

"Great, isn't it?" Stacie sat beside her and positioned the tray behind them where both could reach it. "I wander down here a lot whenever I have to be on the phone for a long time. It's like my second office."

Cathryn couldn't imagine working like that. She preferred the structure that came with being an essential cog in the corporate machine. In fact, what she'd miss most about her job at Nations Oil was the prestige that came with such a prominent position. "I never understood the appeal of working from home. I actually enjoy getting up in the morning, putting on a suit that says, 'Take me seriously,' and driving into a parking space with my name on it. It's just who I am."

"Don't you ever wish you had more autonomy?"

"In the corporate world, autonomy comes from being good at your job. I liked being the 'go-to' person for the press at Nations Oil. It was an adrenaline rush to have microphones and cameras in my face, to know all those people saw me as the expert. They were hanging on my every word. And it wasn't just the press. People I worked with—Hoss Bower even—used to come into my office all the time and ask my advice on how to handle the media. That made me feel important…valuable. I don't know if I'll find that again."

"Sure you will. When you're good at what you do, people want you on their team." Stacie refilled their mugs. "What about the other parts of your job? Did you like managing people, watching them develop?"

"Some more than others. I liked it a lot better when they were people I hired instead of those whose daddies played golf with Hoss. I must have been pretty good at training them since they kept getting stolen by other companies." The main reason her assistants left for other opportunities was because everyone was looking for advancement and it was clear Cathryn had a lock on the top communications job for another twenty years.

"Would you consider yourself detail-oriented or more of a big picture type?"

"When you're dealing with a whole lot of information—to say nothing of all the competing personalities—you have to be both. Sometimes you have to get down in the weeds, but you can't ever lose sight of your mission."

With her voice muffled by the large melon cube in her mouth, Stacie summarized what she'd heard, ticking each item off with her fingers. "You're looking for a high-profile job where you get to dress nice every day and interact with the media about important matters. You want to hire your own staff, and have people look up to you and admire what you do. And you want a nice office and your own parking space. Did I leave anything out?"

When she put it that way, it sounded hopelessly out of reach. That's what she'd thrown away by turning on Nations

Oil, and it was unlikely she'd ever get another opportunity like that. "Yeah, pretty much. But the problem is that the oil industry is all I know, and it also happens to be the one place I can't work anymore."

She'd scorched the earth behind her on the way out of Houston. If Stacie was right—and she likely was, since Karl Depew had several clients—all of the oil companies were united in their mission to run roughshod over opposition to expansion. None of them would be interested in hiring someone who had sold them out, and even if they were, she couldn't bring herself to work for them again, not when Stacie was so passionately against it.

The optimism she'd felt when she first rolled out of bed had all but vanished. To make matters even worse, Stacie was apparently oblivious to her distress, grinning as she presented a strawberry at the end of her fork.

"Why are you smiling? This is serious. I have absolutely no prospects for a job, and I don't care how much money you've got. I can't just sit here all day and watch this river run by."

"I'm sorry, sweetheart." She pushed the food aside and scooted closer, taking Cathryn's hand. "I heard every word you said, and I know you're anxious about what you're going to do. I'm smiling because I happen to know of an organization that desperately needs somebody with exactly your skills. Someone who presents herself well and speaks with authority, and who isn't afraid to step under the spotlight on the national stage."

It took Cathryn a moment to piece together what she was talking about, and it filled her with frustration. "Stacie, I know you're trying to be sweet and make me feel good, but who are we kidding? CLEAN doesn't need a spokesperson. You guys hardly ever talk to the media as it is, and when you do it's always through the back door."

"Who's talking about a spokesperson? I want you to be executive director." Stacie hopped up to plead her case face-to-face. "Who better to lead the fight against these bastards than the brave whistleblower who pulled back the curtain on their fraud and corruption? You'd scare the crap out of them because they know you'll cut right through all their bullshit and throw it back at them."

Cathryn rested her elbows on her knees so she could bury her face in her hands. "I can't believe you're saying this to me after all the times we've argued about the oil industry."

"And look how often you were wrong. I'm not saying that to rub your nose in it, but now I want you to look at all of it again in a new light. It's not about talking up your company or looking out for jobs in Texas. It's about reading the research again objectively and considering what's good for the planet. I know if you do that, you'll see it the way it really is."

Executive director, the head of the whole network.

Her pulse quickened with excitement but she dialed it back thinking Stacie was simply making a gratuitous offer. "I thought you wanted Jenn for this. You can't just push her aside because I'm your girlfr—your wife. You'd tear your whole network in half."

"I love Jenn to pieces, but you could run circles around her in this job. Besides, she doesn't want to be the ED anyway. She likes being in the field with the volunteers—that's what she's good at. We need someone who can elevate us in the public eye…in the donors' eyes. Someone who knows the oil industry inside out, who can put on the power suit and sit down in front of Congress and get them to listen."

Congress. That was a great deal more responsibility than being a corporate spokesperson, and though she'd been dismissive at first, Stacie's enthusiasm was contagious. "What about you, Stacie? CLEAN is your baby, and you've always been the boss."

"Because I've had to be, but we both know I'm not very good when it comes to getting up there on the stage. If there was someone else I could trust to handle the day-to-day operations and political duties, I'd put all my energy into building a board of directors who could help us win the support of everyone in America who cares about clean energy. Celebrities, dot-com billionaires, retired public officials. Difference makers. The fact that I have a lot of money gives me access to those people. I want the name CLEAN to strike fear in the hearts of everyone in the fossil fuel industry, and especially in all the legislators who do their bidding."

Cathryn grinned to see Stacie pacing the dock, waving her hands wildly as she talked.

"We got lucky at Lake Bunyan, Cathryn. Nations Oil screwed up big-time and we just happened to be there to shine a light on it. Now the spotlight's on us, and with you taking over the top spot we'll make a splash they can't miss. The press will eat it up. You have to say yes. There's never been anyone more perfect for a job in the history of the universe."

Could that possibly be true? She had all the knowledge and skills Stacie was looking for, but not the leadership experience. Her confidence could make up for that, especially with Stacie providing direction.

She drew in a deep breath, held it for several seconds and then began nodding her head rapidly. "Okay, yes."

Stacie let out a yell Cathryn was sure they heard in Ohio.

"But not till the trial's over. They'll say my testimony is biased."

"They're going to say that anyway once they find out we're married. But I'm okay with holding off on the announcement until it's over because we've got a lot of planning to do in the meantime—like deciding where our headquarters will be."

Already Cathryn was seeing herself in the job, even imagining what it would be like to go to work every day in an office where she was the boss. "What are our choices?"

"Wherever you want. I have meetings here in Pittsburgh for the shipping company, but that's why God invented teleconferencing. What matters most to me is you being happy."

Cathryn stopped Stacie's hyper pacing by grabbing the belt loop on her shorts and pulling her back to the table. "Don't you think it matters to me that you're happy too? You built this house. Isn't this where you want to be?"

"I'm not so sure. Pennsylvania's not as conservative as Texas, but neither state recognizes you as my wife. I don't know about you, but I'd resent paying taxes to a state that considered us second-class citizens."

"So we should move…"

"Maybe back to Minnesota. I've never been anywhere that treated me with more respect and dignity." She raised both hands as though she'd just had an epiphany. "That's it! Minnesota. Let's do it."

Minnesota. Friendly people…blizzards. "Doesn't it get really cold there?"

"Yes, but you'd look awesome in boots. I'm talking three-inch heels with skinny jeans, and one of those long scarves swirled around your neck a couple of times." Stacie fanned her face. "Lord have mercy."

"You're serious."

"Totally, but not Duluth. I'm more of big-city gal, like maybe Minneapolis, where we got married."

"I'm with you on that one," Cathryn said. "There's more going in a big city…and you get more hits on SappHere."

"Don't even think about it. Marlene will be canceling her membership, and she expects Cate to do the same."

"I knew there would be a catch."

"Let's rest up a few days and then drive over and start looking around for a place to rent. After couple of years we'll know if Minneapolis is the right place."

It was only then that Cathryn realized her anxiety was subsiding, replaced by anticipation. She was eager for a new career challenge and excited they were moving someplace where they could build a whole new life together. "Are you sure you're ready to give up this place? It's really beautiful, and you've got family here."

"My family is you now. Get used to it."

As they kissed on the dock, a passing barge sounded its approval. An omen, she decided, for her new mantra. *Make Some Waves.*

Bella Books, Inc.

Women. Books. Even Better Together.

P.O. Box 10543
Tallahassee, FL 32302

Phone: 800-729-4992
www.bellabooks.com